Merry Friggin' Christmas

MERRY FRIGGIN' CHRISTMAS

AN EDGY CHRISTMAS COMEDY

BY

JOSEPH CILLO, JR.

Infornuity Publishing, LLC

Merry Friggin' Christmas is a work of fiction. Names, characters, places, and incidents either are the products of the author's imagination or are used fictitiously. Any resemblance to actual persons, living or dead, events, or locales is entirely coincidental.

For Marianne, John, Bob and all my atheist friends.
Merry Friggin' Christmas!

"What evidence would you have of my reality beyond that of your senses?"

"I don't know," said Scrooge.

"Why do you doubt your senses?"

"Because," said Scrooge, "a little thing affects them. A slight disorder of the stomach makes them cheats. You may be an undigested bit of beef, a blot of mustard, a crumb of cheese, a fragment of an underdone potato. There's more of gravy than of grave about you, whatever you are!"

-- Charles Dickens, *A Christmas Carol*

1

Caught Dead in Jersey

I wouldn't be caught dead in Jersey. That's what I used to say. And then I was. Twice. You know that bit they say Hemingway said? All true stories end in death. Well, it's a lot of bunk. I know that from experience. Death is never the end of the story. Put that one down to me, Carlton St. Michael, if no one else ever said it. But I wouldn't call my story a true story. I don't see how it could be. More like the most outlandish, superstitious nonsense ever contrived. That's what I would have called it when I was alive. Or, at least, before I died the first time.

Life goes on and on, or so it seems. And having died twice, you would think I would have more confidence about it, but, well, I keep wondering if I might wake up and find out I was right all along, before the madness inspired by my first death. And maybe I never died at all? Not the first nor the second time? Maybe I'm just in a coma or dreaming, and the dream will end? Maybe I'll wake up? Or, maybe I'll die, and the nothingness I always expected will finally take over?

They say my story is one of the all-time top-rated shows on the Undying Rerun Network. Yeah, that's right, URN. That's their idea of a joke around here. That's one of the things that makes me skeptical. Really? URN?

My life as depicted on the URN (if there is such a thing) is a Christmas comedy, of all things. Even though I spent most of my life mocking the fools prancing around in their red and green holiday sweaters, with all their ho-ho-hos and hallelujahs, the whole fat fantasy of Christmas.

They say my story is Rod Serling's favorite and he watches it over and over. Well, if this is real, and it all really happened, I wonder if he kibitzed on the script, and that's why he likes it so much? I'll have to look him up, if I ever get all these toilets cleaned.

Oh, but I've gotten way ahead of myself. Do I owe you an explanation? The dead don't owe. The twice dead owe less. And, if I'm dead, how is it you can even read what I'm writing, never mind make demands for explanations?

Proof, I say! Proof that this can't be real. But then, how do I know you are reading? If dead men can't write, or even if they can, can the living read a word of it? But there's not much else to do but clean toilets, so write I will. I feel I must, like an irresistible compulsion, like somehow it will all make sense if I write it down and something will finally come to an end. Something that is aching to end, like pain or grief, but which must be suffered. But I have no idea who the audience will be? Perhaps it is not meant to be read, only to be written?

There is a peculiar thing, however, about writing in this particular hallucination (I'm not sure what else you would call it). This laptop they gave me is defective. Most of my all-time favorite words just don't come out right. Like, all the letters work fine, so I can write "fire truck" with no problem, but when I take out the "ire tr", I get "#@*!". So, I tried writing, "George Carlin's seven dirty words are $#!!, piss, #?@!, @?#!, @*#%$?@!!, #@%#&?#?@%!!, #!#$". I guess there are only six dirty words here?

So, I tried to use the "P" word in my favorite context, which I used a lot because I spent most of both my supposed lives irked by a great many things. So, I typed the expression with the p-word and it came up,

"This really *boils my eggnog* off." The point is, I'm being censored, and some of it is contextual. I don't normally talk like Ned Flanders, but that's just how it comes out. I would never type the words *boils my eggnog* in any context.

I know these words are offensive, but it's hard to do comedy today without them, and my act was full of them. I suppose if you know Carlin's act, you can use this as a kind of key? Hey, I don't make the rules. I'm typing what I mean, and that's what's coming out. I checked the computer settings and found a note saying, "*Holly-Jolly* censoring enabled," and try as I might I could not disable it. If I weren't pretty certain this whole thing is a stupid dream, I'd try to contact the system administrator and give him a piece of my mind, using as many of the dirty words in a single sentence as I could, like, "Hey #@%#&?#?@%!!, you really *candy my cane* off with this bull $#!! 'Holly Jolly #?@!ing censoring'." Yeah, so, I missed a few. I don't want to use those other words, anyway. If what I am experiencing is not some screwed-up dream, and you can actually read what I am writing, I'm sure some ambitious soul may eventually undertake to translate the symbols and produce a *naughty edition,* so look for that one if it bothers you.

Maybe one day, you will be able to catch my story on the URN, if there is such a thing, but most likely, you will not want to pay the price of admission. You have to be dead. And, I know those Hollywood guys, they ain't touching what's hot in heaven, not when they've got so much hotter stuff from the other place. Oh, yes, I've seen that other place, too. So, if true stories don't end in death —and I'm not sure how you could be reading this if they do— well, you may want to think about that a bit. You may not get the chance to come back and go mad like I did. So, read my friends, if you can, and consider well if death may not be the end. Still confused? Not sure how you could read what a dead man writes? Well, for now, let's just call that a mystery.

2

Laugh Out Loud

Mon, Dec 5, 2011 - The Last Day of My First Life

I,Carlton St. Michael, was a man on the verge of success. Fame and fortune awaited. I had found just the right material, with just the right edge, that would *jingle the bells* (I warned you about this censorship!) off just the right people, inspire all the needed controversy, and catapult me to the top. Laughing with the sinners in the pre-Christmas of the year of our Lord 2011, testing out my new act, I could feel it. The Laugh Out Loud Club, the small, Greenwich Village former speakeasy, was packed, unusual for a Monday night. I liked to try out new material on Mondays because there would likely be fewer people to notice if you bombed, and, as my manager Lenny Gold had taught me, if you can make them laugh on a Monday night, they'll be putty in your hands on a Friday or Saturday night. The local crowd had had their two-drink minimum, and most had more. New Yorkers out on a Monday night were the serious party crowd and would know how to get home without operating any dangerous machinery like an automobile. The most difficult mechanism they might need to manage was a turnstile for the subway.

A general improvement in mood set in after the Thanksgiving holiday when the Christmas shopping season started in earnest. Maybe there was something in all the helium released by the floats from the Macy's Parade? The pre-Christmas jollies, I called it. Come December, folks were ready to laugh. Not that I bought into that Christmas crap. No merry friggin' Christmas for me. The generally happy mood made for a softer Monday trial-by-fire for my new stuff and I could feel the excitement and anticipation in the larger-than-normal crowd. I was primed and ready, having downed my Vicodin and glass of wine. I could feel the electricity as if the stage lights were somehow supercharging me with their heat and light. My mind was sharp, completely focused, completely confident. Each word of my act was finely tuned and ready. I was in that high-performance state, where everything was just bigger and brighter, more perfect than perfection. I was on! Looking out over the crowd, my eyes darted around the room. Lenny, my manager, looked apprehensive. Chico, my fellow comedian, smiled and nodded, and the pretty young blond sitting at the front table looked awestruck. I winked at her and began my act.

"I used to be a Catholic. I was actually quite a good little Catholic boy. Right up until the time I found out that I had no tolerance for 'mysteries'."

I paused here. A kind of false punchline. A setup. I could see their confusion. I could feel it. I let the tension build. Then, I continued. "Now, don't get me wrong, I enjoy a good mystery just as much as the next guy, so long as a mystery is something to be figured out and resolved. Like, Sherlock Holmes, you know, 'Elementary, my dear Watson, it was Colonel Mustard in the living room with a candlestick'."

I mocked the great detective with an exaggerated accent, which got a few laughs, but it was still setup. I rolled my eyes and continued.

"But, you see, that's not what Catholics mean by 'mystery'. Oh, no, no!"

I paused again here, my timing was perfect.

"To a Catholic, a mystery is something that doesn't make any #?@!ing sense."

The audience laughed, and I gave them time. Lenny shook his head. I rolled my eyes and shrugged my shoulders. "I don't know, man? It's a mystery." I shook my head.

"I see some of you laughing. You must be the Catholics. Right?" I gave a confused look, scratching my head, "Like, 'I don't know why I'm laughing?'"

I shrugged my shoulders again. "It's a mystery."

I waited for the laughter to quiet.

"Ok, so some of you look a little confused, probably because you're not Catholic. I get it. You're like, 'What's this a-hole talking about? What mystery? It was Colonel Mustard. Elementary, man.'"

I rolled my eyes again. "You have to understand the Catholic idea of mystery, and I'm telling you, it makes no #?@!ing sense, so you have every right to be confused. Let's see if we can clear things up with an example. A Catholic believes that Jesus was fully God and fully man at the same time. Now, a rational person might suggest that this is a contradiction. The reasoning goes like this: God and a man are two different things. Since fully means 'entirely' or 'completely', to say that someone is fully God and fully man, well, hmmm."

I used my arms like a balance.

"Let's see, fully God." I weighed down one side of the scale.

"Fully man?" I tipped the balance the other way.

"Well, that doesn't make any #?@!ing sense!"

I gave that confused look scratching my chin and paused.

"But if you ask a Catholic, he would tell you..."

I paused, shrugging my shoulders, making that confused face, milking the timing.

"It's a mystery."

The audience laughed, again. I waited for the laughter to die down and adjusted my pose.

"Now, let's consider the implications of this mystery. Suppose Jesus is fully man and fully God, as the Catholics contend. I know, I know it makes no #?@!ing sense, but let's just go with it."

I rolled my eyes and paused.

"Ok, Jesus, fully God, fully man. Ok. Well, that would mean that Jesus, being fully man, well, he would need to eat and drink, right? Fully man, eat and drink."

I motioned to my mouth as if eating, and then as if drinking.

"Ok, so Jesus is fully man, and he's eating and drinking, so what are the implications of that? I mean, what else does he have to do? Why it's elementary. Of course, he would have to. Of course, he would have to fart and $#!!."

The audience laughed. Lenny glanced up at the ceiling. Chico nodded approvingly. I glanced at the pretty blond, then quickly away. Likely, she would not be into bathroom humor.

"Why sure? Wouldn't he? I mean, he's fully man! I mean, he has to."

The audience laughter died down.

"But, he's also fully God. So, as fully God, I would assume he wouldn't do any of these things."

I folded my arms and rubbed my chin, then opened my arms like I was pleading to make some sense of it.

"I mean, I just can't imagine God, the creator of the universe, laying down a large, smelly turd. At least not any kind of God I would worship!"

I rolled my eyes, with an exaggerated smirk. The audience laughed, and I waited for them.

"So, what would happen when this guy, who is fully God and fully man at the same time, when the man part of him has to take a dump. It leads to the inevitable question."

I put my hand to my chin, again, as if in thought. My timing was perfect here. I waited for a moment, until total silence slowly crept over the place.

"Did Jesus' $#!! stink?"

I shrugged my shoulders looking confused, again. That one got a big laugh, but Lenny rolled his eyes again. What's eating him? I'm killing it here and he looks like he's about to $#!! a grenade or something. I smiled, shook my head.

"Well, if you're thinking of Jesus as fully man, you'd say, 'Sure, he's a guy, he's got to be laying down smelly ones.' But if you think of Jesus as fully God, you'd say, 'Of course not! There's no way God is laying down smelly turds!' But what do you think a Catholic would say?"

I paused and shrugged my shoulders, looking up at the ceiling with palms up. I milked the pause perfectly. I was on fire!

"It's a mystery."

The audience applauded and laughed a bit louder. I waited for the laughter to dissipate.

"Now, let's suppose that Jesus' $#!! did not stink. Well, he lived for thirty-three years, he must have produced quite a lot of the stuff. Let's suppose that on a dig in Israel, an archaeologist discovers one of Jesus' turds. I can see the headline, "Archaeologist Discovers Mysterious Turd, Still Steaming, but with No Discernible Smell."

The audience laughed louder and longer.

"And, what do you suppose they would call this discovery? Why, it's obvious! There's only one thing you could call it. It's inevitable."

Here comes the big one. Wait for it! Wait for it!

"The 'Holy $#!!!'"

The audience erupted in raucous laughter. They were eating it up, so to speak. I guess it may be a bit disgusting to think about eating up holy $#!!, but there you have it! But, I was not done.

"And what would the Catholics do?"

I paused just a beat, then lit into the climax with a crescendo of volume and speeding up the pace.

"Why, I'll tell you what they would do! They would build a church on the site, the Church of the Holy $#!!! Pilgrims would come from all over the world to worship it, and contemplate the mystery, and take a whiff of the odorless feces. They would have processions and vigils in honor of the holy turd. There would be stories of healing and miracles, how leprosy was healed by the Holy $#!!. The lame would walk. The blind would see. Just one whiff of it would raise the dead back to life!"

I paused a beat, then gave them my mock Christian routine.

"Lord, oh Lord, I was healed! Healed by the power of the most Holy $#!!! Praise Jesus!"

Yeah, they were rolling in the aisles. I had them. One of those nights when everything just clicked. Just have to wrap it up, now. I waited for them to quiet down. I reduced the volume and spoke solemnly.

"And so, I have renounced Catholicism. At least until they take the mystery out of it. You've been a great audience. It's been my pleasure to be here with you tonight. Thank you and good night."

The audience stood and applauded. I took my bow and exited the stage. What a night! My new material was killer. I just had to break it out into bigger venues. No doubt, I was heading for the big time!

I headed backstage, the rush from the adulation taking over where the wine and Vicodin left off. Backstage at the Laugh Out Loud Club was an old storeroom where they used to keep the booze in the thirties, with false walls to hide the stuff, and an emergency shoot to dispose of the bottles if they were ever discovered. Oh, the good old days of legislating morality that made all the criminals rich and famous. The room had a permanent musty scent combined with stale beer, and, always, the faint scent of vomit. Stage fright accidents were common among some of the inexperienced acts. My buddy Chico Chinico, all smiles greeted me.

"Congrats, man! You really killed them!"

We touched elbows.

"Still afraid of the germs, eh, Chico?"

"Hey, man, I know where your hands have been!"

I laughed and looked over at my agent Lenny Gold. What's with the sourpuss? I mean, jeez, I just had the best set of my life. He's my agent. You'd think he'd be happy.

"Edgy stuff, Carlton. I'm not sure I like this."

"Oh, come on, Lenny, you're always so uptight!"

"This anti-Catholic stuff." He shook his head. "Could be dangerous."

"George Carlin made a lot of fun of Catholics. Never hurt him any."

Lenny shook his head and smirked. "George Carlin did bits about irreverent Catholic school kids. He didn't come out and say a major religion doesn't make any #?@!ing sense!"

"You see, you never listen. I did not say that Catholicism doesn't make any #?@!ing sense, I said that when something doesn't make any #?@!ing sense, the Catholics call it a 'Mystery'. Now, how are you supposed to represent me properly when you don't understand my material?"

"Don't give me that smart-ass $#!!, Carlton! You know what I mean. Catholics take these 'mysteries' pretty damn serious."

"Seriously, Lenny, seriously."

Lenny looked confused, tilting his head. "Seriously what?"

"Catholics take these mysteries pretty damn seriously."

"You're damn right they do!"

I laughed, shaking my head and rolling my eyes. Lenny was a good egg, but he was a Jew and had a bit of a persecution complex when it came to Christians, in general. He was an older guy, who had been in the business for years and seen a lot of how things worked, but his perspective was dated. Johnny Carson was no longer the king of late night. Prime time had gotten edgier and comedy more biting. The entire society had gotten coarser. And Catholics? Those anti-abortion, anti-gay, even anti-contraception relics? Oh, they were everybody's favorite target, and I was not going to miss that bandwagon. Not with the inside dope I had!

"Listen, Lenny, I know these people. I used to be a Catholic. Hell, they probably still claim that I am, baptized and confirmed. Now there's a real mystery for you. Anyway, trust me, the only Catholics that will be *jingled* off are devout Catholics, and the more devout they are, the more they will turn the other cheek. Oh, they may protest. But that will just be good publicity. The most devout will pray for me, heaven forbid. Most of the ordinary Catholics will be on my side, getting a good laugh at themselves."

"Turn the other cheek, eh?" Lenny made his typical snide retort. "Tell that to Torquemada."

"Torquemada, man?" Chico jumped in. "Wasn't he the dude with the big stick diplomacy?"

"That was Teddy Roosevelt, Chico." Lenny rolled his eyes. "Torquemada's the dude who tortured heretics and Jews in the Spanish Inquisition."

"Oh, man! The Spanish Inquisition? Like, no one expects the Spanish Inquisition, man."

"And, neither do I!" Okay, so Chico steals his lines from Monty Python. I still like the guy. Then I changed the subject, "Let's go to McGinty's and get a drink. Lenny, how about a nice glass of wine? If it's prepared in that special way, it will forgive all your sins."

"Leave me out of your blasphemies, Carlton. This may make you rich and famous, but mark my words, it won't end well. And remember, you've got an interview with the *Today Show* tomorrow, so don't stay out too late."

I shook my head. Man, Lenny could really be a drag. "You make me rich and famous, Lenny. Let me worry about the ending, and the *Today Show* tomorrow."

3

McGinty's

I know what you're thinking. *The Today Show?* That's the big time, national network show. But, that's not the *Today Show* we scrappers on the New York comedy scene were talking about. We just called it that to make it sound like the big time. *The City, Today* was a local morning show on the *Citywide Network,* a local cable channel without even a broadcast license, and no network at all, though they claimed to be a network. There was no trademark infringement with the big network show, as only local entertainers called it the *Today Show,* as a joke. We welcomed a legal challenge, as it would provide publicity that could not be bought. Imagine a big network issuing a cease-and-desist to local entertainers, the nub of which would come down to referring casually to a show called, *The City, Today* as *The Today Show?* Morgan Shaunessey and Vicki Knight likely dreamed of reporting on that one. Their news division was scrappy, and they hit local items hard. Morgan hosted in the studio and Vicki roved, hopping over to the Jersey side, when necessary. The thing both of them had, and the main reason for the popularity of *The City, Today,* was that they were off the scale on the hot-meter. But they focused on the local, so local comedians like me could break in. You didn't need to be a big celebrity to make news with them, but in having attained a large, local following, even big celebrities liked to get coverage from them to promote local happenings. For me, it was a big interview, and Lenny was right to be concerned that I be ready.

So, we arrived at McGinty's Tavern, this pre-celebrity hang-out next to the Laugh Out Loud Club. Decked out with Christmas decorations, the usual colored lights, Santas, reindeer, elves, tinsel and pine wreaths cluttered up the place. I rolled my eyes at the superstitious stupidity, recalling how my father tried to dupe me with that crap. Oh, yeah, I was always on the naughty list with that guy. I was probably the only kid who ever actually got coal in his stocking. I wondered where the old fart had gotten it from? But, the old bastard never missed Mass on Sunday and made sure I got a good Catholic education, if that's not a contradiction in terms.

But not even all the Christmas crap could bring me down tonight. I was onto something big this time that was getting me to the top. And, then I saw it. The little brat lying in the hay in a manger. Well, now that was just going too far. I could take the fat bearded falsehood in the red furry suit riding around on a sleigh pulled by reindeer, but that crap about a savior being born? Well, it just *burned my cookies off* and reminded me of why my act was so important. I had to rescue people from this nonsense. An apostle of atheism, I was spreading the bad news that there was no God, no Savior, and certainly no virgin birth. I would go out to all the world and tell the bad news that the Christians were a bunch of lying hypocrites and not to be trusted. Virgin birth? Perhaps a lesson in biology is in order. Resurrections? What's dead is dead and stays dead. Friggin' mysteries, that's what they called them. Merry Christmas? Yeah, right. Merry Friggin' Christmas.

We pushed our way into the crowded tavern. I checked out the performers' pictures hung on the wall. Yeah, amidst the festive Christmas crapola, my grinning mug was still hanging there, along with

Chico and even a picture of Lenny, from back in the day when he was a ventriloquist. Lenny's act got to be pretty big for a while, playing in Vegas and Atlantic City at the Casinos, doing cruise ships sometimes, when he wanted a working vacation. Actually, Lenny was the most successful of the three of us, having landed a gig on the Tonight Show back when Carson was big, but that was long ago, and his star had faded as ventriloquism just lost its appeal. Then, Atlantic City went downhill, and he decided to work on developing new, younger talent as an agent. He looked happy in that old photo, with that silly-looking dummy on his knee, though, as the straight-man in the act, he typically was his usual critical self. Chastising the dummy, who was always in need of chastisement. That was his shtick. And, he had been good at it. It occurred to me that I was his new dummy, but there was no way I was sitting on his knee.

McGinty's was crowded that night, more than usual. Something about Christmas time brought people out. Maybe people came home for the holidays or were tired from shopping and wanted to blow off some steam? Some of the extra crowd came from my strong draw at the Laugh Out Loud Club, which spilled over to McGinty's after the performance. The pre-Christmas revelers, wherever they all came from, were bundled against the cold and took up more room than normal. We would need to work our way to the bar. But there was something I had to do first.

"I gotta make a pit stop," I shouted over the din of the crowd. "I'll meet you at the bar."

I made my way to the men's room, slipping through the sweaty, over-clothed bodies dressed for cold outdoor December in the warm, overcrowded room. As I got there, I took out my cell phone and called Maury Stanowitz. Now, Maury was a putz. Not sure there was a better word for him, but, he was a top entertainment agent. He got results, and did not have moral or ethical qualms, like Lenny. Sure, he was a straight-man like Lenny, but he did not waste time chastising his clients. He had influence with venue owners and media that came from a

"It's important, Carlton." I felt the menace in his voice. I imagined a scene from a gangster movie, the gun to my head and a pen in my hand to sign the contract for an offer too good to refuse.

"Yeah, yeah, just make me rich and famous, that's all I ask."

I pushed the button to end the call. Freaking putz! I knew I had to tell Lenny. Just had to get the right moment.

I snaked my way up to the bar where Lenny and Chico waited. They had a glass of red wine waiting for me. They knew I didn't care much what wine it was, just so long as it was red. Chico and Lenny were drinking draft beers. Lenny handed me the glass of wine.

"Here you go. Just say the magic words and all is forgiven."

"That's the spirit, Lenny," I chuckled.

"Holy Spirit, Carlton?"

"Holy Spirit, Holy $#!!, what's the difference?"

"No discernible smell, either way, man," Chico chimed in.

"Don't you start down this road, Chico." Lenny had found a new dummy to chastise. "You can't afford to tick off the Catholics."

I rolled my eyes and didn't try to hide it. Eye-rolling was becoming my favorite comic motif, and, it was almost out of my control. I'd have to be careful if I ever went to Jersey. Roll your eyes at the wrong character there, and you end up in a barrel at the bottom of a river. But then, I had vowed never to go back to Jersey, so I figured I was safe. I waved the sign of the cross over my glass of wine with my right hand and then raised the glass and took a sip.

"There. Now, my sins are all forgiven. Okay, time to dirty up the old soul, again. Which vice to indulge this time?"

The attractive blond from the front row of the show walked up to me. Her long hair danced hypnotically on her shoulders as she swayed drunkenly in that I'm-so-available kind of way. When women had this tipsy look about them, like they are having difficulty focusing, well, it was like ringing the stupid bell and making the dog in me drool. I looked her up and down.

"Lust, it is."

Lenny's eyes went iris-less, again. It had become a motif less comic for him. It suited his dummy better than it suited him. The girl pointed to my picture on the wall behind the bar.

"Hey, that's you!" The girl slurred her words and blinked a couple of times.

"Well, now that you mention it, that does look like me. You know what's funnier?"

I pointed to Chico's picture.

"That one kind of looks like him!" I pointed at Chico.

"And that one?" Pointing at Lenny's picture with the ventriloquist's dummy. I imagined the dummy with my face.

"That one kind of looks like him!" I pointed to Lenny. "Only much younger. I wonder if the dummy looks any older? Hey, Lenny? What ever happened to that dummy anyway?"

"He was burned at the stake for heresy."

"Now, now, you're scaring the girl." I turned and smiled at the blond. "Now, how would you like it if a soon-to-be-rich-and-famous comedian bought you a drink?"

"Carlton, just don't forget about the *Today Show* tomorrow." Lenny pointed to his watch. I wondered if he thought there was a string he could pull to open and close my mouth.

The girl looked confused. "How can today show tomorrow?"

"Oy," Lenny sighed and turned away. Chico slapped his hand on his forehead and laughed.

I looked at the girl with the seriousness of a saint.

"I think it has to do with the sunrise." I waved my hand across the imaginary horizon. "That's when today shows tomorrow. Have you ever seen the sun rise over the Hudson?"

"Any day I wake up early enough, which isn't often." The girl hiccupped, then continued. "It's just a few blocks from my apartment."

"Now, that's something I would like to see!"

4

Accidents Happen

Tues, Dec 6, 2011 - The First Day of the Rest of My Life

My arm jerked under her neck as I woke in the darkened bedroom. The woman next to me lay warm and breathing the breath of heavy sleep, thankfully undisturbed by my sudden movement. I closed my eyes. Who was she? It didn't matter how attractive she was, but I could not help noticing she was attractive. Blonds! They were my downfall. She was here, and I had someplace I had to be. Where was that? Oh, yeah, the _Today Show_ interview! I looked at my watch. 6:45 AM. Ugh, I was late! I got quietly out of bed. Leave a note, I figured, that would be the best way. Just, let yourself out, honey. I gotta go. I found my clothes and dressed quickly in the dark. She rolled on the bed and woke.

"What's your hurry, Tiger?" she brushed her long, blond hair from her face.

"I'm late for the _Today Show!_"

"Today show tomorrow, you mean. I don't think the sun is up yet?"

"I don't have time for this. Take your time, let yourself out whenever you're ready."

"Let myself out? This is my apartment, you lousy $#!!! You said you wanted to watch today show tomorrow?"

"Yeah, yeah, today show tomorrow. Sorry, gotta go!"

"Well, don't bother coming back, you lousy creep!" She threw a pillow at me and hit me in the head. She must have been some kind of athlete because she threw it hard. My senses came back in slow motion. A time bomb clicked forward toward detonation culminating in the explosive pounding of my head. Hungover, I winced in pain.

"Sorry, baby! It was really great. But, I gotta go."

I hurried out the door of her apartment and ran down two flights of steps to the street, buttoning my shirt as I went, my coat slung over my shoulder. The slowness of my wits allowed only a creeping realization that I had no idea where I was. Yeah, the pretty blond from last night. That was her. A few blocks from the Hudson. That would be the West Side. How did I get here? I could hear the memory of the clacking of the subway cars, that awful screeching of its brakes. I remembered. The PATH train? Did I take the PATH last night? Why would I do that? The blond, that was why. Today show tomorrow. Yeah, she had a view of the river. The West Side. The PATH. Not the West Side. The PATH. The thought pierced my mind like a bullet in my pounding brain: *Holy $#!!! I'm in Jersey!* How the frig could I make it to *The City, Today* in midtown? Well, Merry Friggin' Christmas!

I scrambled out the door and ran down the sidewalk past a Catholic school, Saint Friggin' Nicholas Catholic School, if you can believe it. I wondered if that was where they taught elves to make toys? Buttoning my shirt, carrying my coat, I glanced around trying to get my bearings. Some of the Christmas lights around the area were still lit in the predawn light, which just *boiled my bells* off the more. A plastic Santa glowed at me. "Ho, Ho, Ho." Yeah, have another Ho-Ho, you fat bastard. What I would give for a magic sleigh to get me across that river and back to my city. Friggin' reindeer. Never around when you need one! Lenny warned me about not staying out too late. Yeah, the damn blond. Lust again. I felt like a dummy on the old bastard's knee. "Now Carlton, I told you. You have to stop chasing blonds." *Uh, huh, huh, huh, okay, Lenny, so next time a redhead! Uh, huh, huh, huh.* I could feel him pulling my string. I needed a freakin' cab or a train or some other way to get across that stinking river and back to my city. Lust! What an evil sin! Ugh!

I saw a cab drive by the intersection ahead. Salvation. Where there's one, there's usually more. I had to get there! I started jogging, then running. I passed a church at the corner and noticed the Lady carved in stone, palms up in benediction. *Our Lady*, the Catholics called her, but she wasn't *my* lady. She was just a hunk of rock.

I quickened my pace and reached the corner. I turned right which would take me past the front of the church. Friggin' church. Why couldn't the cab have come from the other direction? I started to run as fast as I could manage past the church and *bam!* What the frig was that? I glanced about and saw the soccer ball bouncing toward the street. The pain registered slowly in my dulled senses. A young, athletic African-American kid sprinted through the gate to the park across the street. He nimbly darted across the street not watching at all for the traffic which greeted him with an insufferable blare of horns and screeching of brakes that pounded my hungover head almost as badly as had the soccer ball. He grabbed the ball and gazed at me apologetically. I screamed in pain.

"Are you okay, sir?" the kid asked, as he bounced the soccer ball on the sidewalk.

I looked down at the little bastard. "Christ, kid! Watch where you kick that thing! What are you doing play soccer in December, anyway? That ball is frozen like a brick."

"Sorry, sir. Coach says we should practice whenever we can, if we want to get scholarships. We play in the park before school."

"Well, just keep playing in the street, kid. It's a great way to get yourself eliminated from the gene pool."

"What's that, sir?"

The roll of my eyes intensified the excruciating pounding of my head. Perhaps, this therapy would help train me off this habit, that now that I was in Jersey, would likely land me dead, in a barrel at the bottom of a river.

"The gene pool! The gene pool!" I shouted. "You know, Darwin, the survival of the fittest? Oh, Christ, you're a Catholic. You don't believe in Darwin."

"Oh yes, sir. We learned about Darwin in science class. Just not sure what that has to do with playing soccer."

"Just keep playing in the street, kid. You'll figure it out." I turned and hurried toward the intersection, again. "Damn Catholics, there's too damn many of them, anyway. They should all go play in the street!"

I finally realized I was half freezing to death and managed to get my coat on. And here's where things got a little interesting. I ran past the portal entrances to the church as fast as I could manage and slowed as I reached the corner. The cab had come from the right, so I wanted to cross the street to be on the side of the road that taxis would more likely be on. What made me glance to the right? Why would I glance to my right after I passed that infernal church?

Past the parking lot, the great mural glowed iridescent. The Resurrected Christ at the empty tomb radiated its own light, the light of the world, with Christ as its source. Then, from right to left, the scene traveled backward through time, the backlit Crucifix against the setting sun and the nativity scene with its brilliant star. The sun and star shone impossibly in the morning darkness, like some dual star system in some alien landscape where time overlapped. The slow realization of the foreground image materialized in my mind last, most oppressive of all. The bread and chalice of the Eucharist beckoned in front of the central Crucifix, inviting me into its mystery. The mystery I hated. The mystery I mocked.

The whole friggin' fantasy of the Catholic faith condensed into a single friggin' painting impossibly visible at this distance in the predawn glow. I had to get across the street and as far from the wretched thing as I could.

If you ever get the chance to catch my story on URN, remember, the Undying Rerun Network, you would get to see the things I had no way of seeing. Well, here's where they made a big deal about showing one Mr. Nicholas Penneymoore, in the cab of his truck flipping through the channels of his radio as he waited for the light to change, and every damn channel had that infernal song on about some old woman getting run over by a reindeer. Well, old Nicholas was a born-again, Bible-believing Christian, like a lot of those watchers of the Undying Rerun Network, and he had a bug up his butt about that stupid song, and a Perry Como Christmas CD just out of reach on the floor of the cab of his Guaranteed Overnight Delivery truck. Yeah, they just loved this part. So while I was making a dash to the corner, Old Nicholas, a large, muscular, truck-driving Christian, with a long white beard, which he treasured since it gave him an ability to play quite the genuine Santa Claus, once they stuffed him up with padding to make him look fat, well the light turned and he put his old crate into gear. His truck started rolling, down toward the intersection where I needed to cross. But Nicholas, bless his Christian heart, kept looking at that Perry Como CD and not so much the road, as that infernal reindeer-accident song drove him mad. And they gave Nicholas a speaking role in the good old URN production.

"Dad blang it! This ain't even a real Christmas song! What in blazes does an old woman gettin' run over by a reindeer have to do with the savior gettin' born!"

Sometimes I think this scene was what made my story the all-time highest rated program on the URN. Man, those heaveners just ate this stuff up.

So, as I made it to the corner and began to cross the street, good old Nicholas Penneymoore made a grab for the Perry Como Christmas CD, keeping one hand on the wheel, but both eyes off the road. And there I was in the crosswalk, with the right of way, staring up at this truck with the oversized abbreviation on the front of the cab, G.O.D., bearing down on me, and apparently no one in the cab. And, genius me, oh so clever and smart, did I even try to get out of the way? No. I shouted at what looked like a driverless GOD truck, in a fruitless and foolish effort to demand that it obey the rules of the road. No ventriloquist would ever make his dummy do something so stupid.

"I have the right of way, you schmuck!"

Well, I heard a screeching of breaks and then felt a crushing amount of pain, as my body was launched forward and the truck came to a stop, thankfully before treading me under its wheels.

"Now, Carlton, I told you always to look both ways," I heard Lenny's pedantic, straight man voice.

But I had the right of way.

"You're damn right, you did...Dead right!" The bastard grabbed the punchline of his cheap joke. I felt my jaw go slack. If I were really on his knee, he'd have spun my head around.

I looked up and saw the large letters, G.O.D. and the backlit form of the muscular Christian, with his long white hair and beard waving in the breeze, looking like a vision of the Almighty, Himself, come down off some Michelangelo painting. But, I was an atheist, and I was sticking to it.

"You don't exist," I said.

Welcome to my first death.

5

My First Death

Now, being dead was nothing like I thought it would be. I was an atheist, so I was thinking it should be like, nothing. You know, you're dead, so your brain doesn't sense anything anymore, so nothing at all is going on. Like you're passed out at a party, and the party keeps going on, but you just have no awareness at all. And then you wake up and find your friends had dressed you up in ski clothes or something. Only, if you're dead, the joke's on them because you don't wake up and they have to explain to the cops or the EMT's why your corpse is dressed for skiing. But, it was nothing like that. There I was, Carlton St. Michael, caught dead in Jersey, and I found myself fully aware and looking down at the scene. I was aware of everything, except, maybe, the fact that I was dead, or at least, people would soon tell me I was dead. I'm still not all that sure. As I looked down, I saw that oaf of a Christian standing over my body, while that kid with the soccer ball administered CPR. But, then like some kind of slow-motion fade-out, everything drifted away into a kind of gray fog, and I could not see the scene anymore, nor my body.

Ouch! Something horrid bit my leg. Cripes! something else clawed at my arm. I could not see clearly what they were, but a dread came over me, like nothing I could explain.

"Holy $#!!! What the frig! Get off me!" I threw a few elbows.

But, whatever they were, they kept coming. They were swarming me, like something out of a zombie movie. The flesh-eating kind of zombie, not the witchdoctor kind. I threw more elbows, I kicked, I punched, I twisted away from their grasp. I tried to focus in the dim light to see, to understand, to know. And then, I saw one. A hideous, red face leered through the gloom, with rows of pointed bloody teeth, horns like a goat, talons like a raptor. The thing grabbed hold of me. The foul, sulfurous smell of it made me gag as it drew me closer. I struggled and turned away as it opened its maw to bite. I hadn't the strength to free myself nor to push it away.

"Jesus Christ!" I gasped. The friggin' thing shrieked horribly and backed away. All of them backed off. I sensed they were circling, preparing to strike again, though I could not see them clearly.

"Oh, you don't like that? Okay, Jesus Christ! Jesus Christ! Jesus Christ!"

A hand reached down from above and started to pull me up. I looked up to see who it was, and it was Him, the one from the cross. The one with the wounds in His hands and feet and His side grasped my hand firmly, no hint of weakness from his wounds. He wore a white tunic over his wounded flesh, the crown of thorns atop his head. The suffering Jesus, not the resurrected glorious Jesus who had glowed iridescent in the mural at St. Nicholas' Church, nor the baby Jesus lying in the hay, who had *frostied my snowman* off just the night before, but the tormented and crucified Jesus held me in his sure grip and raised me up away from the swarming throng of hideous creatures. He pulled me atop of a cloud of some kind, or something. Just a haziness, but a much lighter haziness.

"You don't exist! I mean, you did exist, but you died."

"Yes, so did you."

"I did? Oh, yeah, well, I guess I did. Friggin' GOD truck ran me over. Did you see that? I had the right of way!"

I swear to you. The Suffering Jesus, crowned with thorns, rolled His eyes at me.

"I thought you were calling me?" Jesus leaned his head, quizzically. "That you might need my help?"

"Help? Well, no, I just thought it was a way to keep those bastards away from me."

"Oh, okay. In that case..." Jesus began lowering me back down.

"Wait a minute, wait a minute! Let's not be hasty. We all can use some help sometimes."

Jesus laughed and pulled me back up.

"It's just that I didn't know you ever existed." I looked away into the gray of the mist around us. Why couldn't I just look in his eyes?

"Oh, really, Carlton?"

"Yes, I'm an atheist. This is all, uh, very disconcerting."

Jesus shook His head and rolled his eyes, again. I wondered if it were the fully God or fully man part that so disdainfully regarded me? If I believed such nonsense, likely the fully man part would be preferable. Anyway, whether fully God or fully man, the dude seemed disgusted with me. "Carlton, you have hated me and my church for a long time. You cannot hate something that doesn't exist."

I paused a moment. I felt a kind of weight upon me, like some invisible burden.

"Well, it's just that they make up all this stupid stuff about you. Like you were born of a virgin and all."

"So now you're insulting my mother? You know She's queen of heaven and earth, don't you?"

"Holy $#!!! You mean it's true?"

Jesus winced in pain. He took a breath and shook his head.

"Yes, Carlton, it's all true. And, would you please not use that word here? This is heaven, you know."

Jesus paused a moment, and took a deep breath, as if he felt some deep emotional pain and was considering his words carefully. "Carlton, you'll have to forgive me, but it is a bit difficult to converse with you, or even to look at you, while you are in an unrepentant state. It pains me deeply to see you like this, here, in this place."

Jesus took another deep breath and looked at me. He managed a slight smile, shaking his head. "Carlton, they don't make up stupid stuff about me, they believe the truth about me. It seems to me, you're the one who has been making up stupid stuff about me."

"Holy $#!!! You heard about that?"

Jesus looked pained again and paused.

"Would you *please* not use that word? Yes, Carlton, I've seen your act. Why do you think you are here?"

Now, how was I supposed to know why I was there? I figured if I were dead, I'd just be rotting in the ground, in friggin' New Jersey of all places. There should just be nothing. It made no sense that I was anywhere, other than freakin' Jersey, dead in the street. Well, they say God has a sense of humor, so I figured I might as well try a joke. I shrugged my shoulders and looked confused.

"My eternal reward?"

Jesus chuckled, shaking His head.

"You *are* a comedian! Let me introduce you to someone. He's about the funniest guy we have up here."

Jesus turned and called out.

"Chesterton?"

A jolly old fat guy with unkempt hair and a bushy mustache appeared as if from nowhere. He was dressed in a three-piece tweed suit and carried a walking stick. He knelt before Jesus.

"Yes, Lord?" the fat man answered.

"Finally, some respect. Did you know that I saved this guy from the pit of hell, and he didn't even say, 'thank you'?"

"Well, Lord, he is not yet ready for heaven or hell. Perhaps some manure will help him bear fruit."

"Oh, I think he's quite full of manure already. Unholy manure."

"The worst kind."

I listened to this interchange, and well, it just started to rub me about as raw as sandpaper on a hemorrhoid. Who did these jokers think they were? Unholy manure? That's a b-rate line, at best. I knew I could do better.

"Well, excuse me! I guess I was just supposed to bend down and kiss your holy ass!" Now that's comedy.

Jesus glared at me, looking pained again. Well, I guess that one went over like a lead turd. Then, Jesus shook his head and smiled, wryly.

"Carlton, Carlton. And, I guess I was just supposed to turn the other cheek?"

I chuckled, forgetting where I was and who I was talking to. "Hey, that's a pretty good one!"

Jesus shook his head and turned toward the fat guy he called Chesterton.

"See what you can do with him. You're going to need a lot of manure."

"Yes, Lord, Holy manure. Still steaming but with no discernible smell."

"Alright, alright! I get it. I'm full of $#!!. Let's get on with it."

Jesus winced and took another deep breath. He motioned to formally introduce me to the fat man.

"Carlton St. Michael, G. K. Chesterton, the funniest soul in heaven."

I shook hands with this fat Chesterton guy. This guy was a comedian? Maybe he did physical comedy? Pie-in-the-face stuff?

"I'm sorry, I've never heard of you."

Jesus shook his head, sadly. "None of the really funny comedians seem to make it here. Or, if they do, they're no longer funny once they get here."

"Perhaps I can hear a sample of your material?" I always liked checking out the competition.

Chesterton looked up, turning his head, in thought. His expression brightened, as he smiled and showed his crooked British teeth, "Oh, ah, here's a witty one. The Bible says we should love our neighbors and love our enemies because, generally, they are the same people."

"That's it?" I said, incredulously. That was the best comedy they had in heaven? Oh, man, imagine an eternity of jokes like that? That's not heaven, man. No way! More like the other place.

Jesus shrugged.

The unfunny fat man answered. "Well, Carlton, you see, we don't make fun of people here. Comedy is a lot more difficult when you introduce that constraint. Think about your act. Is there a single joke that is not at someone's expense?"

Chesterton glanced in Jesus' direction. I looked at Jesus and saw Him bleeding on the cross. I kid you not! And I realized that my entire act was at the expense of Jesus and His church. Shame filled my soul. I bowed my head.

"But it doesn't make any #?@!ing sense," I muttered, softly.

Jesus winced again and took a deep breath. "I heard that Carlton. Please don't use that language." Jesus shook his head, dubiously. "I am leaving you in Chesterton's hands. You will find him witty, intelligent and what you might consider a know-it-all and a bore. But, I want you to consider the fact that he might just know it all. You will not see me again until you have made your choice."

Jesus vanished in a great flash of light. I blinked my eyes, gawking incredulously.

"Well, yes, I guess that was a bit of a dramatic exit. You really must stop using that language, Carlton. Jesus died for our sins. You wound him with such words. Especially here. Unrepentant sinners are typically judged outside of this place."

"You mean he actually feels physical pain?"

"When we sin, we crucify again to ourselves the Son of God. Jesus chose to show you His pain so you will better understand the love of

God and His sacrifice, and the consequences of what you were doing. By His wounds, we are healed. Let me show you."

Chesterton waved his hand, and a vision of Christ scourged and bloody, being mocked with the crown of thorns and the purple robe appeared on a cloud bank, like a great movie screen. Roman soldiers bowed down in mock homage, pointing and laughing.

"All hail! King of the Jews!"

"Did you think you were being clever when you mocked Christ in your act? Did you think you were coming up with something new and original? They mocked Jesus in a similar way when He still walked the earth. How are you any different than the jeering, scoffing crowd?"

The scene changed to Christ being nailed to the cross.

"The wounds of Christ. His hands, and His feet."

The cross was raised with Jesus on it. The crowd continued to jeer. Mary and Saint John were at the foot of the cross.

"Jesus suffered for hours on the cross, while the crowd jeered and mocked him. They nailed a sign above him saying, 'Jesus of Nazareth, King of the Jews'. Did you think they did that to honor him? Or, do you think they thought it was funny?"

One of the people in the vision called out, "If you are the Christ, come down from that cross."

Jesus on the cross said, "Forgive them, Father. They know not what they do."

Jesus winced, and gasped for breath.

"It is finished."

Jesus died.

"And, the last wound, in His side."

The vision showed the spear piercing Jesus' side.

"When we sin, we crucify Christ. He pays the debt for our sins. He dies the cruel death, that we may have life. Yes, Carlton, when we sin, He feels the pain."

Chesterton waved his hand and the vision on the cloud ended.

I took this all in and felt a tear welling in my eye. Did my many sins cause this pain? When I mocked Jesus, was I like that crowd? But, then, how could any of this be real? I was hit by a truck. My body was lying in that street in Jersey, with that kid trying to revive me. Superstitious nonsense, wasn't that what I always thought about this religious stuff? Hadn't I mocked it because it didn't make any #?@!ing sense? Mysteries? Unexplainable mysteries?

Then I remembered all those shows about near-death experiences and the scientific explanations. Lack of oxygen to the brain, the release of endorphins, all that scientific mumbo-jumbo explained this kind of thing. That's what was happening to me. No Jesus. No Chesterton. And, no demons, or whatever they were, that clawed at me before Jesus grabbed me. It was just some wild hallucination. And I nearly fell for it!

"Wait a minute, wait a minute! I get it now. I'm having a near-death experience. My brain is short on oxygen and I'm hallucinating."

"My guess is that your brain is short on something," Chesterton smirked. "I'm not sure that it's oxygen, however."

"Now, now, Fatboy! I'm onto you. You're nothing more than one big, fat hallucination."

"Fat jokes, Carlton? Is that the best you can do?"

"Listen, G. K., cripes, you think I would have a hallucination with a real name, at least."

"It's Gilbert, Gilbert Keith."

"Okay, Gilbert Keith, everything has a rational explanation, and the rational explanation is that you are a figment of my imagination."

"Yes, a bit of undigested beef, perhaps?"

"Don't give me that Dickens crap! I'm either going to croak off or wake up. Either way, you'll cease to exist."

"A perfectly legitimate point of view." The fat delusion almost sounded reasonable, but there was nothing reasonable about any of this. "If you would not mind indulging me, mere figment though I am, I'd like to introduce you to someone."

"Some moldy old saint, I suppose? Going to convince me of the errors of my ways so I'll wake up a new man, ready to dedicate my life to some phony-baloney religion? I'm onto you, Fatboy!"

"Oh, no, no. I want to introduce you to someone who thinks a lot like you do. Everything has a rational explanation and all."

"Bring it on, Fatboy. You can't flap me, I'm unflappable."

Well, now this imaginary Chesterton dude dragged a finger along the cloud-covered floor, and the ground split open as if it were being unzipped. And, I, Carlton St. Michael, peered down into the most horrifying scene of torture and mayhem, beyond anything I would have thought my imagination capable of. The overpowering fumes of sulfur and burning flesh assailed my nostrils and burned my throat. The tormented screams of anguished souls clamoring to escape, a hideous screeching tore at my eardrums. The demons laying their torturous devices to the flesh or spirit or whatever of those agonized beings that looked human enough, yet not human at all, fueling the noxious vapors and raucous cacophony of torment. The overwhelming vision staggered me, and I swooned, dizzied at the appalling spectacle.

One hand over an ear, the other covering my nose and mouth, I turned my face to look away, at anything else, then back at Chesterton. His grimace, blurred in my watered eyes, faded to a look of pious pity, a kind of sorrowful love for something very dear that had been lost, lost forever, with no hope of being found. And I realized I had been flapped. I was not so unflappable, after all.

"Holy $#!!!" I shouted, almost a scream, as I backed away from the foul-smelling, clamorous scene, more fearful than death.

"No, Carlton. There's nothing holy about it. Unquestionably, there is a most discernible smell."

I waved my hands to push away the fumes, "You're telling me!"

"Friedrich Nietzsche, I summon you in the name of the Most High, Jesus Christ."

Shrieks and howls emanated from the depths of this hell as the Nietzsche dude emerged from the pit. This phantom of what was a man, or whatever it was, came up from the depths, drawn by some unseen force into the clouds. Behind it, the gaping opening of the clouds sealed up concealing the pit.

"Carlton St. Michael," Chesterton motioned, making a formal introduction to this most pitiable creature. "May I present Friedrich Nietzsche."

"Pleased to meet you." My mouth gaped, dumbfounded.

"Likewise, I'm sure." It dusted itself. Ash and smoke floated from its clothes.

"This is the poor soul who declared, 'God is dead'."

"I may have been wrong about that." It glanced furtively to each side and added, "Could I trouble you for a glass of water?"

"Now, Friedrich, you know that's against the rules. And besides, 'That which does not kill us, makes us stronger'. Isn't that what you said?"

"I may have been wrong about that, as well." The soul of Nietzsche gasped and coughed out smoke and ash. I gaped at him in horror.

"Oh, give him a glass of water, for Christ's sake!"

A terrifying shriek came from the thing, like nothing on earth could make. I covered my ears and closed my eyes, my entire body tightening and quaking. My God, just stop this!

"Not for His sake!" the ungodly, forsaken thing screeched.

"Holy $#!!!"

"You see, Carlton, Nietzsche was condemned by Christ. The idea of doing anything for His sake is a source of great pain to him now."

"What kind of a God would condemn a soul to that kind of everlasting torment?"

The soul of Nietzsche smiled, wryly. "I like the way he thinks."

"A just God. You see, Jesus did not reject Nietzsche, Nietzsche rejected Jesus. In fact, Nietzsche was given the same chance we are now offering you, but he chose to persist in his unbelief."

Once more, a vision was projected on a cloud, and there was Friedrich Nietzsche talking with Jesus in the clouds, looking fully human and little resembling the wraith-like phantom that watched with us.

"You don't exist!" the more human Nietzsche said.

The vision dissipated as quickly as it had appeared.

"It's just not rational to believe in a vision of the afterlife that leaves no physical evidence." The hell-raised spirit of Nietzsche shrugged.

"No, it is not," Chesterton agreed, "It is a matter of faith. You chose not to believe, even having seen. You were given forty days to repent and accept Jesus, having seen a vision of the consequences, but you decided to hold fast to your pride. And what did you get for putting your faith in your own sense of rationality? Only madness. Writing letters calling yourself 'The Crucified'. What folly."

"I may have been wrong about that."

"Ok, Friedrich, do you have any last words for Carlton before you go back?"

"Do I have to go back? It's so nice and cool here…"

"Unfortunately, eternal damnation means eternal damnation. We thank you for your assistance. Do you have any last words for Carlton before you go?"

"First Corinthians, chapter 8, verse 2: 'If anyone supposes that he knows anything, he has not yet known as he ought to know.' Learn this, Carlton, or I'll see you in hell."

"Very prophetic, Friedrich. It saddens me greatly that it is too late for you."

Chesterton motioned for me to join him, as we walked a few paces from this pitiful soul. The clouds swirled around Nietzsche becoming a whirlwind, resembling very much the swirling of a toilet bowl. The whirling torrent of cloud took the poor soul of Nietzsche in its grasp, carrying him round and round, then drawing him down, down, like an immortal turd flushed from the heavenly toilet.

"Holy $#!!!"

"So much for the philosophy of the superman. Pride, Carlton. Pride is the sin ever to be hated. You know, Nietzsche himself was never directly guilty of murder, but his prideful philosophy inspired the murder of tens of millions. Once God is dead, why not murder? Why not weed out the weak from the gene pool? Why not conduct experiments on the inferior to better the lives of the master race?"

Perhaps my pity for the wretched thing was misplaced? I shook my head. "Yes, the Nazi bastard deserves to burn."

"Do you make yourself his judge? And what do you believe you deserve, Carlton?"

"Well, wait a minute. I haven't inspired people to murder, have I?"

"Not yet, Carlton, not yet. Nietzsche was not a Nazi. He actually spoke out against antisemitism and German Nationalism in his day. But when you plant the seeds of Godlessness, you can neither predict nor control what monstrous crop might take root. How is your philosophy so different from Nietzsche's? Do you not believe in survival of the fittest? In weeding the weak from the gene pool?"

"But that's scientific fact!"

"No, Carlton, that's scientific theory, and there is some truth in it, but it does not disprove the existence of God. Nor is it a model for how people should treat each other. I remember having this debate with Clarence Darrow."

"You debated Darrow? The guy from the Scopes Monkey Trial?"

"Long ago, Carlton, long ago. He was a lot like you. Intelligent but completely wrong."

Chesterton shook his head, pensively. "Carlton, you will have forty days to make a decision. Now, it is time for you to go."

"Go? Go where? You don't mean? No!"

The clouds began swirling like a great toilet bowl again. I struggled to grab something, but it was all just so much mist, ethereal, without any substance. My body was taken round and round, swirling in the great heavenly toilet bowl, flushed like a smelly turd, sucked down, down, down.

6

Resurrection

I opened my eyes and gathered in the surroundings. I blinked a couple times, my eyes adjusting to the light. People in green gowns and matching green caps hovered over me. Machines connected to me made beeping, clicking and whirring sounds. A hospital operating room, I recognized it. The excruciating waves of pain screeched all over my body. I was alive. It had all been a near-death hallucination. I heard a startled voice.

"Holy $#!!! He's back! Welcome back, Mr. St. Michael. Lucky for you that kid knew CPR. He saved your life."

"Take him to the recovery room. We've done all we can do here. He's in God's hands, now."

"Not His hands!" I called out, with all my strength.

Then, everything went black.

Mon, Dec 12, 2011 - The Seventh Day

So, for a week I lay in the hospital, from the recovery room to intensive care to the step-down unit and then to a regular room. Nothing much to think about. Just, whether I had really died? Had I gone to heaven and met Jesus? Was that fat guy more than just a figment of my imagination? And, whoa, what about that vision of hell? If it were real, I only had forty days to make some kind of decision. What decision? But how could any of that nonsense be real? It's just not rational to believe in a vision of the afterlife that leaves no physical evidence. Holy $#!!, that's exactly what Nietzsche said! But, my mind was all foggy from the pain killers, so the thoughts were scrambled and jumbled and made more sense now in hindsight than they did at the time. I did remember the pain, however. Oh boy, did I ever! My right leg was shattered. My right arm was broken. Both were elevated in traction. Who knows how scrambled up my guts were? Oh, I suppose the doctors knew, in all that medical mumbo-jumbo on my chart. I felt the pain from an incision in my abdomen, so they had been mucking around in my guts. But all I knew about it was the pain.

"Nurse, Nurse!" I screamed, "Give me some damn pain meds!"

I frantically pushed the call button for the nurse. A pretty nurse came in, Jameson, it read on her name tag, Nurse Jameson. Not a blond, this one, though. But it didn't matter. Dark hair, pale skin, blue eyes, I took her in. Even in my pain, I would remember a pretty woman's name. Especially when she shares a name with my favorite whiskey. Now, that's a match made in heaven.

"You really shouldn't need any." She looked puzzled. "Unless you have a tolerance..."

"Where's my damn Vicodin?" I screamed.

The nurse administered more pain meds and wrote something on my chart. She looked about as good going as coming. Amazing how a pretty girl changes everything. But, her memory faded quickly in the haze of the new dose of painkillers. My mind went once again to the vision of hell and the soul of Nietzsche coughing up smoke and ash. I felt something touch my elevated elbow and opened my groggy eyes.

Chico had his Mets cap angled, the way he wore it in his act. Chico often tried too hard to be funny, but he did have a face for comedy. I never could quite figure out why, but most people just started laughing when they looked at him. Mostly, I think it was because he always looked so confused. I saw him blink several times as his face came into focus.

"Holy $#!!, man! Did you know you was dead for over twenty minutes?"

"Chico, Chico?"

"Yeah, man?"

"I had the most horrible dream. I dreamt the Catholics were right!"

"The Catholics were right, man? Right about what?"

"Right about everything! Heaven, Hell, Purgatory, virgin birth, Immaculate Conception, everything!" The grogginess receded as I blinked and focused on details of my nightmare. The Catholics were right? My father was right? Now that's a nightmare! I felt my body shiver.

"Whoa, man, maybe I should have paid more attention in Sunday School."

There was that look of confusion that made most people laugh, but I was not in the mood for that brand of comedy.

"I dreamt that God ran me over with a truck."

"He did, man! You was run over by a truck that said, 'G.O.D.' on it, *Guaranteed Overnight Delivery.* But it wasn't really God, man."

"Holy $#!!! Well, that explains that part."

I looked up at the T.V. my roommate was watching. That fat bastard Chesterton was on the tube. How could that be? The same three-piece suit, carrying a cane, with the same bushy mustache and unkempt hair, he spouted some boring nonsense about religion in a pedantic British drawl. Was I still dreaming?

"Holy $#!!, that's him!"

"That's who, man?"

"Chesterton! He's on TV!"

My roommate, an older guy, had his broken leg up in traction, as well.

"I'm sorry, my son." The old dude waved the remote. "It's just EWTN, the Eternal Word Television Network. I'll turn it off if it bothers you."

"No, no! Leave it on!"

"Chesterton, man? Who's Chesterton?" Chico raised his eyebrows.

"Evidently, he's the funniest soul in heaven."

"He don't seem too funny, man."

"That's what He said!"

"That's what who said, man?"

"Jesus! He said that really good comics don't get in."

"Get in where, man?"

"Heaven! Apparently, only squares get in."

"Well, that guy seems pretty square, alright."

"Yeah, how can somebody so round be so square?"

"Hey, that's a great put-down, man! I'll have to remember that one in case I get any fat hecklers."

"Evidently, you're not allowed to make put-downs in heaven. No jokes at anyone else's expense. That's why nobody funny gets in." I blinked a few times.

"Who says, man?"

"Chesterton, in my dream. Made me think about my act. You know, I'm always making fun of people."

"Hey, man, it was just a dream. Don't let it screw you up! I mean, you can't really believe that you visited heaven? Like, that's just not rational, man."

"Holy $#!!! That's what he said!"

"Who said? Chesterton?"

"No, Nietzsche!"

"Nietzsche? Wasn't he the dude who said, 'God is dead?' How did he get into heaven, man?"

"He didn't get into heaven. That fat dude, Chesterton, raised him up out of hell to talk to me!"

"Holy $#!!, man! That must have been some wild dream."

"Unholy $#!!, unholy $#!!." I shook my head.

"Excuse me, son," my roommate joined the conversation. "I'm Father Murphy, a Catholic priest. I couldn't help overhearing. I believe you have been given quite an opportunity."

"Father," I glanced up at the ceiling, then blinked, steadying my vision. "I understand you might think of it that way, but all I believe is that I was run over by a truck and had some kind of near-death hallucination."

"Well, that may be, but let me ask you this. Had you ever heard of G. K. Chesterton before?"

"No."

"Well, you must have quite an imagination to dream up a guy so well that you can recognize him on TV?"

Now, when a priest says something like that, well, it just *snits my snowballs* off. I don't know why.

"Yes, Father." I made no effort to disguise my irritation. "I do have quite an imagination, but I did not recognize him on TV. I mistook an actor on TV for him. Now, will you please change the channel!"

Father Murphy changed the channel. A scene from "It's a Wonderful Life" appeared. Clarence was jumping to save George Baily. I rolled my eyes. I forgot it would be Christmas soon. I wasn't sure how soon, but soon. I hated Christmas. Friggin' Christmas!

I looked toward the door, as Lenny entered carrying a video tape. It was good to see Lenny, but it made me feel like crap. I wasn't sure why. It was like I felt I owed him something, but I couldn't remember what.

"Hey, Carlton. You look better and better every day!"

Yes, Lenny. It really is a wonderful life."

"Listen, Carlton. I have a video tape of the news coverage of the day of the accident. I really think you need to see this."

Lenny put the tape in the VCR and pushed the play button.

"You taped the news coverage of my near-death accident? How thoughtful of you."

"I was taping your interview on *The City, Today*, wise guy. Remember, that's where you were heading?"

As the video tape began, I really regretted missing that interview. The host of *The City, Today*, Morgan Shaunessey was a babe! Redheads! There was something about hot chicks with red hair. Okay, Lenny, so next time a redhead! Man, it would have been cool chatting up that chick. But, Lenny was immune to the whole hot-chick thing, so there must be something important he wanted me to see. So, I started doing more listening and less gawking.

"Well, we were supposed to have irreverent comedian Carlton St. Michael on this morning, but we've just gotten word that he was in an auto accident in Jersey City, while on the way to the studio. We go now to Jersey City Medical Center where our correspondent, Vicki Knight, will interview the brave little boy who may well have saved Carlton St. Michael's life. Vicki?"

"Holy crap, I'm still in Jersey? What the frig!" I was so disoriented by the accident and pain meds, I never figured out more than I was in a hospital. I knew they must have hospitals in New Jersey, but I was quite sure I never wanted to be in one.

Lenny laughed. "Yeah, Carlton, you're still in Jersey. You chased that drunk blond across the river. Just keep watching."

The reporter Vicki Knight, a tall attractive blond, held the microphone, and smoothly delivered her story. The kid who hit me in the head with the soccer ball stood next to her, outside the emergency room of the hospital.

"Yes, Morgan, I have here little David King, 11 years old, sixth grader at St. Nicholas Catholic School in Jersey City. David, will you tell us what happened this morning?"

The kid looked up at her and answered. "We were playing soccer and the ball got kicked over the fence, so I ran through the gate and grabbed the ball outta the street, and threw it back over the fence, and I was just about to run back through the gate when I heard the tires squealing, so I turned around and I see the guy hit by the truck. I ran to him to see if I could help. Nobody seemed to know what to do. I just got my merit badge in first aid, so I started to do stuff."

"Stuff? What kind of stuff?" The reporter moved the microphone back toward the kid.

"Well, I saw his leg was bleeding badly, so I used my belt for a tourniquet. I saw his arm was broken, but there wasn't anything to do about that. Then, it looked like he was going into shock, so I put my jacket over him to keep him warm. I tried to get a pulse on his neck, but there wasn't one, so I started CPR. I did that for a while until the ambulance came."

"And, did you do anything else, once the ambulance came?"

"Oh, yeah. I put my rosary beads in his pocket and asked the Blessed Mother and St. Luke to pray for him and make him well."

"Well, there you have it, a hero indeed. As for Carlton St. Michael, our prayers are with him, as are the prayers of St. Mary and St. Luke. Back to you, Morgan."

Carlton used the remote to shut the TV off.

"That's all I need. Dead people praying for me."

"There's more. I think you should see." Lenny moved to push the button on the TV manually.

"Sorry, Lenny. I just don't think I can bear the smarmy emoting that will inevitably follow."

"Carlton, when they pray for you, it's just their way of wishing you well. They're not trying to provoke a theological debate. I mean, they're certainly not trying to insult you."

"Listen, I grew up with these people. They're all superstitious fools. Imagine the presumption of this kid. Shoving rosary beads in my pocket and asking Saints to pray for me!"

"Dude? You gotta chill out!" Chico chimed in. "The kid saved your life."

I liked Chico better when he looked confused.

"Yes, I'm grateful that he saved my life. Just keep God and prayers out of it!"

I glanced over at the priest in the other bed. He had his face buried behind a newspaper, but I imagined he smiled smugly, and it *irked my icicles* off.

"Carlton, you were run over by a truck that said, 'G.O.D.' on it, and the kid is on the news praying for you. You were dead for over twenty minutes..."

"Lenny, Lenny, I know where you're going with this. I was run over by a Guaranteed Overnight Delivery truck and revived by a kid who knows CPR. Prayer didn't have anything to do with it."

"I'm your manager, Carlton, and as your manager, I'm asking you to think about your act and about this accident. Can you continue to go on stage and rant about how the Catholic religion doesn't make any #?@!ing sense?"

"You're my manager, not my priest, for God's sake. You worry about making me rich and famous, and let me worry about my material and my soul."

I glanced again at the priest. He had put his newspaper down, perked to attention, his ears like those of a service dog noting some potential hazard, when I mentioned my soul. Perhaps, he would come slobbering over like a Saint Bernard with a cask of brandy around his neck? I could use a drink, but I had no need of dogs or saints. Perhaps, he thought the Hound of Heaven from that old poem my father used to read would be sniffing me out like a bloodhound. What else would a priest spend his time fantasizing about? He certainly would not fantasize about what I fantasized about. At least, I hoped not. But, then again, why would I give a crap?

"I'm talking business, not religion." Here comes the Lenny finger-wagging, like he's chastising his dummy. "Group-based mockery can get you a quick audience, but it's a dark audience, and things can quickly turn and then you're done. Remember Vinnie the Dateman? All those crude jokes about women? Priding himself on being a bad date? He was huge for a year, and now, he can't get work even trying to redefine himself."

Lenny was *licking my lollipop* off with that one. Vinnie the Dateman was a pig, and I resented the comparison. I put my good hand behind my head like I was yanking a string and let my mouth clap open and shut, and ended with it open, gawking like an idiot, letting my head list to one side. Lenny glared at me. He never got this frustrated with his dummies, but then he always knew what they were going to say.

"Sure, that's a concern. But women get offended and protest. Catholics? They pray for your soul. So, if they're right, the best thing I can do is make fun of them. I'll get more prayers that way."

Lenny gaped at me without speaking. I really pushed his buttons with the dummy imitation. I would have thought he would have been ready to throw his voice into my mouth.

"You're the guy who taught me how to write a routine around a theme, and to write what I know. That's all I'm doing. I know this Catholic crap, and everybody's making fun of them. Sure, it will cheese some people off, but that will be good publicity."

Lenny shrugged in exasperation. "I feel like Obi-Wan Kenobi warning about the dark side of the force."

"I really think you need to lighten up."

"Carlton, I'm not a religious man, but even I'm going to pray for you."

"Please don't."

I glanced over at the priest again. He kept his trap shut, but I could tell he was praying. "That goes for you, too, Father."

"What's that, my son?" The priest assumed that smug innocence pose that I always imagined they would have behind the screen of a confessional. But at least there, I would not have to look at it.

"No prayers for my soul," I glared at him.

The priest laughed. "Why should you be so concerned about people praying if you know there's no one there? I surmise that you are an atheist, but if your atheism is certain, why would you care? If you had doubts, you might welcome prayers in case you are wrong? Your attitude appears to be less than rational."

Now, having been run over by a G.O.D. truck and being doped up on meds, I really was not prepared to banter theology with a priest. I leaned my head back and looked up at the ceiling. "Just, no prayers for my soul, Padre. No St. Mary, no St. Luke, no Easter Bunny, no Santa Claus."

"How about St. Jude? Patron saint of hopeless causes?"

I couldn't think of anything snarky to say about the patron saint of hopeless causes, so I refocused on Lenny. "Please, Lenny, the act is fine. Even Father here would likely get a good laugh, if he let his guard down and snuck into the sacramental wine to loosen him up a bit. And, his only response would be to say some prayers to St. Jude, because I'm such a hopeless cause."

"Okay, but are you planning to work in a bit about that foolish kid who saved your life? Even the most dedicated atheists are liable to see that as ingratitude."

"Look, of course, I'm grateful. I wouldn't be human if I wasn't grateful that the kid saved my life. But there wasn't anything miraculous about what happened to me. A little boy scout who knew CPR and the good doctors here saved my life. It had nothing to do with rosary beads, St. Mary or St. Luke."

"Well, it would be much better publicity if it did."

"Just make sure they spell my name right."

Maury Stanowitz popped his head into the hospital room and spied us. Maury was a presence. A large, athletic man, with dark curly hair, a large mustache, and the gravelly voice of a gangster. He walked and talked with purpose and determination. He entered the room carrying his briefcase like a spy on a mission to disrupt an assassination plot, or to execute one.

"Well, looks like I've found the right place. Lenny, Chico, nice to see you."

Maury shook hands with Lenny and reached out his hand to Chico, but Chico offered him his elbow. Maury squinted suspiciously and pulled his hand up behind his head mimicking Chico. Chico awkwardly touched his elbow with his own. After shaking Maury's hand, Lenny wiped his hand on his shirt.

"Hi, uh, Maury." I said, "Chico's a germaphobe. He doesn't shake hands."

"Oh, guess that explains it. Surprised to find a germaphobe in a hospital. No place to find more germs than in a hospital."

Chico turned white with fear.

"Sorry, man, gotta go."

Chico hurried out the door.

"Now look what you've done!" Lenny said, shaking his head in dismay, "I had him up for a part in a sitcom playing a hospital orderly. No way he's doing that, now."

"Well, that's the problem with managing undeveloped talent. That's why I specialize in mature acts."

"More like, specialize in stealing clients. What are you doing here, anyway? Do you make a habit of skulking around hospitals, looking to steal clients while they're too doped up to know what's going on?"

"Carlton, you haven't told Lenny, yet?"

"Told me what? What's going on here?"

"Jesus, Lenny, I was going to tell you after the *Today Show* interview. Holy $#!!, I forgot all about it. I signed a contract with Maury." Now, I knew why I felt so sick seeing Lenny. I forgot that I had totally screwed him.

"You signed a contract with Maury? What do you mean, you signed a contract with Maury? When did this happen?"

"Well, it hasn't actually happened, yet." Maury laid his briefcase on the hospital serving table. "That's why I'm here. We completed our negotiations and Carlton was going to come to my office and sign the contract after the *The City, Today* interview. The papers are all drawn up."

Maury opened his briefcase and took out a contract.

Lenny glared at me. I felt like a rat. "How could you do this to me? After all I've done to get you this far, on the verge of hitting it big, you're dumping me?"

"Oh, Lenny, don't take it that way. It's just good business. Maury has the contacts and the influence to get me to the top. I appreciate all you've done for me. You're a dear friend to me, but you just don't have the juice to take me to the top."

"I can't believe this!"

"Oh, don't be like that! I need someone who is ruthless. Someone who will pull out all the stops to get me the best deals. Frankly, Lenny, you're too nice a guy for that."

"Too nice a guy? You think about that, sometime, when things get tough and you get shoveled to the bottom of his pile. Remember Vinnie the Dateman? Maury pushed that guy right to the top, and when things got hot, he dropped him. And, on the way down, all the established comics in his stable mocked him right out of the business. Is that really the kind of representation you want? That ruthlessness you want can go both ways, Carlton."

"Well, I guess we'll see what happens."

"We'll see what happens? If you sign that contract, that's it. There's no 'seeing what happens'. It's goodbye for good."

"I'm sorry you feel that way, Lenny. I'm signing with Maury."

"I'm outta here. Break a leg, Carlton."

Lenny left in a huff. I glanced at my cast. Break a leg? Been there, done that.

Maury's expression reflected about as much empathy as the brute was capable of. "Uh, on Vinnie the Dateman. Uh, his fifteen minutes of fame were up. He made all our other acts uncomfortable. The female acts couldn't stand him, and the male acts were hearing from their wives and daughters. I don't see that happening with your act. I don't think Catholics are so sensitive."

"Yeah, I tried to explain that to Lenny. That's why I have to make a change. He thinks I'm Darth Vader or something."

"You better not be. Darth Vader wasn't very funny."

I chuckled and felt the pain in my stitched incision. I was starting to like Maury, which scared me. He gave me the contract to sign. And sign, I did.

"Ok, Carlton. We'll start working the public relations angles right away. With all the free publicity you've gotten already, we should be riding high in no time."

"Just make me rich and famous."

Maury put the signed contract in his brief case and closed it.

"Will do, Carlton. Just rest and heal up. By the time you're out of here, you'll be well on your way to fame and fortune."

Maury shook my hand, and, after he left, I wiped my hand on the bed sheet. I was doing what I had to do, but man, I just didn't like hurting Lenny like that. We'd been through a lot together. When I first came to New York, all I knew about comedy was that it made you laugh, and I had some talent for making people laugh and a ridiculous backstory of a father trying to shoehorn me into some biblical parable. The guy had taught me how to build a theme into the routine, and have the whole thing work together for some ending payoff, rather than just getting laughs with disjointed gags. Even his dummies were themed, and when he came up with a new routine, it usually meant a new dummy and a new voice. The guy knew comedy and knew how to build an act that would have staying power, not just timely jokes that got stale. But, I had learned what I needed to learn from him, and now I needed to exploit what I had learned. And one thing Maury was good at? Exploiting. I looked up at the ceiling, then closed my eyes.

"Pretty tough business, show business?" The priest from the other bed was like an emotional sponge, soaking in any bit of pain. And then, he would wring it out and strain through it looking for some opportunity to sell his soap or drain cleaner or whatever. I fully expected a late-night infomercial for his new salvation brand soul cleaner.

"It's cutthroat, Father. I bet it's not as cutthroat as the Vatican, though."

"Oh, they don't cut throats at the Vatican. They mostly use poison. Less of a mess that way."

I glanced over at the priest. He grinned like a dog who had just peed on my leg. He was obviously another New Yorker with a sense of humor trapped in New Jersey. New Jersey comedy was all about baseball bats and brutal murders. They didn't use poison jokes in Jersey. I know, it sounds crazy, but it's just a sense you get when you're around comedy in the tri-state area. I was confident enough in my assessment to go with it.

"What the heck are you doing in Jersey, anyway?"

Father Murphy laughed. "Stationed here for my time in purgatory. Likely, not much different from you."

"Oh, no, Father. I'm not stationed anywhere. And I don't believe in purgatory. I was caught dead in Jersey. Now that I'm resurrected, I just need to cross over or go under that friggin' river and I'm back in my city and no stinking drunk blond will ever lure me back here, again."

"Next time, maybe a redhead?"

Could the priest have known that was an old Lenny joke, one from his gig on the Tonight Show, back when Carson ruled the late-night?

"That's an old joke, Father. And, not exactly one I would expect from a priest."

"I wasn't always a priest."

A couple of doctors walked into the room. I took a deep breath and turned my head to face them. The two of them wore those green pajamas doctors wear when they operate on people. I was relieved to see they weren't wearing those dopey hats they wear when they operate. One was taller than the other, but they both had grins that made them look more like soap opera doctors on a break than real doctors dealing with real illnesses. I wondered for a moment if they were prescribing themselves medication.

"Carlton!" the shorter doctor greeted me, "I'm Dr. Stein and this is Dr. Santangelo, we met you briefly in the emergency operating room. Well, how is our miracle man today?"

"Miracle man? Why would you call me that?"

"You were dead for over twenty minutes!" Dr. Santangelo gushed, "And look, you don't seem to have any neurological problems. In my line of work, that's a miracle."

"Now, come, come, Doctor. Don't be so humble. Isn't it more a testament to your good work?"

Dr. Santangelo looked over at Dr. Stein.

"Mr. St. Michael, Dr. Santangelo and I have discussed your case. We have never seen anyone recover so completely from the state you were in when you arrived. Between us, we have over fifty years of medical experience working on trauma cases. Medically speaking, we cannot fully explain why you are alive."

"Yes," Dr. Santangelo added, "you were gone, Mr. St. Michael. I thought there was no way to get you back. But we had to try. That kid worked so hard to keep you. He came with you in the ambulance and kept praying for you. We just couldn't give up."

"If it wasn't for that kid, you wouldn't be here. We would have given up and declared you dead." Dr. Stein had stopped smiling and shook his head.

"Are you sure it wasn't because of the Virgin Mary and St. Luke?" I replied sarcastically.

Doctor Santangelo glanced at Dr. Stein, then back at me. "Who can say?"

"All we know is that you were gone. I was about to record the time of death, and then you were back."

"Yes," Dr. Santangelo said, "you came all the way back and were conscious for a moment. I said that you were in God's hands, now."

"And, I said, 'Not His hands!'"

Dr. Santangelo and Dr. Stein looked at each other in astonishment.

"Come on, now!" I said, "You're men of science, aren't you?"

"As men of science," Dr. Stein said, "perhaps we are best able to know a miracle when we see one."

"I can see we are upsetting you." Dr. Santangelo nodded, as he began his turn toward the door. "We'll come back later and examine you."

The two doctors walked slowly out of the room, shaking their heads.

"Jesus Christ! Even my damn doctors are religious fanatics."

Father Murphy had been silently taking it all in. "You don't have to be a religious fanatic to believe in miracles."

"Was I talking to you, Father?"

"I'm sorry, I thought you were. Who were you talking to? Jesus Christ?"

I looked about. The priest and I were the only ones left in the room.

"I suppose I was talking to myself, or Jesus Christ. It's really the same thing, isn't it?"

"No, my son, it's not the same thing at all."

"Father, I'm really not in the mood. Please, just leave me alone." I looked back up at the ceiling.

"Mr. St. Michael?" I heard this high-pitched voice say, but I took no notice of her, annoyed to have yet another interruption of my ceiling watching.

"What is it now?"

"Hi, Mr. St. Michael, my name is Sharon Stewart. I'm a social worker assigned to the hospital."

I rolled my eyes and looked over to see an attractive young woman glancing down at her clipboard. She was another cute blond, dressed in a white nurse's dress, which highlighted her long, smooth legs. I was beginning to wonder if this were indeed a soap opera set? Beautiful women, goofball doctors talking miracles, screwball priest for a roommate, and that ridiculous drama with Maury and Lenny. Maybe one of the beautiful women would pull the divider for privacy and jump into bed with me, with the priest over there trying to sneak a peek? We were all set for a full-on soap opera scene, and I was ready. Bring on the blond! I looked up into that bright-eyed cherub face, surrounded by her wavy blond hair, and all my troubles just seemed to lighten up. Amazing, how that happens.

"Yes, Sharon, how nice to meet you."

"Mr. St. Michael, the nurse has reported that you may have an addiction to pain killers and has recommended counseling."

Well, I guess that puts a damper on my soap-opera expectations. Not likely we'll get a sneak-peek for the priest if we're talking addiction. I rolled my eyes.

"Oh boy, here we go again with the giving over your life to a higher power crap."

"Oh, so have you already been in rehab?"

"No, no. But I know all about it. I don't believe in any higher power, though."

"Well, that's okay. The program is voluntary. It's just a recommendation. We also have counseling available that doesn't involve a twelve-step group program."

"Oh, I thought the twelve-step program was the only way?"

"Well, it's the way that seems to work best, but there are other methods."

"Okay, I'm always interested in new methods. What would it involve?" This was a complete lie. I didn't care a wit about new methods of treating substance abuse, but I cared a good deal about talking with pretty blonds. It didn't matter much what the subject was. Except maybe, if it involved talking about a higher power.

"You could have one-on-one counseling with a psychiatrist to try to understand why you feel it necessary to self-medicate. The idea is if you remove the underlying pain, they can convince you that you don't need drugs anymore."

"And, how does the psychiatrist get an understanding of the underlying pain?"

"He will talk to you about your experiences and, perhaps, interpret your dreams."

"Interpret my dreams, huh, that might be interesting."

"So, would you like me to make an appointment for you?"

"Sure, but I'd really like to make an appointment with *you.*"

"An appointment with *me?*" Sharon looked confused. She shook her head a bit to clear the hair from her eyes.

"Sure, maybe for dinner sometime?"

"I'm sorry, Mr. St. Michael, I don't date patients."

"I won't always be a patient."

"I'm sorry, Mr. St. Michael. I don't think I'm interested."

"Why not?"

"I believe in a higher power."

Sharon turned and walked out, her clipboard under her arm.

"Another religious fanatic!"

"Yes, they seem to be everywhere. Next time try a redhead." Father Murphy tossed his two cents in.

"Was I talking to you, Father?" I stared at the ceiling, again.

7

Christmas in the Hospital

Sunday, Dec 25, 2011 - The Twentieth day

Christmas in the hospital! When they told me, I was giddy as a school kid on a snow day.

"I'm very sorry, Mr. St. Michael, but it looks like we can't get you home before Christmas." Dr. Santangelo delivered the news like a soap opera doctor diagnosing some exotic fatal condition to a handsome actor, while some beautiful nurse wept for fear she had slept with the dude before knowing what he had was catching.

"You mean I don't have to be around while all those idiots are ho-hoing, and exchanging gifts they know the other person won't like?" I once had one well-meaning Bible-believer give me a leather-bound King James Bible. I think he thought the sight of it would bring on some miracle conversion, that the Holy Spirit would descend from the heavens and drop a load of bird crap on my head or whatever. Hallelujah! Anointed by the Spirit! Now, let me at those heathens! The idiot had to know the last thing I wanted was a Bible.

The doctor looked at me strangely, like I had told him I was happy to be dying of the dreaded, exotic disease because it meant I wouldn't have to live with his sister anymore. Gotta love those hospital soaps.

"Well, yes, Mr. St. Michael, I guess. I mean, you will be staying here in the hospital, so if you would like visitors, they can come see you here."

"Just fine with me, Doc. Nobody I want to see on Christmas, anyway."

And there wasn't. Who would I want to see? My father? No way. The bastard had disowned me. He had felt called, he had told me, to deliver to me my share of the inheritance and sent me on a journey to a not so distant land, less than fifty miles then across a bridge into Manhattan, encouraging me to squander my birthright on loose living. He hoped that one day I would come to my senses, being in want from some famine or other calamity, so he could accept me back with open arms and throw some big party while my older brother brooded about how unfair it was. He had twisted the parable as a way to get rid of me. My brother would never brood, though, which the old man well knew. The dead don't brood. They just rot.

My brother died when I was eight years old, and he was ten. An act of God, they called it. That's what they called getting struck by lightning while riding your bicycle trying to get home before the storm. The new bike he had gotten for Christmas the previous year allowed him to shift down and keep peddling up the hill, while I had to push mine, not having the strength to keep up. If he hadn't waited for me at the top of that hill, he would not have been in so very wrong a place at so very wrong a time. Snippets of the memory still haunted me. I would see him at the top of the hill, urging me to hurry. But I had learned to repress it, so I would not have to relive that horrible moment.

Something so senseless and horrible had to be the work of the Almighty. But for me, it proved there was no Almighty. My father buried himself in faith to relieve his grief and did all he could to make me fear Him. But what God of love strikes a boy dead with a lightning bolt? Only a random, screwed-up universe did that. Or a God not worthy of worship.

But my father had not counted on me being clever enough to score a rent-controlled apartment under some dead dude's name and being funny enough to tell jokes for a living. Barely well enough, until now. Now I was on the verge of mocking his treasured church all the way to the top, represented by the top New York talent agency. Sure, he likely waited by the phone for me to call and invite him to Christmas dinner at the hospital beaten and broken, but he would be expecting repentance. And, that wasn't going to happen. If anything, the old man should repent for filling my stocking with coal and blaming it on Santa Claus. And, my mother, well, she was gone. Lenny, I yanked his yarmulke, so he was pretty *Hanukkahed* off, and he was a Jew, anyway. Maury? You've got to be kidding. Chico? Well, I wouldn't mind seeing Chico, but he had his own family and Christmas stuff to do.

No, I was looking forward to the perfect, atheist Christmas, in the hospital and alone. But something I could not explain and did not expect gnawed at me. I started feeling alone and left out like people should want to visit me on Christmas. But, why? Why would I feel that way? And why would they want to? For goodness sake, it was just another day, wasn't it? I'm an atheist. There was no God. There was no Christ. Sure, there may have been a Jesus, but why should I get all jollied up about his birthday? He was just a guy. Fully man. That fully God jive? That was all bull. So, what's the big deal?

I pushed that lonely feeling out of my mind. Stuck in the hospital, away from the kids, the presents, the reindeer, the churches, the Virgin Mother, the baby Jesus, the idiot shepherds, the three friggin' stooges, Moe, Larry and Curly bearing their gifts for the newborn brat. "Hey Moe, there he is, in the hay, nyuk, nyuk, nyuk." But, at least the little brat slept quietly in the hay. *Silent* Night, don't you know. The old fat idiot, with all the jingling bells and the ho-ho-hos and the Merry Friggin' Christmases? The thought of him gave me a headache. How did all that ruckus get mixed up with the silent night, anyway? Peace and quiet, in a warm hospital bed, reading back issues of Mad Magazine. The perfect atheist Christmas. Maybe, hanging out with that pretty Nurse Jameson, or that Bible-believing social worker Sharon what's-her-name, who wanted nothing to do with me. Get that hospital soap opera story going. Oh, crap, they even celebrated Christmas on those soap operas, didn't they? Maybe, there was no friggin' escaping it?

"There are some people who like to visit the sick on Christmas." Dr. Santangelo appeared all concerned and pitying. "They like to bring gifts and bring a little Christmas cheer to those who can't be at home for the holidays. Would you like us to put you on the list?"

"No, no, Doctor, please don't. I'm looking forward to being sidelined for Christmas. It's like a dream come true. Trust me."

The doctor left, shaking his head. Christmas is tough for atheists. We're trying to have a nice, peaceful normal day, and the whole freakin' world just closes up, bowing down to some superstitious nonsense, some ridiculous tradition. Imagine my father, trying to pull that con on me? Santa coming down the chimney? He must have thought I was an idiot. Especially because we didn't even have a chimney, just one of those high-efficiency natural gas fireplaces. He was the architect who designed it and knew full well it didn't require a chimney. Oh, he built a fake chimney onto the house, so it looked like we had one, just for aesthetics. It wasn't even in the place where the fireplace was and didn't connect to anything. It was all just for show. "But we don't have a real chimney, Pop? It just burns like a gas stove and doesn't need one."

He tried to cover up as best he could, "Well, I'm sure Santa will figure it out." Yeah, I'm sure. It wasn't Santa who filled my stocking with coal that year, you old bastard. It was you, and I always knew it. I might as well be in the hospital. No Santa, no elves, no reindeer, no tinsel, no mistletoe. Well, maybe I would miss the mistletoe? Oh, the sacrifices we make.

Well, having a quiet Christmas in the hospital was not so easy when you have a priest for a roommate. I mean, all day long, visitors coming and going, laughing it up and having a good old time. All the gift-giving and Christmas cheer, and none of the mistletoe. I desperately tried to keep my attention focused on my magazine, but it was just impossible.

"Merry Christmas, Father."

"Merry Christmas. Oh, thank you, you shouldn't have."

"Merry Christmas, Father Murphy."

"Merry Christmas, Father Murphy."

"Merry Christmas, Father Murphy."

Merry Friggin' Christmas, Father Friggin' Murphy!

So, then, this woman came in with her kid. She was a young mother, and a looker, so I looked. Yeah, the old babe-radar went to full alert. So, I looked past the green and red Christmas crap, and there was this hottie, blond with everything perfectly in the right places. I mean, this was the one you dream about catching under the mistletoe. But, man, it was hard to look past the Christmas in that outfit, the red dress, the green tights, and the little girl accessory she had with her, dressed up in the same way, like a mini version of herself. I mean, these two were the picture of what I can only call cute, which is a word I hate, but there was no other word for it. And, something about it just really *partridged my pear tree* off. It set off the cynical comedy reel of my mind, and in this company, I had to keep it in and keep my mouth shut.

"Merry Christmas, Father Murphy!" they said together, as if they rehearsed it, practicing to maximize the infernal cuteness of it.

"Oh, Merry Christmas! Aren't you two just darling in your Christmas dresses!"

"Thank-you, Father Murphy," they said in their sing-songy unison. I'm telling you, they must have practiced it.

"Little Angela made you a card." The mother handed the card to Father Murphy. I tried desperately to hear something sexy in that sweet motherly voice, but I just couldn't make it happen.

Little Angela gave Father Murphy the hand-drawn card, then described it. "You see, here's the Virgin Mary, and St. Joseph, and little baby Jesus."

I rolled my eyes and tried to focus on my magazine, but I couldn't. The scene of ultimate Christmas cuteness was playing out in my hospital room, and that old itch was screaming to be scratched. You know it's all real. The virgin birth. You met Jesus. He told you. And all the snideness and cynicism was rebelling against it, dying to spew forth from my mouth. Virgin birth? Not a chance! Did you see that babe? She didn't become a mother at the word of some angel! As much as I needed to scratch the itch, my soul rebelled. She was a mother, and I couldn't sustain her as a sex object. Not with that cute child with her. The frustration of not getting the thing sufficiently scratched, only made me more desperate to scratch it. I felt like my brain was about to explode, like an egg yolk busted up while still in the shell.

"Oh, Angela, you're so talented! Oh, I just love it!" Father Murphy spoke in that affected way people speak to children when they are praising them. I felt as though I was gagging, drowning in a sea of cuteness, and I could not escape. Trapped in my bed with my leg tied up and elevated. No way out.

"Thank-you, Father," Little Angela giggled. "See the dress that Santa gave me? Just like Mommy's."

Now, the thing about New Yorkers, we pretty much say whatever we have a mind to and don't really give a crap about what people think. But, I was in a hospital in Jersey, with Bible-believers who likely were connected with people who knew where bodies were buried because they had buried them. How hard would it be to end up a corpse in a barrel somewhere, likely under a river or some sinkhole in the Meadowlands if I grinched up Christmas for the wrong person? Even the gangsters here loved duping their kids for Christmas. But, the Santa lie people told kids, that was a madness button for me. That was the lie that set me off into a rage, every time. More than an itch now, I was burning like fire. I just wanted the infuriating scene to end. Santa gave you the dress? *Ho-ho* off! It was that hot mother of yours, kid, and she did it to make herself look better. So, all her friends could marvel at how damn cute she was. Little girl, you're just a friggin' handbag to her! Santa didn't give you $#!!!

Well, the Hallmark Christmas cuteness moment went on and on for an endless eternity as if time had slowed down and barely ticked ahead. Each syllable, another tormenting itch that needed scratching, cynical comic lines building within, needing to be expressed to bring the infernal scene back to reality. It wasn't that I didn't want to be rude. I just didn't want to *crush the candy canes* off any Jersey guys, especially while I was vulnerable. I couldn't even make it to the toilet and had to crap in a pan, how would I escape some Jersey Giovanni or whatever? I wanted to hold it all back, to keep it all in. It was all stuff to write into my act, and spout about in front of a safe, adult, New York audience, not stuff to blurt out in front of a child, a woman and a priest in friggin' New Jersey. If ever there were three groups some goombah wise-guy would want to protect, those were the three, other than some made-man or whatever. But, I was about to blow.

Finally, the two left.

"Good-bye, Father Murphy." They waved good-bye together in their choreographed cuteness. "Merry Christmas!"

"Merry Christmas." Father Murphy beamed his Christmas smile.

The two of them skipped, yes, that's right, they skipped out of the hospital room. I had survived it. I had made it to the end, the end of time, it seemed. I had suffered through the Christmas cuteness and had not spouted off and got myself killed in friggin' Jersey. It was finished. But the itch was still there. You know it's true. The virgin birth. Jesus told you. I didn't know anything of the kind. It was a stupid dream.

And then it happened, friggin' Santa came ho-ho-hoing into our room. If I wasn't strapped up in that ridiculous traction contraption, I would have gotten up and kicked his butt.

"Ho, ho, ho! Merry Christmas!"

"Merry Friggin' Christmas to you, you fat bastard! Go check your list twice! I'm on the naughty one, so leave me the #?@! alone!" I couldn't hold it back, anymore.

Santa did a double-take. His eyes widened, his mouth dropped open, and he dropped his bag to the floor. Sure, it was a look of recognition. The bastard knew me. Did I owe him money or something? I was in no condition to defend myself. Holy Moly, would he stab me with a scalpel or something? He walked to the side of the bed. Was this it? Would I be murdered in Jersey, stuffed in a barrel and tossed in the river? That was the kind of crap they did in Jersey. How would he get away with it with the priest in the next bed? Wouldn't he have to kill the priest, too? Hopefully, I hated that friggin' priest. The bastard fell on me with all his weight and I screamed, "Ahhhh!"

The man backed off and looked surprised and alarmed.

"Oh, sweet Jesus," he said, "did I hurt you, again? Oh, I'm so sorry. Maybe you don't recognize me? I'm Nicholas Penneymoore. I drove the truck that hit you."

Well, Merry Friggin' Christmas, Nicholas Friggin' Penneymoore! Holy Crapoli, imagine that. The sonofabitch that ran me over.

He fell to his knees and wept at the side of my bed. I didn't mind the weeping so much, but then he started praying.

"Lord, oh Lord, forgive me for what I done to this poor man! I was inattentive and careless. Help me to make up for what I done."

"Oh, for goodness sake, stop your damn praying." I rolled my eyes, in disgust.

"I'm so sorry, mister! I'm just so sorry," he blubbered, and hugged me, trapped as I was in my bed, with no escape.

"Ouch, ouch, ouch! You big oaf! I'm busted up and in pain, here!" It didn't really hurt that much, but I wanted the fool off me.

"Oh, I'm so sorry. How can I make it up to you?"

"You can't."

"Oh, but there has to be something I can do?"

"No, nothing. You screwed me, and I'll probably never walk again without a limp. There's nothing you can do about it."

"Well, mister, I can pray for you! I can always do that."

"You pray for me, you sonofabitch, and I'll hunt you down and kill you!"

"But I have to do something," the bearded fool begged.

Now, sometimes my mind went so quickly to meanness it scared me.

"Okay, I got it. Here's what you can do. You can shave off that ridiculous beard, and never play Santa Claus, again."

"What?" The man was totally devastated.

"You heard me. No more Santa. You want to make it up to me? That's the only way."

"But, I have to play Santa. That's what I do."

"Listen, buddy, you said you owed me. You do that, quit the Santa biz, and we're even."

Nicholas closed his eyes and shook his head. "You don't understand. I visit sick kids at Christmas time. I grow this beard year-round, and look like an idiot, so as it's real for them. They pull on my beard and can see it's real, so they think I'm the real Santa."

"Well, if you want to make it up to me, someone else will have to do that."

"Don't you see? Many of those kids are dying. If they can believe, even for a moment, that some mystical foolishness like Santa is real, maybe they can believe in heaven, and not be so scared when they die. I'm not doing it just because it's fun. It helps those poor kids. Oh, Mister, please, please don't make me stop."

I saw the tears in the old fool's eyes. A weirdly sad, perfect Santa, with a true flowing beard, plaintively begging me to allow him to continue doing something I had no real authority to deny to him. But, if I insisted, I knew he would shave his beard and never play Santa again. He felt that much guilt for running me over. Now, I've had a bug up my butt for a long time about lying to kids about Santa. Duping kids with that stupid fantasy? I thought it was just cruel. Eventually, they would be disappointed when they found out it wasn't true. But kids dying of cancer, or some other dread disease? Why not lie to them? Why not help to soften the touch of the bony finger of death for children who were dying? It was an argument an atheist could not disagree with. A child dying with the false hope of heaven and a loving God was surely better than a child facing the eternal blankness of oblivion. And, I, more than anyone else, had reason to believe that heaven was not a fantasy at all, yet I was demanding that this man stop giving these kids hope that heaven might be real because Santa was real?

For the first time, I saw myself as just as bad a moralist as a fire-and-brimstone preacher. Was I really the guy taking away the Christian punchbowl and ending the party that would soften the blow of death for kids with cancer? I took a deep breath. Part of me still wanted to make the fool suffer for what he had done to me, but a much larger part saw that it would be just plain meanness. All it would do would be to cause more suffering. There weren't any scales that could be balanced.

"Okay." I rolled my eyes in resignation. "You can keep doing the Santa thing. Just, don't pray for me. If I hear that you're praying for me, I'll come shave that damn thing off myself!"

8

Back to Normal

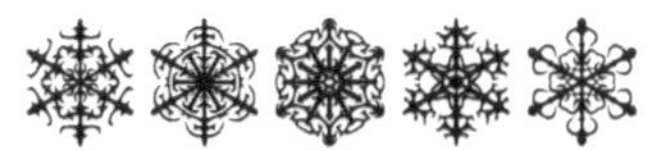

Well, I spent three weeks in that hospital recovering, which included my crazy Christmas visit with Mr. Nicholas Penneymoore. Now, four days after my Christmas in the hospital, it was time to go home. It had been easier to push the marching calendar of days to the back of my mind while I lay in the hospital and on painkillers. The merciless crossing off of days counting to forty, by which time the fat fantasy had said I would have to make a decision, continued whether I thought about it or not. Three weeks, more than halfway, spent in the hospital, trying to avoid running over in my mind those crazy events of my dream. I was happy to be alive and healthy, but the possibility began gnawing at me more, now that I would be released. Had I met Jesus? What about this Chesterton dude? He was a real guy. I saw him on television. Or, at least an actor playing him. I would have to look him up, just to see who he really was. He said things I could check, that stupid joke, for one. Love our neighbors and our enemies, because generally, they are the same people? What a tool, if he really said something like that. Well, I would just have to check it out. But for now, there I stood, leaning on my cane, a walking cast on my leg and my arm in a sling, looking like a survivor of a lost battle. Nurse Jameson was talking over the discharge instructions with me. She looked up from the checklist on her clipboard.

"Okay, Mr. St. Michael, you will need to use your cane for the next couple of months, even after they remove the cast. You had quite a bad break."

"You're telling me!" I tried to get her attention off the stupid checklist and onto me.

"Yes, well, it's quite a good break that you are even alive." She turned her head away then and looked back at her clipboard.

"I was only kidding." I could see she was the serious type and wasn't going for my silly jokes. I'm sure she had patients try to flirt with her all the time, so why should I be the exception? Gratitude was a better angle for the serious ones. "I'm very grateful for the care I've gotten here."

"Well, you're very welcome. Your friend Lenny made sure everything got handled for you. He really is a good friend." Sure, that worked, she looked right into my eyes, but man, why'd she have to bring up Lenny? I sighed, and Nurse Jameson looked puzzled but continued.

"You should continue using the sling on your arm for another two weeks or so. We have scheduled physical therapy for you and they will advise you on when you can stop using the cane and sling."

"Thank you very much. That physical therapy is torture, though."

Nurse Jameson smiled. I think she liked the idea of me being tortured. Was she that evil, scheming soap-opera nurse? "Well, my guess is that it beats the alternative."

"You're telling me! You know, I was dead for twenty minutes."

"Yes, you have been given a second chance. You should make the most of it." She looked back down at her clipboard.

"Oh, I plan to. I'm not letting any opportunities pass by. So, I was thinking..."

She was focused on her checklist, and finding another item, interrupted me. "Oh, and, one more thing. We have arranged an appointment for you with Dr. Freundheim, to evaluate a possible substance abuse problem."

Well, now that she thought I was a dope addict, there was not much hope. But, I kept swinging.

"I don't really think I have a problem with substance abuse, but I am looking forward to having my dreams interpreted."

"Well, Mr. St. Michael, I would take this substance abuse thing seriously, if I were you. It can really complicate things." Yeah, the serious types were not going for the dope addicts. But I kept swinging.

"I kind of like complications." I shrugged my shoulders.

"I don't think you'd like these kinds of complications." A knowing earnestness pervaded her speech, her blue eyes cutting into my soul. But I kept swinging.

"Why don't you join me for a drink sometime and we can discuss this further?"

"I'm sorry, Mr. St. Michael, I'm afraid that's not possible." She squinted at me with an intensity I did not understand.

"Why not? Don't date patients? I'm not a patient anymore."

She pulled the clipboard down to her side and spoke to me as if I were a foolish child. "I don't drink. I have a substance abuse problem. If you'd like, I could take you to a group meeting, maybe be your sponsor?"

"No, no. Just can't deal with that higher power stuff right now."

I didn't mind so much striking out when I went down swinging, but something about this one made me ache. It was like there was iron in her words and she had slapped me with them. And, worse, I felt I deserved to be slapped. I limped awkwardly on my cane, heading for the door.

"Good-luck, Mr. St. Michael. I'll pray for you," I heard her call from behind me.

"Please don't." I didn't turn around as I hobbled out of the hospital.

9

Psychiatrist Appointment

Fri, Dec 30, 2011 - The Twenty-fifth Day

So, life was back to normal. Home at last in my Greenwich Village Apartment. No more Jersey. No more hospital. No more nagging priest roommate. Just, a hobbled leg, an arm in a sling, and an appointment with a psychiatrist. Yes, well, I had to go up to midtown for that one, but I was looking forward to it, because life was anything but the normal it was supposed to be. I had an insane deadline looming, issued by a near-death hallucination that was driving me bonkers. That fat load Chesterton kept popping up in my mind. "You'll have forty days to make a decision." To decide what, exactly? To decide to believe that crazy vision was all real? Right. Like that's gonna happen. But, man, it bugged me. Maybe the psychiatrist could help shake me from this bull $#!! dream.

Dr. Freundheim, they had made my appointment with him from the hospital. I wondered if he took up psychiatry because his name contained the letters to spell. "Freud." Not sure I would go to a proctologist named Freundheim, unless my brains were in the wrong place. All I had to do was show up for the appointment, but, I had this queasiness in my stomach about visiting a shrink. My noodle was my business, and it needed to be a little cracked for me to be funny. I just had to get help with this crazy dream. That hot social worker said he could interpret my dreams, and why wouldn't I take the advice of a pretty young thing like that? Now, if she were some old hag with a wart on her nose... Who am I kidding? If she were Jack the Ripper, I'd have to see somebody about that crazy dream! That dude Nietzsche, coughing up ash and smoke for all eternity? Begging for a glass of water? Holy $#!!! But, what if this head shrinker decided I was insane and locked me up with the fruit cakes? I was a short step away from that on a good day. And that would lead to the moment my father was waiting for—the call from the hospital about the prodigal son in the nuthouse.

The journey to midtown was a long walk for a healthy person, but hobbling all that distance on a cane with my walking cast? Not a great idea. I called a cab and waited until the driver rang at the door.

"Taxi," the intercom speaker called out.

I pushed the speak button. "I'll be right down."

The elevator clanged and rattled its usual clunking way down to the lobby. I met the driver at the door, a skinny, young African American, whose eyes looked a little glazed and bloodshot. Likely some kind of drug user. Not a good sign. His eyes seemed to dart back and forth, searching for some hidden threat behind every possible hiding place. Cab driving in New York did not promote mental health, even if you weren't taking drugs.

"What happened to you?" The driver looked me up and down with suspicion. "Get hit by a truck?"

"You got it." I leaned forward on my cane. "Got killed by a truck in Jersey, but I came back."

Now, this spooked the driver. Sometimes I wish I could just keep my trap shut.

"Mister, you better get you another cab." He took a step back and glanced quickly over his shoulder, back at the cab waiting on the street. He looked ready to flee or possibly fight if I threatened him in any way.

I raised my hands slowly. "I didn't really die. My heart stopped, and they started it up again. There's nothing spooky about it. It helps me to deal with it when I joke about it."

"Ok, but just so you know, I got me a gun in the glovebox, and I take no chances with zombies. You get one in the brain, you tries anything."

I consciously struggled to keep my eyes focused respectfully on the cab driver, feeling a magnetic like pull in my orbital cavity toward the top of my head. Show disrespect to a nut-job like this and you would likely get shot. "Okay, I don't have time to wait for another taxi."

I limped to the car. The driver opened the door and watched suspiciously, giving me a wide berth. I slowly managed to get myself awkwardly into the car, given the limited use of my arm and leg. Zombies? Why not? I was dead for twenty minutes in Jersey, I guess that could make anyone a zombie. But, I hadn't noticed any urge to devour human flesh. At least, not yet.

I thought about Nurse Jameson, as the cab made its way up to midtown to 46th Street, stopping and going at all the lights. She looked right into me with those steely blue eyes, warning me about that substance abuse stuff. Did I have a problem? I didn't think so. At least, not with substances. My problem was this crazy dream. There was something about that woman that spooked me, though. I was never that serious about anything, not even death.

The cab came to a stop at the office building on 46th Street.

"That's twenty-three dollars, boss."

I leaned my body awkwardly, struggling to get my wallet from my hip pocket. A twinge of pain traveled down my shoulder, and I groaned.

"Whatchu doin' there, boss?" the driver asked, opening his glove box.

"Relax. Please just relax. I'm getting the money out of my pocket. It's not easy with a busted-up arm and cast on my leg."

"You just move yourself slowly, boss. You ain't bitin' me."

I rolled my eyes. I figured I could get the money easier once I got out of the car. I opened the door and struggled to get out.

"Where you goin' boss? You ain't paid yet."

"I can't get the money out of my pocket while I'm sitting. I have to stand up."

"You just keep those chompers away from me, you hear?"

I sighed and scooted my body awkwardly out the door. I leaned my cane against the cab and got two-twenties out of my wallet to pay. But something must have spooked the driver and he took off before I could pay him. My cane rattled onto the pavement and I limped to pick it up, shaking my head. I was getting a feeling like I was somehow not meant for this existence. Like, maybe I had not come all the way back and was in some weird space between life and death. Oh, that was madness. The shrink would interpret my dream and clear this mess up, once and for all. I wondered if other near-death survivors experienced this kind of thing. My instinct was to joke about it, but people did not seem ready for that. Somehow, I had to find a way to cope that would not get me shot in the head as a zombie.

I hobbled into the building and found the directory. Yeah, there it was. Dr. Freundheim, Psychiatrist, room 1720. That was pretty high. I wondered if anyone had ever jumped from there? I took the elevator up to the seventeenth floor, and half expected the doors to open to some weird alien planet or some other alternate plane. I was a bit relieved that the elevator would be ascending rather than descending. My imagination was out of control. It was not a good day to see a shrink.

I made my way to the waiting room and approached the receptionist's desk. The receptionist was a gum chewer whose name tag read Betty.

"Hi, Betty. I'm Carlton St. Michael. I have an appointment with Dr. Freundheim."

"Why are you calling me Betty?" She appeared more suspicious than confused.

"Oh, I'm sorry, I thought that was your name?"

"It *is* my name."

"Well, then, that's why I'm calling you that."

"Most people don't call me by my name."

"Oh, so what do they call you?"

"They call me Betty."

"Uh, okay, then, my name is Carlton St. Michael, and I have an appointment with Dr. Freundheim. Am I supposed to sign in or something?"

"Oh, yes, I see, you're Carlton St. Michael. I'm Betty. Please have a seat."

So, now I assumed that Dr. Freundheim must be one of those kindhearted psychiatrists who hires his patients. I looked about at the other patients in the waiting room. One dude, an older man, with a thin, scraggly gray beard unworthy of a Santa, kept sticking his finger in his ear and sticking out his tongue as if the pressure from his ear would force his tongue to come out. Another patient, a middle-aged woman, kept mumbling to herself, something about needing to feed her cats but having no mice to feed them. I had hoped to find some Woody-Allen like neurotics who might be a little less delusional, but I suppose mental illness is not like the movies. Or, maybe it's more like *One Flew Over the Cuckoo's Nest?* I supposed Nurse Ratchet would make an appearance soon.

The door from the doctor's area opened, and a middle-aged woman with short, dark hair smiled with a false pleasantness, in that okay-I-know-you're-all-nuts-just-don't-stab-me kind of way. She wore those nurse's pajamas that made me see her more as an inmate in an asylum than a nurse. Her green eyes seemed to shift back and forth, scanning for sudden threats. Nope, nothing like Nurse Ratchet.

"Carlton St. Michael?" She looked first toward the guy with the finger in his ear and tongue stuck out.

"That's me." I struggled to stand, using my cane for assistance.

"Ok, sir, just follow me."

She showed me into an examining room and motioned toward a couch.

"Please take a seat. The doctor will be with you shortly."

I nodded, careful not to make any sudden moves that might convince her I was bonkers. Man, what was I doing here? I looked around the examining room, which was set up to look like an ordinary room that might be in any normal house. The overly ordinary appearance made it more creepy. There were family pictures on the walls, interspersed with some wall art that you might find in Walmart. The room was carpeted, rather than having the clacking tiled floors of most doctor's offices or examining rooms. But, for all its attempts to pretend to be normal, the chair that sat close to the couch made it clear that this was a headshrinker's office, and despite all my efforts to act normal, I felt a dread fear that my head would be shrunk. The horror of my situation set in, as I realized my head probably *needed* to be shrunk. And it was not that big to begin with. The realization bridged the gap between knowing that bad medicine existed and knowing that I would soon be dosed. I scrunched my face, as I imagined the nasty taste of it.

The doctor came in, looking over my chart. He was a balding, graying man, tall and thin, with a neatly trimmed goatee. He wore a white lab coat and looked like he could have been called in from central casting at any moment to play some mad scientist in a low budget horror flick. Or, perhaps, he could have pulled off Sigmund Freud himself if you put round glasses on him and a cigar in his hand.

"Carlton St. Michael?" He looked up over his half-moon reading glasses. "I'm Dr. Freundheim."

"Pleased to meet you." I struggled up from the couch and extended my hand. I was relieved that he did not have some phony German accent. But, even his name, which I knew from my two years of high school German translated to "Friend Home," seemed a phony attempt to put me at ease. Man, I was getting to be about as paranoid as the zombie-hunting cab driver. And, if you act paranoid in this place, you might get locked up and never let out. Okay, so that was a paranoid thought, but wasn't that the point? I was freaking out.

The doctor shook my hand and looked at me suspiciously. He looked back down at his chart. "Please, Mr. St. Michael, have a seat."

The doctor motioned to the couch and I sat down, trying my best to look sane, but not knowing really how to do it. Which, ironically, likely was the best way to appear *insane,* but I could not stop myself.

"Am I supposed to lie down on the couch, like they do in Woody Allen movies?" I asked, like an idiot.

"If you would like. Just make yourself comfortable."

"I think I'll just sit, for now."

"So, your chart indicates that you may have a problem with pain medication, Vicodin, in particular."

"I really don't think I have a problem. I take a Vicodin with a glass of wine before I go on."

The doctor looked puzzled. Not a good sign.

"Go on? Go on what?"

"Go on stage. I'm a comedian."

"Oh, I see."

"But I really don't want to talk about that. I was wondering if you could help me make sense of a dream."

"A dream? Well, perhaps."

The doctor tilted his head and rubbed his goatee. I was quite certain he thought me a lunatic.

"Yes, well, I had this dream, see, that I went to heaven and met this guy there named Chesterton. And, well, when I woke up, I see this guy, Chesterton, on TV. Only it's not really him, it's an actor playing him. Chesterton died many years ago."

"I see."

"Yes, well, I had never heard of this guy, Chesterton, and well, I was wondering, could I have dreamed up a guy who actually lived but who I have never heard of?"

"I see, you met this guy in a dream, and then you found out he was a real person."

"Yes, yes. Is that possible?"

"Well, not exactly. The mind is a tricky thing, though. It tends to fill in gaps to make things make sense. Are you quite certain that you never heard of him?"

"Yes, yes, quite sure."

"You said that you saw him on television? Could you have seen him on TV before?"

"Well, I don't think so."

"How did you come to see him on TV when you awoke?"

"My roommate in the hospital, that damn priest, was watching him on TV."

"Well, there you have it. You probably picked up on him while you were sleeping. And who knows, you might have seen the program before while you were flipping channels and never consciously noticed him."

"Yes, yes! That must be it. I knew there had to be a rational explanation."

"There always is. Tell me, did this Chesterton say anything notable in your dream?"

"Yes, yes! He said that the Bible tells us to love our neighbors and our enemies because generally, they are the same people."

Dr. Freundheim chuckled. "Oh, that's quite amusing. Well, you said you were a comedian."

"That's not my joke; it's Chesterton's."

"I think you'll find that it is your joke. Check and see if Chesterton ever said such a thing."

"Yes, yes, I imagined the whole thing! That's really not my kind of joke, though."

"Our minds can do amazing things in our dreams."

"Yes, yes! Thank you, Doctor."

"You're very welcome. Now, how about that problem you are having with pain pills?"

"Pain pills? Oh, I don't have a problem with pain pills. I think you've cured me of the only problem I have. Thank you, Doctor, thank you so much!"

I shook the doctor's hand and beat it out of there.

10

Finding the Fat Boy

❅ ❆ ❅ ❆ ❅

Okay, so the shrink said to check out Chesterton, that my own noodle came up with that lame joke. Off to the New York Public Library. Check the fat bastard out. If he never said that stupid line, maybe I could put this trouble behind me. Just a short walk over to Fifth Avenue, a few streets over toward 42nd street. Sure, it was a bit painful limping along with my cane, but I loved walking in my city. Wandering along with my people, all the hustling and bustling. Well, you know, there used to be a lot more hustling on 42nd street, back in Lenny's day. I'd say it used to be the hedonistic center of the universe, just the place to forget about a guy like Chesterton and that stupid dream. The sex shops, the hookers, the live nude shows, but always also the library.

Yeah, the great lion statues of the library proudly gazed out across 5th Avenue, guarding the portal of knowledge against the encroaching prostitutes wandering by from the corner at 42nd street. Ah, the good-old days, before New York started electing Republicans as mayor, and the Disneyfication of Times Square. Now, it's all clean theaters and legitimate commerce. No more peep shows and live sex acts. No more Playland. But through it all, the New York Public Library remained, and still stood, now keeping watch against the cartoon mice and goofy dogs. And, I had a library card!

I limped on up the steps into the lion's den, confident that I would resolve this Chesterton hallucination once and for all. I struggled up to the librarian's desk, where a woman in her mid-fifties looked up at me over her reading glasses. Her hair was graying, and her face had begun its sagging and wrinkling, advancing as it would, to settle her into the most perfect image of a librarian, given another ten years or so. Her frame, thin and frail, and her reading glasses balanced on her pointed nose. She smirked as if she had known me as a child and would never expect to see me once I had graduated high school and was none too happy to see me now. Everything about her said, "SHHHHH!"

"Hi, I'd like to see all the books by G. K. Chesterton."

"Fiction or non-fiction?" she whispered, with an intimidating intensity.

"Well, my guess is that it is probably all fiction, why don't you show me them all?"

"Well, yes, why not just ask for a tour of the library? Are you at all familiar with Chesterton? He wrote essays, religious commentaries, literary commentaries, mystery novels, poetry, plays, and I believe he also did illustrations."

"Just show me the books!" I wasn't going to be intimidated by some middle-aged shush-monster.

"All of them?" she said, twisting her face skeptically, accentuating her not-yet-fully-librarian wrinkles. "Ok. Let's look them up."

The librarian typed something into the computer, and rolled her eyes, then shook her head, smirking again.

"Looks like the author search of the library holdings for Chesterton, G. K. returns two-hundred ninety-seven references as author, and ten as illustrator. You'll need to complete a call slip for each one you would like to see."

"Holy $#!!!" My volume was too loud for a library, but not quite a shout. "Prolific little bastard, wasn't he?"

"Shhh! Well, prolific, but not so little."

"Yeah, well, he's not so little, is he?"

"No, he wasn't. You talk like you know him personally?"

"Me? Oh, no. He's dead, you know. We had that in common for a while."

"What? You were dead?"

"Shhh!" I delighted in shushing the not-so-old bat. "Yes, I died and met him in heaven. Now, let's see those titles. I'm particularly interested in the ones on religion."

The librarian rolled her eyes. Sure, she thought I was a nut. But I was close to getting what I needed from her, so I didn't much care.

"Well, Chesterton poses a little bit of a problem there. We really don't have a way to limit the search by subject once it is limited by author. Typically, that's not a problem, but with Chesterton, well, he wrote so many different kinds of things..."

The librarian punched a few keys on the computer, and several pages printed off. She handed me the printed pages.

"There you go. Most of the holdings discussing religion are here, in Room 315. I think you'll be most interested in the ones with call numbers NCZ."

"Holy $#!!! There must be a hundred of them!"

"Shhh!" Oh, yes. There it was! The full librarian finger to the lips glaring and shushing. "Yeah, you met him in heaven!" she added, sarcastically.

I looked over the books. It would take a lifetime to look through them all!

"Jesus Christ! I'm looking for a single quote. Do you have a book of quotes of some kind?" I asked in an intense whisper, hoping to avoid another shushing.

The librarian tilted her head and smirked again. Or, maybe, she just always looked like she was smirking?

"Ah, well, if you're looking for a quote, why don't you search the web?"

"Holy $#!!, the internet! Why didn't I think of that?"

"Maybe, they don't have the internet in heaven?" Smirk, smirk! Yeah lady, why don't you go read a book? But really, I must have hit my noodle hard in the accident not to realize I could use the freakin' internet. I didn't have the internet on my phone like some people did these days, but I could easily have checked from my computer at home.

I glared at her. She chuckled to herself, in a most unlibrarianly way, and pointed over at a row of desks with computers on them.

"You may access the internet from the computers over there. But, you'd better be careful."

"Be careful? Why is that?"

"If you start reading Chesterton, you're liable to end up a Catholic."

"Don't worry. I'll stay away from his works in the Mysteries section."

"Oh, Chesterton wrote lots of mysteries."

"Yeah, I bet he did." I rolled my eyes. Mysteries!

I sat behind one of the computers and googled "love our neighbors and love our enemies". And, sure enough, there was his fat face, unkempt hair, bushy mustache like a rat on his upper lip, and those awful crooked teeth.

"Holy $#!!!" I exclaimed, much too loud for the library.

11

Back to the Psychiatrist

Well, I stormed, if limping on a cane can ever be considered storming, on back to that quack psychiatrist's office. "Oh, Carlton, I'm sure it's your joke." I told that idiot I wouldn't make a stupid joke like that. That's not an atheist joke. That's a Catholic joke if there ever was one, or at minimum Christian. I barged into the waiting room in time to catch him escorting the woman in search of mice for her cat out of the examining room. At least it wasn't the idiot with his finger in his ear. Some new psycho was in the waiting room, mumbling something unintelligible. He wore a navy blazer, dress shirt and gray slacks, and would have looked rather normal, if his eyes hadn't appeared to roll around like dice on a craps table, never quite settling down to snake-eyes. The man with his finger in his ear appeared to watch him intently, as if he had his last dollar on the pass line and a craps roll would send him to the poor house. I threw a print-out of the web article with Chesterton's face on it at Dr. Freundheim. The patients in the waiting room looked on, agitated. The mumbling man looked up at me blinking and fell silent, his mouth falling slackly open, his eyes settling into the feared two-craps. The man fingering his ear stuck out his tongue. A nervous quiet focus became palpable, as the mental patients seemed intent on hearing what I would say.

"He said it, Doctor!" Disdain and disgust colored my voice in the blood red and bilious green of an atheist's Christmas. "It wasn't my joke."

"Easy, easy, Mr. St. Michael. You're upsetting the other psychotics."

"I'm not a psychotic, Doctor! He said it!"

"Who said what?"

"Chesterton! He made that stupid joke about enemies and neighbors."

The mumbling man got all excited by this talk and seemed to piece together a special message delivered by God, or maybe that other fellow or one of his minions. "Yes, yes. My neighbor is my enemy. I must kill my neighbor."

The mumbler scrambled up and hurried out the door.

Dr. Freundheim shook his head. "Now look what you've done!" He took out his cell phone and speed dialed the police. "Harvey? Dr. Freundheim here. It's Mr. Howard. You better pick him up before he tries to kill Mrs. Hollander, again. Yeah, that's right. One of my other patients set him off. He'll likely use the squirt gun, but you'd best be careful. It's very real to him."

Dr. Freundheim hung up his cell phone and glared at me. "Now, Mr. St. Michael, what's all this about?"

"Dr. Freundheim, the fat bastard actually said it. Word-for-word, just like in my dream!"

Dr. Freundheim glanced at the piece of paper.

"Now, Mr. St. Michael. Please step into my office and let's discuss this."

I went with Dr. Freundheim back into the examining room.

"Please have a seat, Mr. St. Michael," Dr. Freundheim said, looking at the printout of the article I had thrown at him. "Okay, so he said it. So, what? You probably heard it on that show while you were half awake. You probably just forgot you overheard it. Maybe you picked it up from the TV while you were semiconscious? There's always a rational explanation."

"Yes, yes! That must be it!"

"Of course, there is always the possibility that St. Mary and St. Luke intervened to save your life. I mean, there is always an irrational explanation, as well."

My jaw dropped open in shock. I wondered for a moment if I had stumbled into some alternate reality where everybody was in the business of messing with my mind. It occurred to me that I was in positively the worst place to be having paranoid thoughts. I was certain Dr. Friend Home had a strait jacket stowed in some closet or compartment that would be readily accessed.

The doctor read my panicked appearance and sighed. "I saw the report on the news, Mr. St. Michael. The kid stuffed rosary beads in your pocket and prayed for the saints' intervention."

"Look, Doc, that's not funny! If it's true, I've got to change! Change the way I think about everything. Or, I'll be in hell with Nietzsche. If you had seen it, you wouldn't joke around."

"Nietzsche? In hell? That must have been some dream."

I realized I had said too much. I thought I saw the doctor glance toward the closet.

"Well, I often dream of German philosophers in hell. It really wasn't that unusual." I calmed myself and was the picture of nonchalance.

Dr. Freundheim shook his head and smiled. "Well, you did say you were a comedian. Only a comedian would think it was not unusual to dream of German philosophers in hell."

"Well, it's not only Germans. I once dreamed I tried to ride a log flume with Kierkegaard at Disney World. I think he was Danish. One of the great Danes. But they said they didn't allow dogs on the rides."

I suspected I had not improved my situation. The doctor looked at me like I was nuts. And he was an expert on pecans, almonds and fruitcakes for sure. He shook his head and looked down for a moment. I think he glanced under the desk.

"Mr. St. Michael, millions of people believe in irrational things without having a dream to provoke them into it. When we find rational explanations for events, they make us feel comfortable, like the world is working the way it should. But, things happen all the time where the rational explanation seems a bit of a stretch. People grab onto the rational because it makes them feel safe, like things are happening as expected, by rules we can understand. But that does not necessarily disprove the irrational explanation. It just gives us an alternative to believing in something that may be less predictable and more intentional. Things that are out of our control and yet intentional we find to be threatening, even menacing, if we don't trust the intelligence that is intentionally directing things. We may feel safer in a random chaotic universe, than in a more controlled moral universe, especially if we enjoy activities that may be morally questionable.

"But, some people have very strong beliefs in less rational explanations, like God is in control, and that ironically makes them feel safe, no matter what happens, as long as they live lives that they feel will be pleasing to God. Or, even if they don't, but trust that God is merciful and will forgive. But, which explanation is correct? Well, who can really say? Your experience in your dream is convincing you that there may be a God, and if there is, you expect he will not be pleased with how you have been living, is that correct?"

"Look, Doc, if there's a God, I mean, I was being pulled apart by demons in that friggin' dream! And, Jesus saved me. I can't believe any of that crap. But, if it's true? If it's real? I have to change everything. They told me I had forty days to make a decision. I don't even know what I'm supposed to decide!"

"Okay, so all you had told me before was that Chesterton was in your dream, and he was a real person. And then that Nietzsche was in hell. But, it sounds like you actually have had a profound near-death experience. Many people who have these kinds of experiences find meaning in them and respond by making major changes in their lives. The phenomenon is more common than you might think."

"But I don't want to make any changes! I want to be the person I was, the atheist, the comedian on the verge of stardom. Not some Bible-believing buffoon. I mean, it was just a dream, wasn't it? I shouldn't have to change, should I?"

"You could always just wait forty days and see what happens."

"Doctor, you are not helping!"

"I see I'm upsetting you. I did not mean to. The kid who saved you was pretty religious, correct? One of these Bible-Believers you have such disdain for?"

"Worse. He was a friggin' Catholic."

"That's right, stuck Rosary beads in your pocket. Very Catholic."

"I mean, who does that? Friggin' brat."

"Well, why don't you look him up? It might do you some good to thank him? Get his perspective? If he sounds like a religious nut to you, the rational explanation will seem more plausible. The more you can do to convince yourself that the dream was not real, that it could not be real, the less you will feel that you need to make changes because of the dream."

I reached into my pocket for the rosary beads the kid had given me. Why was I carrying them around with me, anyway? My instincts were right. I needed to disprove that crazy dream, find all the inconsistencies. But Chesterton was a real person who really said those dopey things. Of course, I could have picked it up from that stupid priest watching that television program. The accident, that was real. My friggin' busted up body, that was real. That idiot Nicholas Penneymoore, he was real. And the kid? The kid was real. He had saved my life. I should really thank him. Maybe if I made what was real more real, what was not real would be less real? That dream could not be real, but the rosary beads? They were real. I showed the rosary beads to Dr. Freundheim.

"You know, I've been carrying these around since the accident. Now, why would I do that? I'll go see the kid. I gotta give these back."

"Yes, yes, there's a good idea. You've been through a lot, Mr. St. Michael. These near-death experiences can be very disorienting, and even cause life-altering changes in perspective. Your mind will continue to try to piece things together and make things make sense. That's perfectly normal."

"Thank-you, Doctor. I'm sorry if I was disruptive. I just haven't been myself since the accident."

"Have you thought about getting help with your substance abuse problem? I think we can help you with that, as well."

"One problem at a time, Doctor. If I'm going to hell in a couple of weeks, I'm going to need all the painkillers I can get my hands on."

Yeah, so he looked at me like I was crazy. And, he was a guy who knows crazy, so I resolved to be more careful next time.

12

Returning the Beads

I had to go to Jersey to get to the kid's apartment. Going to Jersey for me was like going to that Nazi dentist from the movie *The Marathon Man* for a root canal.

"Is it safe?" I could hear the menacing German accent.

"Of course not, it's Jersey!"

The kid lived in a public housing apartment in Jersey City, easy enough to get to hopping the PATH train and burrowing under the Hudson, the same way I must have on the night before the accident with the tipsy blond. But, I wasn't going to the dizzy broad's apartment this time. I never did see a view of the Hudson from her place, so I'm pretty sure that was jive. But, if her place was near the church, likely the neighborhood was a bit safer. The part of Jersey City where the kid lived? Well, not so much. I took a cab from Journal Square and looked up at the building. I knew this would be a tough neighborhood, so I went in the morning when I would be less likely to find trouble. And it was December 31st, New Year's Eve. By afternoon, the entire region would be a zoo, especially Manhattan.

It was not cold for New York in December, but cold enough, and difficult to be adequately bundled up with my cast and sling. But what could be done? It promised to be a lot hotter in hell if that dream were real. No need to bundle up when you're breathing smoke and spitting up ash for all eternity. I took off my glove and buzzed the intercom for Mrs. King's apartment, then blew on my hand.

"Yes?" The woman's voice seemed pleasant enough.

"Uh, yes, Mrs. King? This is Carlton St. Michael. Your boy saved my life."

"Oh, yes, Mr. St. Michael. I'll buzz you in."

The door to the building remotely unlocked with a buzz. I entered the building and hobbled my way to the elevator. The elevator door opened, and a large African American man, doubly bundled up against the cold and hooded like a drug dealer exited. The guy could have ripped off my good arm and beat me to death with it before I would be able to dial 9 on my cell phone. He did a doubletake when he saw me.

"Ain't you that dude that got hit by the GOD truck?"

Being caught alive in Jersey was almost as bad as being caught dead. I wanted to be famous and recognized, but being famous for being run over by a GOD truck was not what I had in mind. I just wanted to find the kid and get this over with. Just, return the damn rosary beads and thank him, then get out of Jersey for good. My father was waiting some forty miles west of here, and I didn't want him getting any ideas that I was groveling my way home. I certainly was not in the mood for chitchat with strangers, but it was more dangerous to ignore him.

"Yes, sir. That was me," I said, as politely as I could manage.

"Well, that just dills my pickle! They said you was dead over twenty minutes. And that kid who lives right here, he done saved your life. Don't that beat all. Praise the Lord!"

Well, this guy was friendly enough, a southern kind of friendly from his accent. And he could easily put me back in the hospital if he had a mind to, so why did he *holly-jolly me* off so much? My instinct was to say something snarky, like, "well, praise my fat ass and frozen balls," and I had to hold myself back.

"Yes, praise the Lord." I turned my body to let him pass. I looked up at the big, hooded dude. Praise the Lord? Praise the doctors. Praise the hospital. Praise the kid. The Lord had nothing to do with it. The kid and the doctors saved me, not the Lord. It was just a stupid dream.

Looking past this first man, I saw another man passed out in the elevator behind him. A black man lay propped against the wall. He wore a similar hoodie but was not as large as the friendly southerner. His look of meanness and anger, even in his unconsciousness, struck me with the idea that he had not just passed out from booze or drugs, but had been assisted in some violent way to the land of dreams or nightmares. But I was in an alien place, wary of the possibility of violence, so most likely, it was just paranoia. I did not, however, feel safe riding the elevator with the guy laying there.

"Oh, you don't gots to worry about that brother. He's going to sleep for a while, I'd say."

I nodded and took a deep breath, as I stepped toward the elevator.

"Actually, you know, we should probably get him off the elevator, so he don't scare nobody. Let me get him out of there, for you."

The large hooded man dragged the limp body by the shoulders out of the elevator. Would he stuff him in a barrel and drop him in the river? He propped the man up on a chair in the lobby.

"There, he should be right comfy there. He should give you no trouble, now."

Something was totally off about this scene. I thought I would be the vulnerable one. A well-to-do white New Yorker, wandering into an almost entirely black, public housing building in friggin' Jersey? And, this guy, so polite, considerate, and respectful? I thought I was on another planet, or something.

"Thank you." I nodded.

"Merry Christmas, Mr. St. Michael."

It seemed odd that he would use my name, though I guessed he got it from the news reports. I hoped they spelled it right. I felt bad, though, that I thought the guy might kill me. I wondered if having died once, I was more worried about dying again.

"Merry Fri... Christmas," I returned the greeting. I almost added the Friggin' but thought better of it. He might be one of those psychos who could flip from friendly to fierce at the drop of a semi-dirty word. I just had to get this over with. I got in the elevator and took it up to the fifth floor. Talk to the kid, friggin' Dr. Freundheim. He's liable to get me killed.

I got to the kid's apartment and knocked on the door. The kid's mother answered.

"Yes?" she said, as she opened the door, keeping the inner chain locked. A look of recognition spread across her face. She closed the door, took the chain off, and opened it fully, with a big, toothy smile. She was an attractive woman, I guessed in her forties, with skin so dark that the whites of her eyes and teeth glared by contrast, giving an exaggerated level of joy to her expression.

"Oh, Mr. St. Michael? How are you doing?"

"Well, still limping around, but okay. Alive, thanks to your son."

"Yes, yes, that is good. What can I do for you?"

"Well, Mrs. King, I'd like to talk with David, thank him for saving my life, is all."

"Oh, yes, sure, sure. Come in. Where are my manners? David? Mr. St. Michael is here to see you."

The boy sheepishly peeked in from behind the doorway into the kitchen. He moved fully into the doorway.

"Yes, sir?"

"I'll give you your privacy." Mrs. King nodded and headed off to one of the bedrooms.

I looked the kid over. Hard to believe this little kid saved my life. He was small for his age and thin, but athletic.

"Well, uh, kid, uh, thank you for saving my life. Anyway, here, here are your rosary beads back."

For some reason, I felt like the servant from the parable returning the talent he had buried. That's not something an atheist should ever feel.

"No, no, Mister. You keep them. You're gonna need them more than me!" The kid waved his hand and shook his head.

"What's that supposed to mean?"

"I'm sorry, sir, I forgot my manners. You're very welcome. Please keep the rosary beads. You would honor me if you would keep them."

"Look, kid, I don't believe in God. These beads can't do me any good."

"Just because you don't believe in God, doesn't mean that He doesn't believe in you."

"Listen, kid, I don't need the beads. I came all the way to Jersey to return them. I don't want them. I wouldn't know how to use them."

"Well, mister, why don't you just keep them for a while? If there's no God, it can't hurt anything. Just do me a favor. I saved your life, I think you owe me that much. Just keep them forty days."

"Forty days? Forty days? Why forty days?"

"Jesus was in the desert without food or water for forty days. I'm just asking you to keep the beads in your pocket for forty days. Just do that, and you don't owe me anything."

"Well, okay, kid. But just for forty days. Then, I'm giving them back."

"Okay, mister, I'll see you in forty days."

I put the rosary beads back in my pocket and left. Why would this kid want me to keep his rosary beads? And what was with this forty days business?

13

Admitting a Problem

❋ ❋ ❋ ❋ ❋

I stomped as best I could in a walking cast out of the apartment, not waiting to exchange any pleasantries with the kid's mother. I was *red-nosed as a reindeered* off! I had come here to give the friggin' rosary beads back and thank the stupid kid. What did Dr. Freundheim say? If the kid seems crazy the dream will seem less real? Well, the little brat was nuts, alright, but the mysteriousness of his request made the creepy dream seem more real. Forty days? Keep the stupid beads for forty days? Make a decision in forty days? It was just creepy. And, I would have to come back to Jersey. Ugh! I guess I could just mail the beads to him. Just send them with a note. "The forty days are up." I would have to work hard to resist adding something snide. The kid did save my life. For most people, it would not be hard to be polite. Had that dream actually made me harder and coarser? The doctor said these near-death hallucinations might lead to major changes. Maybe it was making me more of an ungrateful, self-centered jerk? That's pretty major. I could deal with that, as long as the rich and famous part came through.

I made my way to the elevator and down to the lobby. The large friendly doubly bundled southern guy opened the door from outside and stepped in, filling the door so very little light could get past him. The eerie effect of his long shadow in the morning light made me shiver. He clapped his hands together, then rubbed them inside his gloves.

"New Jersey winters. Cold as hell!"

"It's not cold in hell. I've seen it. I know. Trust me." The memory of Nietzsche coughing up ash returned unwelcomed to my mind. "And, it's just as cold in New York."

"Don't I know it! How do you northerners deal with this?"

"Mostly, we have central heating."

"The big guy laughed. "So, did everything go okay with the kid?"

"No. The friggin' kid wouldn't take his rosary beads back. Told me to keep them for forty days. I'm going to mail them to him. No way I'm coming back to Jersey. No offense, but I hate it here."

"None taken. I hate it here, too. Especially the cold. No matter how much I bundle, my balls still freeze."

"Actually, it's been a mild winter." I thought of the kid playing soccer in December. Even in January, it was still mild enough for the little fool to knock me in the head, again. I winced at the memory. But, I was never coming back to Jersey. Never.

"Mild for you Yanks, maybe. Colder than a banker's heart on foreclosure day for us Southerners."

"If you hate it here, why do you stay?"

"Can't afford Manhattan so I'm staying here with a friend. I got business in the city. Research at the library. Just a couple bucks and that screeching train ride, and I'm in the greatest city in the world."

"You said it, brother."

"At least in the summer time. Ball freezin' cold in the winter, though."

I got a cab back to the PATH station, and limped in, using my cane to steady myself. The PATH train cars screeched and clattered and just plain *stuffed my stocking* off, as I waited for the train to arrive. I would have thought the sound would have been more welcome, since it was the sound that enabled my leaving Jersey, the place I never wanted to be caught dead in, again. Maybe, the sound irritated me so much because it reminded me that I had come here for nothing? Friggin' kid.

Take it from me, Carlton St. Michael, if you ever get a chance to go to New Jersey, don't. The screeching wreck of a beast came to a stop in front of me and the doors opened. My mind tried to put things together to make the dream less real. My hand in my jacket pocket, I fingered the rosary beads. Miserable, freezing Jersey, sure, it was real. But that guy at the elevator, clearing out that passed out man, and being so polite? The kid not taking the beads back? No, this screwball reality didn't make anything in the dream less real. I mean, it wasn't screwed up in some straight-out, nightmare-like, twilight zone way, it was just off. It was off enough that it made the dream seem more real. What was it that friggin' doctor said? We feel comfortable when things happen the way we expect? That's why we like rational explanations? Well, I expected that kid would take his stupid beads back, and I expected that big guy with the hood would have murdered me and stuffed me in a barrel just for being in that freakin' building. "Merry Christmas, Mr. St. Michael?" Really? From that behemoth of a man? Maybe his passed-out friend would have murdered me, if he were awake and the gentle giant wasn't there. I just don't expect guys like that to be researching crap at the library. Everything about this excursion to Jersey was unexpected. None of it reinforced a rational view of the world.

I struggled through the doors with my gimpy leg. My leg was killing me from all the walking. I took a seat near the door. The crowds that would be taking the PATH into the city for the New Year's celebration would not start until later in the afternoon. The PATH train made its less then comfortable way through Jersey City, under the Hudson River, and back to my city. I took it to Christopher Street. I had no intention of getting any closer to the great hole where the twin towers used to be, my least favorite place in Manhattan. I thought of that place whenever I rode the PATH, which wasn't often. The tomb of the unknown, or at least, unidentified. I wondered if it was better to die crushed under a Manhattan icon murdered by some terrorist bastards than to die in Jersey run over by a G.O.D. truck? I hadn't figured out what it really meant to die and stay dead yet, so I figured it didn't matter much. As I pulled myself up by the handrail to get off the train, my cell went off. I hobbled as fast as I could through the doors and answered it. Maury Stanowitz. I flipped the phone open.

"Hey Carlton," Maury said, in his gangster-like growl.

"Yes, Maury"

"*The City, Today* called. They want you to come on and talk about the accident."

"No, Maury, no way! I'm not interested in talking about the accident."

"They'd like you on tomorrow. It's a great opportunity."

"No way, not tomorrow, not next week, not ever!"

"Don't you think you owe them one since you missed the last interview because of the accident?"

"No, I don't believe I owe them anything! Just because I was in an accident on the way to their stupid show does not mean I'm obligated..."

"They really want to talk about it," Maury interrupted me. I felt a twinge of regret for screwing over Lenny for this prick.

"Listen, I don't want to talk about the accident, ever!"

"Come on, Carlton! They booked the kid. You can thank him for saving your life in front of millions of people."

"The kid? What do you mean, they booked the kid? I was just with the kid. When did this happen?"

"I just got the call. The kid's on for tomorrow."

"Tomorrow? Tomorrow's New Year's Day, Maury? Are you friggin' cracked? No, no way! I will not do a show with the kid. And tomorrow?

Don't they have some New Year's crap to blab about? Why freakin' tomorrow?"

"Wait, did you say you were with the kid? You shoulda told me. We could have gotten some free media."

"Maury, I don't want free media on this. It's personal. Look, the kid is friggin' crazy."

"Works even better if he's crazy. People can't take their eyes off crazy."

"Maury, I'm not going on any friggin' show with that kid."

"Carlton, baby, it will do wonders for your career!"

"I don't care what it will do for my career! Look, Maury, I'll do their damn show, but no kid! I'd rather have them talk to me than that crazy kid. You tell them no kid and not tomorrow. I'm going to be so hung-over tomorrow, I won't recover for a week. Tell them I'll do their friggin' show next week. After the new year. I need some time to think. But no friggin' kid!"

I hung up the phone. I looked around to get my bearings. I had managed to limp all the way to the doors of the PATH station while I talked with the putz. I pushed open the doors, I looked up the stairs and sighed. Not going to be fun climbing all these stairs with this stinking leg. Freakin' A. The last thing I wanted to do is go on television and talk about this. Thank God, oh, well, thank whatever, it was New Year's Eve. I had the best excuse ever for getting blind drunk, not that I really needed one. But, at least, I would have lots of company.

I struggled up the steps of the PATH station, wanting nothing more than to find the first bar, and just get loaded. But I was on friggin' Christopher Street and was in no mood to get hit on by gays. It wasn't even 11 am yet, so most of the bars weren't open anyway. I hobbled along and came to a package good store. A small place conveniently located near the PATH station, my guess is they did a great business serving people who didn't want to go to Jersey sober. If I hadn't gone so early, I would surely have stopped before I left. They had a nice variety of liquor and refrigerators with beer and white wine along the wall. But,

I did not look much further than the liquor. A surly looking woman with green spiked hair and a pierced nose sat behind the counter, eying me suspiciously. I found a pint of Jameson.

I stepped to the counter and paid the cashier. I opened it keeping it in the brown paper bag and took a swig.

"Hey, you can't drink that in here!" Little Miss Punkrocker spit the words out as if she were waiting to say them all her life.

"Oh, *sleigh* off, It's New Year's Eve. You gonna try to get me arrested for drinking in public? Good luck with that."

"Well, if you're gonna drink it here, you could at least offer me some."

I passed her the bottle, tilting my head. "A little early to be hitting the hard stuff, isn't it?"

She laughed and took a swig. "You be careful out there. Lots of amateurs drinking tonight. Nothing but trouble."

"I died in Jersey. I don't scare easy."

Yeah, well that spooked her. Nobody wants to party with some ghost, or zombie or whatever unnatural thing I was, especially not one coming from Jersey. Of course, I was just a guy who had a #?@!ed up near-death experience, with an edgy sense of humor and a need to joke about it. But, you gotta be at least a little weird to like jokes about death, and this one? Well, she was just pretending to be weird.

I turned and limped out the door back to the street. I felt the liquor going to my head. I hadn't eaten anything yet, having been on my failed mission to Jersey. Stupid kid. I still had the damn rosary beads in my pocket. I'll need them more than him? What the frig for?

New Year's Eve in Manhattan. The hoards had already begun descending on the island. Time Square would be the center of the one night only amateur show. The bad karaoke of drinking. The great commercial mess up in midtown. No, not for me. I can get plenty drunk on my own, and I needed to get drunk to put that bastard Chesterton and that stupid kid out of my mind. Not to mention Nietzsche and the pit of hell.

I made it to McGinty's, limping the whole way on my walking cast. I finished more than half the bottle on the way. I saw a homeless guy bundled up against the cold, seeking out tourists to beg from. Not doing too badly from the look of it.

"Happy New Year." I gave him what was left in the bottle.

"You giving me your leftovers?"

"Okay, I'll give it to someone else."

I grabbed to take back the bottle. He spun away with it.

"You trying to steal from me? This here's my bottle. Go get your own!"

"It's your bottle because I just gave it to you, and you acted like you didn't want it."

"You gave me nothing."

I closed my eyes. There's a reason these guys are homeless. Just let it go. "Merry Friggin' Christmas," I said.

"Happy #?@!ing New Year to you, jackass!"

New York, you gotta love the professional drinkers of New York. I wondered if amateur night wasn't a significant step up, even with the hordes of people from Jersey.

I stumbled on into McGinty's Tavern. I figured, if you're gonna get so drunk you can't speak, do it where they know where you live so they can call you a cab and get you home. It was early, so they had just opened for lunch. I sat at the bar and ordered a ham and cheese sandwich. I had planned to just settle in and go on a binge for the night, but something stopped me. Nurse Jameson popped into my mind. "I don't think you'd like these kinds of complications." Wasn't that what she said? It was freakin' haunting me. I thought about her, with those steadfast blue eyes, a deeper, kind of royal blue, not those twinkling light blue eyes, or even those somber gray eyes you see sometimes. And that seriousness. Like she had carried the weight of a cross to the top of a hill voluntarily and had hung on it to save the souls of many. I realized she had foiled my plan to get drunk. I wouldn't be able to do it, at least, not any more than I already had. I asked the bartender for the check.

I heard laughter. She entered the bar with friends, and I turned to see who it was. Oh, it wasn't ordinary laughter. No, it was piss-drunk laughter. My heart sank as I recognized her. What a crappy way to end a crappy year. I saw the look of recognition on her face. I closed my eyes. Would I have the strength for this? Lord, if I believed you were real, I would believe that this was a test. She laughed and staggered over. She smiled.

"Hey, I know you." Her words slurred as her deep blue eyes struggled to focus on me. She was ringing the stupid bell. The same stupid bell that started my misadventure with the blond leading to my first death. Ding, ding, ding! But, the dog didn't drool. Something was off.

"Yes, Nurse Jameson, you cared for me at the hospital."

"Yeah, Carlton St. Michael. The *miracle man.* Back from the dead. But don't give me that Nurse Jameson stuff. I'm Charlie, uh." She covered her mouth and belched. "Charlise, that is, but call me Charlie."

I closed my eyes for a moment. The serious woman, whose memory had just gotten me to put down my drink, was $#!!-faced here, on my home turf. I wondered what was wrong with me? I mean, wasn't this like manna from heaven? The woman who had smacked me down with her iron words was right here, drunk and vulnerable, very likely willing, and my only thought is how can I get her to a meeting? What did I know about getting someone to a friggin' AA meeting? And why did I want to, anyway?

"Well, hi Charlie, so good to see you again."

"Good to see you, miracle man, hah!" She covered her mouth, and turned her head, in that sloppy, inebriated way, that should be making me think of only one thing but wasn't.

"You know, I thought a lot about you since I was in the hospital."

"I've thought a lot about you, too!" she said, poking her finger into my chest.

"Uh, what I mean is, about having a substance abuse problem. You know, it is a complication I don't need."

She blinked a couple times. The deep blue of her eyes submerged beneath the pooling of her tears.

"I can't do it! I tell you, I can't. I tried. God help me, I tried."

"Can you help me find a meeting? I really need to stop."

She looked confused for a moment. She blinked, and a tear traced down the pale skin of her cheek.

"You need a meeting?" She seemed to sober up quickly, given a sense of mission. "Yeah, that's right. Vicodin, right. Yeah, probably booze too. We can start with AA. They have to have a meeting around here. Probably lots of people on New Year's Eve."

She took out a phone and attempted to focus on the display like it was some kind of hypnosis inducing tool. She managed to sloppily punch a few keys.

"There's one at St. Joseph's Church. It's not far."

"Nurse Jameson, will you come with me? I can't go alone. I really need your help."

"Of course, Mr. St. Michael. This is a very important step for you. It's not easy to recog—." she slurred her words, and stumbled on, "recognize you have a problem. Please, let me help you." She did her best to stand up straight.

A very important step. What the frig was wrong with me? I had successfully pulled the Clarence move on her from the all-time sappiest Christmas movie. I knew if I were drowning, she'd try to save me. And, she did. That's how I saved her. Yeah, sure. But, I'm no friggin' angel, so why did I do it?

Oh, I was willing to admit I had a problem, alright. But, I was pretty sure it was not booze or drugs. Something deep within me seemed to have gotten totally spun around. I had undergone some kind of near-death reboot and did not seem to be capable of being who I was, who I wanted to be. I had been fighting to hold onto who I had been, and that made me at times coarser and harder than I was or wanted to be. I thought I could live with that, but I couldn't maintain it. It was a reaction against this magnetic pull toward a moral reality of goodness I wanted nothing to do with but which I was powerless against.

I was swimming against a flood tide that would not allow me to go where I wanted to go, or be what I wanted to be, and I had exhausted myself and now was being carried with the current. I couldn't even get drunk on New Year's Eve! All the marvelous sinful pleasures that used to so delight me seemed to be just, well, wrong, and worse, I did not want to enjoy them anymore. And, let me tell you, bedding down this one, with those royal blue eyes, pale skin and tight body, that was a sinful pleasure to die for. And having died once, I knew a thing or two about what was worth dying for. But, I, Carlton St. Michael, was about to spend New Year's Eve at an AA meeting, so I could sober up a beautiful woman who by the look of it wanted to sleep with me, or at least would only need a little coaxing. The whole thing was unexplainable and infuriating. Sure, I most definitely would admit I had a problem.

14

Amateur Night

We left McGinty's and walked together in the mid-afternoon, New Year's Eve. She staggered against my arm, as I braced my walk with my cane, slowly making our way, just a couple of blocks to St. Joseph's Church. An old neo-classical building, with twin pillars in front, the place looked more like an ancient Greek temple than a Catholic church. I glanced at the church and chuckled to myself. If Lenny could see me now! New Year's Eve and I was going to Church. Charlie held onto my arm as we walked to the corner and waited for the light. Other people were crossing the avenue against the light, as there was a break in the traffic.

"It's clear, we can cross." She looked a bit confused.

"Yeah, I'm not taking chances these days. I don't move as fast as I used to." I tapped my cast with my cane.

She smiled and shook her head. "Oh, of course, I'm sorry, I forgot. That must be hard for you."

"Oh, believe me, that's the easy part. I'm still getting used to being formerly dead. You have no idea. But, I think we need to be extra careful tonight. Lots of drunks on the road. It's amateur night."

Charlie sighed. "Yeah, well, there are a lot of retired pros sitting this one out in the meeting, I'm sure." She pulled my arm closer. "I just want to warn you. These things can be a little weird. Like, emotional weird. People may try to hug you. Just stick close to me."

I let out an exasperated huff. Last thing I wanted was to be hugged by strangers. A pretty nurse? Sure. Strangers? No way. I felt the warmth of her body against mine, the softness of her through her winter clothing. She still believed she was helping me. I had to play along. But, something about it made me uneasy, like I should not continue deceiving her. How would I pull off a believable performance at an AA meeting?

The light changed, and we began to cross. I limped along, my cane on one side, the unsteady nurse holding me on the other. I looked over at her, just wanting to see those eyes again. I wondered if she knew the power of them, or if she was just being herself, without much awareness. Maybe they didn't have the effect on everyone that they had on me? But, as I looked again to those eyes, I no longer saw that iron seriousness. Nor, the unfocused, refocusing drunken flirting when I first saw her at the bar, this afternoon. Nor even the liquid sadness of her earlier despair.

No, a creeping slow-motion terror had replaced the cool, steely blue of them, and any of the other incarnations. I felt the firm push as she moved behind me and thrust me forward. As I staggered forward and fell onto the pavement, I heard a sickening thud and looked up to see her body bounce off the windshield and over the top of the speeding sedan that had run the light. The car never slowed and continued on its way to wherever it was going. I limped desperately to where she lay in the street.

"Charlie? Oh, Charlie. No! I was saving *you*. You, you can't save *me!*"

"Oh, you, okay?" Her last words, not more than a whisper.

I watched the light go out of those deep blue eyes, right there on that New York avenue. No, it's no better than dying in Jersey.

15

Cosmic Mojo

❄ ❄ ❄ ❄ ❄

Well, now that totally sucked. I had to be the biggest failure ever in the angel biz. Friggin' Clarence routine totally backfired! That girl did not deserve that, and I did not deserve to be saved. I should have pushed *her* out of the way and taken the hit. Jeez, I could have died happy in New York, instead of watching that beautiful woman die. Happy Friggin' New Year! Holy crap!

I didn't get out of bed on New Year's Day. I felt numb all over. What was I, some kind of motor vehicle magnet? Was every inattentive or drunk idiot behind the wheel just mindlessly honing in on my position? Friggin' legally in the crosswalk both times, can you imagine?

I had not been out late, especially not late for New Year's Eve, just long enough to give a statement for the cops. They had taken her to the hospital, though she was already dead at the scene. It's a strange thing, watching someone die, seeing the body release, and the person that was, just stop. Did she really go somewhere else when she died, like I did? Would the demons grab and claw at her, and drag her to hell, if she didn't call to Jesus for help like I had? It had to count for something that she died while saving me. What did I mean count for something? If you just die and there was nothing left of you, how can anything count for something? Maybe she had some kind of dream before she died like I must have had, but instead of waking up, the dream would just end? And then, there would be nothing. I hoped she had a pleasant dream.

My friggin' phone rang. I answered it. Maury.

"Hi, Maury."

"*You*, are a genius, Carlton!"

"What the frig are you talking about?"

"Delaying *The City, Today* interview to this week? Pure genius."

"Please, just leave me the frig alone. I feel like crap."

"It's New Year's Day, three quarters of the world feels like crap. But you? You have just pulled off a public relations coup the likes of which I have never seen. They're calling you the Miracle Man!"

"What the hell are you talking about? Who is calling me the Miracle Man?" I thought of Charlie. That's what she called me at the bar. It *melted my snowman* off that anybody else would call me that.

"It's all over the news! They found out you survived another car accident, and they looked up those doctors in Jersey. They called you the Miracle Man, and it stuck. Everybody's talking about it! You, my friend, the Miracle Man, are the number one item on all the local news stations in New York."

A sense of dread and anger built up within me. Me? The Miracle Man? I didn't even believe in miracles. The whole idea of them just *poinsettiaed me* off! Oh, I didn't mind when that sweet nurse drunk out of her mind called me that. It was endearing, and kind of a joke. But that random suck-ass accident, well, doesn't that friggin' prove there was no God and no miracles? What God would sacrifice that beautiful woman to save a sorry piece of crap like me? The same God that would hurl a lightning bolt at a kid on a bike? There just couldn't be a God like that. It made no sense.

"Maury, you gotta stop this. Issue a correction or something. That poor woman saved my life, throwing me ahead of her, so she took the hit. It was no friggin' miracle. It was a crazy, heroic thing to do. But it was not a friggin' miracle!"

"Carlton, baby, *you* have to clear it up! That humble routine will just knock them dead. You'll be bigger than Jesus Christ!"

"John Lennon already tried that, you idiot, remember what happened when he said that about the Beatles? Bigger than Jesus?"

"John Lennon never came back from the dead."

"Listen, I can't talk about this. I need to rest. I'm not sure I'm up to doing that damn *Today Show* interview, either."

"Brilliant! Let's take it away from them. Make them beg for it. You'll be bigger than ever!"

I took a deep breath. "I need to rest. I can't deal with this now. I watched that woman die for me. Do you know what that's like?"

"Yeah, Carlton, you just rest up. Let me take care of things. You are going straight to the top! Like a rocket, baby!"

"Good-bye, Maury." I hung up the phone.

Friggin' putz! Using that woman's death for publicity? I felt dirty. I took a shower and still felt dirty. I went back to bed, wishing I were more hung over. If I had kept drinking, if I had taken her home with me, she'd be here, and alive. If I had followed my sinful instincts, everybody would have won. But, I had to try to play Clarence the angel and got her friggin' killed. If there were a God, then I would have to consider this a test. Yeah, and if there were a God, boy, had he ever raised the stakes! Wow, wouldn't this one be the extra credit question on the test? Why God would let that woman die for me, and then, let Maury use the situation to maximize publicity? What kind of God would do that? The rational explanation? There wasn't a God, and it was all a big accident. The favorite refuge of the rationalist. Accidents and coincidences. Something about the whole thing just freakin' stunk. Either we have a God who's some kind of psychopath, or a random, stinking universe that crushes people without a thought. What kind of crap choice is that?

What would that fat jackass Chesterton say? Joking about holy manure? Was that what this was? God's holy manure meant to make me bear fruit? What a load of crap! Man, even witnessing that woman's death, I mean watching the freakin' life drain out of her, even that could not shake me from thinking about that stupid dream and that fat load Chesterton. My brain had some crossed wires or something from when they shocked me back to life. How was I connecting that freak accident, that woman saving me, with my near-death dream, and thinking they were somehow connected? Only religious people would believe that kind of cosmic mojo existed. Why was I trying to find meaning in these unconnected events, like there was some kind of theme, like life was some stupid work of literature, a fable with some moral? Wasn't it all some bull $#!! random accident, or string of accidents? Why was my brain trying to put two and two together to get four, when there was just a two and another two? Immutable elements, randomly doing whatever immutable elements do, killing one, leaving the other, bringing one back from the dead.

But, it wasn't random. She had raided the game, by pushing me out of the way. She saved me and sacrificed herself. It wasn't random. Not to her. It was purely intentional. I fell to my knees and started to weep.

"Charlie, what the frig! What the frig, Charlie!"

16

Funeral for a Friend

Mon, Jan 2, 2012 - The Twenty-eighth Day

There's nothing like death to take the jokes out of a comedian. If no one important ever said that, then I just did. Someone else's death, though. My own death didn't seem to bother me. I could joke all day about that one. But this Charlie thing, well, I couldn't make myself be funny any more than I could make that Catholic mother sexy when I was in the hospital. Some things didn't work together, even when you tried to force them.

I felt I had to go to her funeral. But it would not be easy. The media were staking it out, hoping to get a glimpse, perhaps a comment, from the Miracle Man. If I were going, I'd have to tell them I wasn't going, then sneak in. Otherwise, poor Charlie's funeral would be all about the Miracle Man, and not about the crazy, heroic woman who had saved me.

The phone rang. Friggin' Maury.

"Yes, Maury?"

"Carlton, baby! Hope you're feeling better."

"I feel like crap, Maury. I have a funeral to go to."

"Yeah, baby, I was hoping you'd go. They want to cover it."

"What the frig are you talking about? They want to cover it?"

"Yeah, you know, the Miracle Man pays his respects."

"Maury, you sonofabitch, if there is any news coverage of me at that poor woman's funeral, you're going to have to deal with the public relations fallout of me punching out a cameraman."

"Perfect! Righteous indignation against the press? Like a rocket, baby!"

"I can barely stand without a cane and I only have one good arm. It won't be much of a fight."

"Even better. If you get your butt kicked, there'll be more sympathy for you."

"I can't do it, Maury. I won't be there. Good-bye."

Friggin' putz! But, that's what I opted for when I screwed Lenny. Ruthlessness. Get me the best deals. Like a rocket. But using Charlie's death for publicity? Man, that was just too crass for me. And, there was no talking about friggin' Charlie without blubbering like a baby, and I wanted none of it. I'm sure that's exactly what Maury wanted. *If they cry, they buy.* If I could be the ruthless jerk I wanted to be, I'd have no problem with it. I just couldn't do it, though. The woman saved my life and her family deserved to pay their respects in peace. But, the scarcity made the media hounds want it more. When the press wanted something this much and couldn't get it, that was when they did crazy stuff like stake out funerals. That poor woman. She should have given her life to save someone who had nothing to do with show business.

I was reticent to even try to slip out of my apartment, for fear that they might be lurking somewhere. But, that was just paranoid. Catching me at the woman's funeral was news. Catching me at a coffee shop? Not so much. Not even the Miracle Man back from the dead could make drinking a latte exciting. My soul ached. All I wanted was to pay my respects to the woman who gave her life for me, like a normal human being. And, all the media wanted was a spectacle. Even at a funeral.

Death may take the jokes out of a comedian, but it held no power to remove the basest instincts of entertainment reporters. Death was their best friend.

My soul on the rockiest of ground, I had a funeral to crash. I set my mind to find a way. I had to sneak in to see Charlie off. Off to where? How would I slip the reporters and get in to pay my respects? Maury had made sure to ask them all to respect my privacy which meant for sure they would be staking out the funeral. They might be waiting just outside my door. Why did I feel I had to go? She was just gone. I mean, I didn't know the family? I couldn't console anybody. What could I possibly say to them? "I was with your daughter. I let her push me out of the way and get run over?" And the funeral would be at a church. A Catholic Church. In Jersey. St. Mary of the Immaculate Conception. Named for one of the infernal mysteries.

How could I sneak all the way there with a gimpy leg and bum arm? How could I hide any of it? I couldn't. If I were going to go, I would have to face them. The best thing to do was to skip it. What kind of miracle man would they think me if I skipped the funeral of the woman who saved my life? It was exactly the right move. Let them think I'm an ungrateful bum. It was better than a miracle man. Sorry, Charlie.

My phone rang. Lenny Friggin' Gold. The guy I had crapped on. Could things get any worse?

"Hi, Lenny."

"Carlton, I heard what happened. I feel awful."

"I'm sorry, man. I think I've hit bottom. I was trying to help that girl, and she saved my friggin' life. And now, I can't even make her funeral without being swarmed by vultures."

"You gotta go! Man up, for God's sake."

"If I step out of this place, I'll be limping along getting pecked to death. Better they just think I'm a total sleazeball. Maybe if there was a way to distract them or something."

"I can't have this conversation with you on the phone. I'm coming over."

An idea came to me. Would Lenny go for it?

"Lenny, do you still have that dummy, what did you call him, the one who was always on the make with the chicks?"

"Sure, Tony Tonelli. But that act is really stale."

"Just bring him along, and lay it on thick with any reporters you see. Make me out to be an ass who doesn't give a crap about the girl. And wear a hat and a scarf over your face so they can't see who you are and ski pants if you have them. It's cold outside."

"If I cover my face with a scarf, they'll think I'm some hack who can't let them see my lips."

Friggin' Lenny. Still so proud of his ventriloquist talent.

"Please, Lenny. You're the best. You don't have anything to prove."

"Yeah, well thanks for the gig, Carlton. It will be fun to be back in the game."

I watched the clock for half an hour, then the door buzzed.

"Hey, yo, Tony here, open up, goombah!"

Tony Tonelli, the dummy. I buzzed Lenny in. He came in with his hand up the dummy's butt.

"Yo, Yo, Yo! Watch where you puttin' dat finga!"

"Oh, sorry Tony, I thought you liked that kind of thing..."

"Bada Bing!" Lenny spun the dummy's head around.

Lenny took off his ridiculous, bright red and green plaid scarf, something I would never wear. His genuine, red Canadian tuque with the pom-pom on top was an even better choice. The hat either had a reindeer or a moose on the front, I couldn't tell which. "So, what's this all about? You never liked this act."

"That scarf is perfect, Lenny! And the hat. Is that a Bob or Doug Mackenzie?"

"My wife gave me them. That's what I get for marrying a gentile. She needles me at Christmas time."

I laughed. At least he had not called her a *shiksa*. He only called her that when he was mad at her.

"I need a diversion, Lenny. That act is so obnoxious, they will be sure to remember it. And, if you did your job right, they will start to believe I'm the jerk I am and not the miracle man they want me to be."

"Oh, no worries. They know for sure you're a jerk. Tony did not hold back."

Lenny moved the dummy's mouth. "My goombah, Carlton? No mooning for him over some frigid broad. Once they've gone cold, what's the point? Plenty more out there with a pulse."

Lenny was right. I hated that act. Almost as much as Vinnie the Dateman. But, I laughed, now. "The ski pants will fit over my cast. I'm going to walk out of here with that dummy and they'll never know who I am. And, that dummy is so rude, they won't want to chase me down for another conversation after you've drawn them away. You can do my voice, can't you?"

"I do you all the time when your back's turned."

"Please, Lenny, no gay jokes in front of the dummy."

Lenny laughed. "It's a mystery!" Lenny shrugged, like in my act.

"Yeah, yeah. Perfect. They'll never know the difference."

"It's hard to stay mad at you when the world keeps dumping karma on you. Run over by a truck, then watching that girl die? Man, sucks to be you."

"I don't believe in karma."

"How about *My Mother the Car?* Oh, well, I'm dating myself. You'll never get that reference."

"Now, when you go out there dressed as me, just act all pissy, like you came up here with your dummy and cheesed me off so much. Tell them you're going to find a blond. The brunettes keep dying on you, or something stupid like that. Just, make me out to be an ungrateful slimeball who would never go to some broad's funeral."

"I never figured you'd go soft on a skirt." The dummy winked.

I laughed. "What's your wife think of that dummy, anyway?"

"Forget about it! He don't let me nowhere near his wife! Jeez!"

"Remember, just make me out to be a real jerk, especially if they start calling you the Miracle Man."

"It will be a pleasure."

I watched from the window of the lobby as Lenny limped out of the door with my cane, my coat, my blue ski pants, my more sensible gray hat and black scarf over his face. I could tell the reporters were eating up as much ham as he could dish. Imagine, Lenny the good Jew, dishing out ham. They would think I was a total dirtbag once he was done. He walked a block to the corner and hailed a cab. I wore his black ski pants and red hat, the plaid scarf over my face, and took the dummy. I limped out and headed the other way as fast as I could, unsteadily without the cane and carrying the dummy, toward the PATH station and Jersey.

"So, you weren't able to cheer him up? Even with that dummy routine?" A reporter called from behind me.

I did my best Lenny, "Oy, the guy's a total pig!"

I couldn't move the dummy's mouth with my bad arm, so I just held him up without turning around and did my best Tony, "Yeah, but all the chicks just die for him! Bada Bing!"

I felt like an ass carrying a ventriloquist's dummy and wearing that ridiculous red hat and plaid scarf to a funeral. At least the ski pants were black. I got a cab from the Grove Street PATH Station to St. Mary of the Immaculate Conception Church.

There was a crowd at the church. I was hoping there wouldn't be. I glanced around for reporters. Yeah, some vultures had gathered, but would they really make a scene at a funeral? A funeral for a heroic woman who had sacrificed her life to save mine? Well, sure they would.

I hobbled out of the cab and up the steps to the church. It was cold, so I hoped the ski pants didn't look too out of place. I wanted to keep the scarf covering my face when I went into the church, but that would be too much, so I took the hat and scarf off once I got to the top of the steps. Immediately, I was confronted by a burly, gangster-looking guy in a well-tailored, dark, pinstriped suit. The guy looked a little like Tony Tonelli, only meaner, and I didn't suppose his head would spin around. I think he was sizing me up to make sure my body would fit into a barrel and figuring which point in the river would be the best to dump me. And beyond him, I saw the television news camera angle for a shot.

"Hey, that's him! You gotta lot of nerve showing up here? And, what's with the freakin' doll? You mocking me? You think dats funny or somethin'?"

"Sir, I mean no disrespect. The girl saved my life. I just want to pay my respects, in peace."

"What the frig was she doing with a piece of $#!! like you, anyway?"

"She was helping me. Taking me to a church. Listen, I didn't run her over. I was trying to help her. And, that's how she helped me. She was always helping people."

The man raised his fist to punch me in the face, but then let his fist drop. "Yeah, she was always helping people." He covered his face and walked quickly away.

I turned to the vulture with the camera and Vicki Knight, the reporter with the microphone. I recognized her from the coverage of my near-death experience. "Please, I just want to pay my respects in peace. Do you really want to disturb these good people at this heroic woman's funeral? Can't you give them a little privacy?"

The cameraman stopped filming. Whatever Vicki was about to say, she stopped and closed her mouth, lowering her microphone to her side.

I entered St. Mary of the Immaculate Conception Church and passed through the narthex into the nave. The blue and violet light gleamed through the great rose windows. I glanced to my right, and there the pieta, Our Lady of Sorrows, in anguish, held the great sacrifice of her son's body. I entered the last pew and knelt, not daring to go further into this space that seemed so inviting and yet so forbidding.

And there, in that church, with all its stained glass shimmering, with its golden pillars, with all the statues of saints and angels, with the Christmas wreaths still hanging and the creche still populated with animals, shepherds, the Immaculate Conception and the Son of God, and the great lamps hanging from the blue of the barrel vault ceiling high above, the same dull, flat deep blue of her eyes once their light had gone out, and the shimmer of blue from the stained glass of her lighted eyes, I sat in a pew in the last row, and wept.

17

Gastric Acid Trip

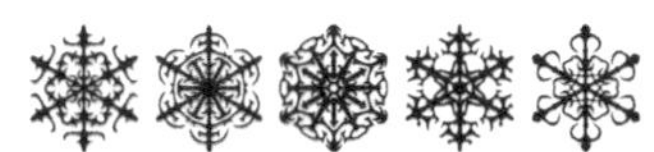

Another restless night, how would I survive this? You would think the resurrected would have more resilience, but I was exhausted, and could not sleep. If the world turned aimlessly, why did anything matter? We all lived. We all died. Why not end run down by a drunk on 6th Avenue in front of a church, saving some worthless comedian? Hadn't I gotten the good end of the deal? Survival? If survival was all that mattered, why wasn't I elated that the foolish girl had thrown me clear and sacrificed herself? Wasn't that what my philosophy added up to? I had more days to eat, drink and be merry. So what if she didn't? But it bugged the crap out of me because of the injustice of it. But why did I expect justice? Why did I look for someone to blame? If I blamed anyone, I should blame the drunk. But, I didn't. I blamed God. Which made no sense. Because I didn't believe in God.

But my moral and spiritual turmoil were not the only factors contributing to my insomnia. Anxiety about the cosmic countdown I was facing, and my big show biz breakout converged in some gastric acid trip bathing my mind in a bilious green vomit. Were I to sleep, I feared I might just dream of vomiting my brains out through my nostrils. How would I be able to do that stinking *Today Show* interview? I was psychologically and emotionally a mess. Maury tried to jerk them around a bit, but I knew he would never actually cancel it. I had to suck it up and get it done. The show must go on, and all that crap. Anyway, I had to clear up this Miracle Man business. There were no miracles. But the more I told myself that, the more something in my rebooted soul objected. *You met Jesus in heaven. You came back after being dead for twenty minutes. How can you say there were no miracles?* My grief overwhelmed my anger, though, and I just felt numb. If there was a God, he was screwing me, that was for sure. If there wasn't, well there was a lot of stuff that was hard to explain. That freakin' dream. Coming back from the dead. Chesterton. Nietzsche. That friggin' kid and his friggin' rosary beads. Charlie saving me, even meeting her at McGinty's. Why had she gone there on New Year's Eve? She fell off the wagon and showed up drunk right there, at my local hangout? So, I could try to save her? What were the chances of that? *I knew if I were drowning, you'd try to save me, and that's how I saved you.* Clarence's words rang in my ears. I marveled at the cosmic jujitsu of the idea. Had she come there to save me, using the friggin' Clarence trick, the same trick I thought I was using on her? How could a random, screwed-up universe pull off that twilight zone $#!!?

These were all serious things, and I could never really be serious about anything. Sure, I was biting and cynical, and you had to be a bit serious in an edgy, comic way to pull that off, but it was all about the laugh. I didn't want to be serious about anything. That would be bad for business. How serious can anything be, if the universe was some random, cosmic accident? If life was just a brutal game of survival of the fittest, why did we get so wrapped up in this moral battle of right and wrong, of justice and injustice, of good and evil? If nothing mattered but survival and passing on your genes to the next generation, why would we try to make sense of anything else? Why was I trying so desperately to make sense of things, if the answer was that simple? Why wasn't I all-consumingly focused on that biological imperative, like most animals seem to be?

I wanted to joke about everything. To show how silly it was to believe in God. But why was that important to my survival and procreation? I wasn't following what I claimed to be the model for the scientific view of the meaning of life. I wasn't dedicating all my efforts to survival and procreation. I didn't want to pass on my genes to some large number of screaming brats, who I would find insufferably annoying. I wanted to understand things, to make the chaotic universe make sense, even if it didn't. And, I could not stop my mind from trying to piece all these events together like some cosmic jigsaw puzzle, to get them to fit into some kind of meaningful plan, rather than a series of wildly random coincidences.

I died in Jersey, run over by a Guaranteed Overnight Delivery truck. She died on 6th Avenue, run over by some random drunk. They were chaotic random events, nothing more. It's just random coincidence. But, somehow, my mind saw them as a test. Part of some great cosmic plan. Isn't that what the psychiatrist said, though? That my mind would continue to try to make sense of things? Didn't he say that was perfectly normal? Wasn't that exactly what I was doing? My mind was forcing some connection between things. Making sense where there was no sense. Finding some mysterious connection. A mystery! Still steaming with no discernible smell. Well, I'd say the whole thing stunk. Colonel Mustard in the living room with a candlestick. Maybe it was something I could figure out? Maybe, it was that kind of mystery, not the Catholic kind of mystery? The fat guy from my dream. Wasn't he the key?

And, then, Clarence, again, "You're not going to like it, George...She's just about to close up the library! Oh, there must be some easier way for me to get my wings!"

The New York Public Library. And, I had a card.

18

Forty Books

✸ ✸ ✸ ✸ ✸

The New York public library has two hundred ninety-seven books by the fat know-it-all, and I wanted them all. The cart was full. I could not have fit another book in it. And, it was heavy. In my hobbled condition, it was hard to push. I wheeled it up to the counter. Every work by G. K. Chesterton I could find, brimming over the edges. The librarian looked up at me from her desk.

"Uh, what are you doing with all those books?"

"I'd like to check them out."

"You can't check out all those books at the same time!" she said, her voice most definitely above library volume.

"Shhh! Why not?"

"The limit is forty."

"Forty? Why forty?"

"Why not forty? You got something against forty? You can only read one at a time, you know."

"Okay, okay, give me the top forty. One for each day Jesus was in the desert. Why does that keep coming up?"

"It's a mystery," the librarian said, with that same ridiculous shrug I used in my act.

The librarian took pity on me and let me borrow the cart. Even with just forty of the books, the cart was heavy for a guy with a gimpy leg and a bum arm. I pushed the cart through the doors and glanced down from the top of the steps at the statue of the lion. Yeah, I'm taking the friggin' books, what are you going to do about it? The lion didn't seem to care. He didn't look all that intimidating either, considering I was talking to his butt.

I looked down the many brown, marbled steps that descended to Fifth Avenue. How the frig was I going to wheel that cart down the steps? The steps were about half as steep as typical steps, so for a normal person, they wouldn't be much of a problem. But, I'm limping in a walking cast, with my arm in a sling. I looked back over at the lion. I'm taking the books, rock-butt! You can't stop me. I pushed the cart forward and let the front wheels clack onto the next step, but the rear wheels were now in the air touching nothing as the cart teetered on the edge of the step. I slid the cart forward until the rear wheels were on the upper step, and the front wheels were beginning to descend the next step. From this position, I had to support the whole weight of the cart. I leaned back and strained, but the walking cast was sliding forward, unable to get a firm hold on the smooth step. The cart was about to pull me down the steps if I didn't let the damn thing go. I looked in panic at the lion. The mother mooned me! I had no choice, I had to let go, or I was going back to the hospital or would be dead in front of a Manhattan icon. At least I'm not in Jersey. But, I didn't think it was worth dying to save the fat bastard's books, so I let them go and fell back on the steps. I closed my eyes. I did not want to watch the top forty Chesterton books careen down the steps and into 5th Avenue. I was surprised when they didn't make a sound. I opened my eyes to see the hulking figure of the man I had met in Jersey, doubly bundled against the cold, holding the cart from the front.

"Mister, you live dangerously." he grinned.

"Holy $#!!! I thought they were going down, for sure!"

"I'm thinking I just saved your life, as much as that kid did. 'Cuz, if you'd fallen with the books, well that'd be bad, but if you'd ruined all those books, that little old librarian? She'd beat you to death with a ruler."

"Or, maybe death by a thousand paper cuts."

"Did you know there's a handicap ramp at the 42nd Street entrance?"

Well if I had known that, wouldn't I have gone that way? It *wrinkled my wrapping paper* off that this guy from Jersey was telling me something I didn't know about my city. But I was polite. "Why, no. I didn't know that. I always like to come in by the lions."

"Patience and Fortitude, the library lions. But you can't get past lions easily in a wheelchair."

"Or, with a cart full of books."

"Let me help you get these down safely."

"Thank you."

The man had little trouble getting the books down the steps for me.

"So, where you off to with all them books?" he asked.

"I gotta get to my apartment in the Village."

"You ain't making it that far, not with that bum leg and all those books."

"I was going to take a cab."

He looked at one of the books. "Mr. G. K. Chesterton. Friend, you read all them books, you gonna be Catholic, for sure."

Well, I needed this guy's help getting the books down, but now he was just *roasting my chestnuts* off. On an open fire, no less.

"No, not me. I'm an atheist. Nobody's making a Catholic out of me."

The man laughed. "I used to say the same thing, except, I was a Baptist. Nobody would make no Catholic out of me! And yet, Catholic I am. My daddy still don't talk to me." He shook his head and smiled, extending his hand, "Mr. J.C. Wiley, former Baptist preacher."

"Carlton St. Michael, Comedian." I said extending my hand. His hand swallowed mine like a shark eating a guppy.

"Yeah, I suppose you are a comedian." He laughed. "You go hail a cab, I'll help get the books in for you. If I try to hail a cab for you, you ain't never getting home."

I hailed a cab and he helped me load the books and cart into the trunk.

"Thanks for your help, J.C., I can't thank you enough."

He shook my hand, again. "You read them books, Mr. Carlton St. Michael, and you see if you don't end up Catholic. That's what done it for me."

I got in the cab. As it drove off toward home, I hoped I'd never have to see Mr. J.C. Wiley, again.

19

Confronting Chesterton

Imanaged with difficulty to limp into my building and get the books up to my apartment. My leg and shoulder ached. But, I was determined to figure out just who this G. K. Chesterton was. End up Catholic? Maybe, if you start off Baptist. But I know Catholics. And I know they're full of bull. My dear old daddy had forced that crap into my brain as soon as I could think. And, Pop, he was a traditionalist. No watered down, Vatican II, touchy-feely, self-discovery Catholicism for him. Oh, no. The Baltimore Catechism, all the questions and answers succinctly laid out. He quizzed me on them every week.

I pushed the cart full of books through the living room on the hardwood floor, then the right-side wheels hopped onto the braided oval rug beneath the coffee table. I pushed the cart past the table, and awkwardly maneuvered my casted leg between the coffee table and the cart and settled into the recliner, then turned on the reading lamp. I glanced at the flat screen television set and recalled seeing Chesterton on that program at the hospital. Could I really have picked up so much detail while I was in a coma? To see him in my dream and recognize him when I saw him later on TV? And, that stupid joke? Did it really make sense that I picked that up? I took out a book and examined it. It looked like an ordinary book. Nothing special about it. Just words. He was supposed to be the funniest guy in heaven, but most of these books did not look funny at all. Okay, fat boy, let's see what you got! I scuffed my cast on the rug, as I pushed the recliner back.

The first book I picked up, *Orthodoxy.* It seemed a good place to start. I opened the book to a page at random and started to read. I swear, I could hear the fat jerk's voice in my head.

> I did try to found a heresy of my own, and when I put the last touches to it, I discovered that it was orthodoxy. I have kept my truths but I have discovered not that they were not truths, but simply that they were not mine. When I fancied that I stood alone, I was really in the ridiculous position of being backed up by all of Christendom.

Well, that gave some perspective. The superstitious fool started out trying to construct a religion. I picked up a book: *The Thing: Why I Am a Catholic:*

> Ours is at this moment the most rational of all religions. It is even, in a sense, the most rationalistic of all religions...A convinced Catholic is easily the most hard-headed and logical person walking about the world today.

I looked up from the book. What the hell was he talking about? Catholics believed in all that superstitious nonsense. They weren't logical at all! The closest they got to logic was a bunch of ready-made answers to questions they chose to ask. I got quizzed on them every week. Miracles and saints, guardian angels and apparitions in French toast. It was all a lot of bull!

I flipped some pages and read on.

> FREETHINKERS are occasionally thoughtful, though never free. In the modern world of the West, at any rate, they seem always to be tied to the treadmill of a materialist and monist cosmos...As a matter of fact, we are the freer of the two; as there is scarcely any evidence, natural or preternatural, that cannot be accepted as fitting into our system somewhere; whereas the materialist cannot fit the most minute miracle into his system anywhere.

Miracles! Superstitious nonsense! When things didn't make sense, it was a miracle. Or, it was a mystery. Atheists didn't call things miracles. We just said we didn't know until we'd figured it out. Catholics were free to call it a miracle. We were free to say we didn't understand it, yet. But, it could be understood. That was the point. It was not some unfathomable mystery. We don't fit miracles into our system because miracles don't happen. What else did we have here? I picked up another book, *The Well and the Shallows,* and began to read.

> I do not feel any contempt for an atheist, who is often a man limited and constrained by his own logic to a very sad simplification.

Well, I feel contempt for you, fat boy! Something deeper within me pondered a little more, though, after my initial snarkiness. Did he have a point? Had I been oversimplifying things? Had I been judging the solidity of something by the obvious scratches on the surface? Had I satisfied myself that I knew something, and looked no further, because it was uncomfortable to deal with the complexity and easier to just dismiss it and move on? Was he talking about something more than memorizing answers to questions? I picked up another book, *A Handful of Authors,* and read some more.

> A strange fanaticism fills our time: the fanatical hatred of morality, especially of Christian morality.

I looked up from the book. I don't hate your morality. I hate your hypocrisy! You talk a good game, but you're just as sinful as everybody else. A Bible verse came to mind. *For all have sinned and fallen short of the glory of God.* And the words of Jesus. *I have not come to call the righteous, but sinners to repent.* I picked up another book, *What's Wrong with the World,* and resumed reading.

> The Christian ideal has not been tried and found wanting, it has been found difficult and left untried.

I shut the book and looked up. You know, come to think of it, I do hate your morality. Who the hell are you to tell people how to live? I picked up another book of essays and read, *Why I Am a Catholic.*

> Nine out of ten of what we call new ideas are simply old mistakes. The Catholic Church has for one of her chief duties that of preventing people from making those old mistakes, from making them over and over again forever, as people always do if they are left to themselves.

Well, what about science? When science figured out something that contradicted what the Church believed, the Church opposed it. Sticking with that phony story about creating the world in six days? Locking up Galileo for teaching the earth went around the sun? Why didn't the Church accept science? I began reading, again.

> It does not, in the conventional phrase, accept the conclusions of science, for the simple reason that science has not concluded. To conclude is to shut up; and the man of science is not at all likely to shut up.

I chuckled at this one. Now, that was kind of amusing. Science was always changing. They just came up with a new theory and declared the old one bull. Something deeper within me raised more concerns. What would I think of the Church, if it had kept changing its mind about everything? What if what was right today, was declared wrong tomorrow, the way science accepted then discarded theories? Wouldn't I declare it all hooey, saying how could what used to be the truth not be true now?

But what about thinking? Religious nutjobs believed all that stupid stuff without question. I flipped some pages and read.

> There is no other case of one continuous intelligent institution that has been thinking about thinking for two thousand years. Its experience naturally covers nearly all experiences; and especially nearly all errors.

I looked up from the book. They might be thinking about thinking, but they believed a bunch of insane nonsense! How was it thinking when you just accepted something as a mystery? But, something deeper within me raised another objection. What if there were things that could not be explained? We assumed that everything could be explained, but what if things existed that simply defied explanation? Like that stupid dream. I was desperate to explain it based on the ordinary things that happen, but what if the real explanation was something beyond the ordinary? What if something supernatural had occurred, that had no explanation based on the logical pieces I was playing with, trying to force it to make sense. What if the irrational explanation was the true explanation, and there was no rational explanation to cling to and make me feel comfortable that things were operating in an ordinary, rational way? What if there were mysteries, and there was no better word for them? I picked up the book, *Orthodoxy* again, and read some more.

> Imagination does not breed insanity. Exactly what does breed insanity is reason...I am not, as will be seen, in any sense attacking logic: I only say that this danger does lie in logic, not in imagination... Poetry is sane because it floats easily in an infinite sea; reason seeks to cross the infinite sea, and so make it finite...The poet only asks to get his head into the heavens. It is the logician who seeks to get the heavens into his head. And it is his head that splits.

> The madman is not the man who has lost his reason. The madman is the man who has lost everything except his reason.

Did he have a point? Was I trying to fit the world into my head? Was I trying too hard to make everything add up? Forcing square pegs into round holes? But it didn't make any #?@!ing sense! You had to believe a bunch of superstitious nonsense! Virgin births, immaculate conceptions, resurrections from the dead! Mysteries, friggin' mysteries! And, way beyond my personal experience of going to heaven. But my soul revolted again. Hadn't I, in a way, been resurrected? Hadn't Jesus, himself, confronted me about his mother's perpetual virginity? If that dream were not just a near-death hallucination and was real, wasn't it all real? A fear began to tense my body. A dread panic seized me. What if it *was* real? I picked up the book and flipped some more pages.

> The real trouble with this world of ours is not that it is an unreasonable world, nor even that it is a reasonable one. The commonest kind of trouble is

that it is nearly reasonable, but not quite. Life is not an illogicality; yet it is a trap for logicians. It looks just a little more mathematical and regular than it is; its exactitude is obvious, but its inexactitude is hidden; its wildness lies in wait.

I slammed down that book and picked up another, *Heretics.*

> The human brain is a machine for coming to conclusions; if it cannot come to conclusions it is rusty. When we hear of a man too clever to believe, we are hearing of something having almost the character of a contradiction in terms. It is like hearing of a nail that was too good to hold down a carpet; or a bolt that was too strong to keep a door shut.

Hadn't I been plagued by my mind attempting to draw conclusions? Conclusions I did not believe? Desperately trying to connect things I demanded must be unconnected random events, with no connection? Hadn't I been struggling desperately *not* to think? Hadn't I been demanding the world have no meaning, while my mind tried to force it to have meaning? Hadn't I been forcing the world to be more chaotic than it seemed to be? Because if it were ordered and there was a God, that God hurled lightning bolts at ten-year-olds on bicycles? There can't be a God like that! I slammed that one down good, and picked up another, *The Catholic Church and Conversion.*

> To become a Catholic is not to leave off thinking, but to learn how to think. It is so in exactly the same sense in which to recover from palsy is not to leave off moving but to learn how to move. The Catholic convert has for the first time a starting-point for straight and strenuous thinking. He has for the first time a way of testing the truth in any question that he raises...What is now called free thought is valued, not because it is free thought, but because it is freedom from thought; because it is free thoughtlessness.

> The outsiders stand by and see, or think they see, the convert entering with bowed head a sort of small temple which they are convinced is fitted up inside like a prison, if not a torture-chamber. But all they really know about it is that he has passed through a door. They do not know that he has not gone into the inner darkness, but out into the broad daylight.

I slammed the book closed and screamed at the ceiling, "I hate you, you bastard! You're making a mess of my life! I can't be a Catholic! I just can't do it! Jesus Christ! Who am I yelling at? What the hell is wrong with me? I need something to distract me. TV, that's it, TV."

I turned the TV on and flipped through lame late-night infomercials. I flipped on in disgust. I hit that infernal Eternal Word Network and there was the fat know-it-all himself, or the actor playing him: "To become a Catholic is not to leave off thinking, but to learn how to think..."

I picked up that book with my good arm and threw it through the television; it crashed and sparked then went dark.

20

The Truth Will Lose You Friends

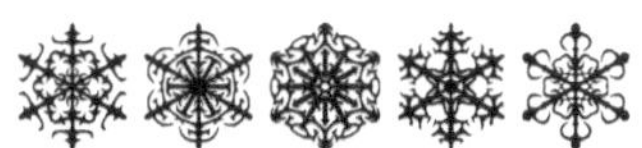

Weds, Jan 4, 2012 - The Thirtieth Day

I didn't sleep that night, either. The swirling confusion of my inner turmoil placed me in a kind of agony. My soul seemed to have accepted something that my mind was in no way convinced of and did not want to believe, and the two were locked in a kind of death match. My stomach churned. I ran that hideous dream over again in my mind. I had to find a way to prove it was not real. The Crucified, the Crucified. He said Nietzsche called himself The Crucified. I googled 'Nietzsche The Crucified' on my computer. Holy crap, it was true. They called them the 'madness letters'. How could I have dreamed that? What else, what else. Uh, oh, yeah, he said he debated that monkey lawyer. What was his name? Scopes, no that was the monkey. The lawyer. Oh yeah, Darrow. I googled 'Chesterton and Darrow.' I read the article. Not only had the fat man debated Darrow, the consensus was he beat him in the debate! It couldn't be a dream, could it? Could I have picked up all that from the TV when I was semi-conscious? I must have. There had to be a rational explanation. I did not go to heaven and meet Christ and

Chesterton, and see Nietzsche in hell. It had been a dream. Then, the fat jerk's words came back to me.

'The materialist cannot fit the most minute miracle into his system, anywhere.'

My mind grasped at any argument it could find. If it were all true, why didn't I believe it when they taught it in Sunday School? If it were all true, why did so many things seem to not make sense? These miracles? Who could believe in them? Virgin Births, Immaculate Conceptions, Resurrections, Ascensions, Assumptions, weren't they all unbelievable? Yet my doctors thought I was alive because of a miracle, so that fit with my experience. This friggin' dream, if I dreamed up a bunch of real stuff I didn't know already, how could it be that it wasn't real? But if I went to heaven and came back, wow, that would be a miracle, and, worse, direct evidence that there was a heaven, a Christ, and a fat know-it-all named Chesterton skulking around up there making stupid jokes. If that miracle was true, and heaven was real, why not all the other miracles? Once there was one that was real, how could you dismiss any of them? If miracles happened, weren't all the dominoes falling? Was any of it far-fetched and superstitious, if some of it were true? If it were true, how could I deny it?

If my dream were true, if it wasn't a dream, how could I do my act? How could I mock Christ, if to do so would be to crucify him? Oh, but how could it be real? It was against everything I knew to be true. And then, I remembered Nietzsche's warning: "If anyone supposes that he knows anything, he has not yet known as he ought to know. Learn this, Carlton, or I'll see you in hell." I don't know. I don't know. That was it! I don't know. There must be an explanation, just I didn't know. That was the answer. I just don't know. I didn't know anything. Wasn't that what they did in science? They had theories. They didn't know. Christians called it a miracle. I would say, "I don't know."

Someone buzzed the intercom at the door. I hobbled over to the intercom and pushed the talk button.

"I didn't order any take out. So, *rip your wreath* off."

I wasn't a person people visited, unannounced. I had a strict "No Pop-in Policy," and was in no mood. Likely it was some stupid kid getting his jollies.

The intercom buzzed again. I pushed the talk button.

"You've got two seconds, talk."

I pushed the listen button.

"It's Chico, man. Let me in."

"Chico? Chico's not here, man."

"That's an old gag, Carlton. Come on, let me in. I gotta talk with you."

"Ok, just busting your chops."

I pushed the unlock button, and buzzed him in. In a few moments, he knocked on the door. I opened the door and let him in.

"If you tell me that your dog ate your stash, Chico, I'll slap you."

"Man, your comedy is getting bitter, dude. You gonna have to chill out."

"I'm on limited sleep. I witnessed a woman killed in an accident, I crashed a funeral, and I spent all night trying to figure out whether I'm hell-bound or just had a bad dream. And, on top of that, I have the biggest interview of my career tomorrow. I guess that can make someone a little cranky."

Chico looked around my apartment, at the books thrown all over and the busted television. "What happened here, dude? Looks like a tornado in a library or something."

He picked up Lenny's dummy, Tony Tonelli, off the couch. "You taking up ventriloquism, man?"

"No, I borrowed that from Lenny. I needed it for a funeral. Nearly got me murdered in Jersey."

"Whoa, man! You live an interesting life. The dummy does look a little like a hitman, though."

Chico had the confused look that made everyone laugh, but I did not find it funny. I think he was right. I had become bitter. And that's death for a comedian.

"Chico, you're a good friend, but I'm tired. Is there something you wanted?" I knew there must be. He wouldn't pop in just to visit.

"Yeah, you know, it's Lenny. He's *stinking my stocking* off! Booked me into that fleabag place, Mickey's Laugh Room. It's disgusting. I just freeze up. Like I'm going to get Legionnaire's disease or get bit by a rat and get rabies."

I sighed. Lenny could not afford to lose any more clients, but Chico was right. Mickey's was a hole. It was the kind of place where they served extra flies in your soup at no charge. I had started out there, and they banned me from the place for making jokes about how unclean it was. I earned a solid chastisement from Lenny for that one, worse than any of his dummies ever got. "Chico, you're gonna have to get over this germ thing. Comedy is a dirty business. You have to be able to make jokes about following your dog around and retrieving your stash from his poop."

"Oh, man! You had to bring up that bit! I hate that bit, man. Just because I'm Mexican, people just assume I do comedy like Cheech Marin." Chico brushed down his arms and shivered, scrunching up his face.

"Lenny's a good man. And he knows comedy. He can really help you. But, you have to be willing to do what it takes."

Chico frowned. He looked more angry than confused, and it was not a good look for comedy. "He can't get me into the good clubs. I just get crap places like Mickey's. I was wondering, maybe you could put a word in with Maury for me?"

I closed my eyes. Maury knew who Chico was and had seen his act. I had seen his act, and, frankly, it was not ready for the big time. If Maury was interested in representing Chico, he would be representing him already, and nothing I could say would change that. "I would stick with Lenny, for now. He can teach you a lot. See a doctor about your phobia so you can play those crappy places, like I did. You have to pay your dues and do what it takes. You need to develop a following, if you want to get Maury interested. He only works with proven acts."

Chico shook his head, disappointedly. "Man, I thought you were my friend. I visited you in the hospital, man. The *hospital!*"

Chico rubbed his arms and shivered again. I sighed. My instinct was to just lie to him and tell him that I would talk to Maury. That was what you did in show business. You just lied, so everybody thought you were their friend, and you got rid of them, and they still thought they were your friend. The show business house of cards was a towering stack of lies like this and everybody knew it, and nobody cared. Lying was as easy as breathing for them. I had already given this idiot more of the truth than I should have, and all it did was *frost his frankincense* off. The show-biz game is to never *bust the Christmas balls* off your friends until you were done with them, which was exactly what I did with Lenny. I resolved to just tell him I'll talk to Maury and have him running home thinking I was going to do all I could to get Maury to represent him and thinking I was his best friend in all the world.

"You know, you are a good friend, Chico. So, I'm going to do a special favor for you. I'm going to give you the best advice I can give you. Stick with Lenny. Learn all you can from him. And stay away from Maury."

It took a moment to register. That was another thing about show business. Everybody was used to hearing what they wanted to hear, whether it was true or not. If you asked a specific favor from a friend, you expected them to say, "Sure, I'll do all I can to help." You didn't expect them to suggest something different from what you were asking.

"You are one cold #@%#&?#?@%!!, Carlton." Chico stormed out of my apartment.

Yeah, well, that was what the truth got you in show business. Another friend off my short lists of friends. But why had I said exactly the opposite of what I planned to say?

21

The City, Today

❄ ❄ ❄ ❄ ❄

Thurs, Jan 5, 2012 - The Thirty-first Day

Do *zombies sleep?* Just one of the nagging ruminations of another sleepless night spent pondering realities that could not be real, incidents that could not have happened, happenings that could not have occurred, occurrences that, well, you get the idea.

If I could think rationally, I would reason that my insomnia was merely a symptom of grief and an expected sequela of a near-death experience. I did not think I was a zombie, but perhaps, having returned from the dead, I was some other kind of eternally waked undead thing, one with no lust to devour human flesh? Some shade of my former self doomed to ponder restlessly in sleepless nights what terrors dreams might bring and what greater horrors awaited if dreams, after all, were more than dreams.

I imagined souls in hell got no rest. And demons, wouldn't they always have some evil to do and no time for sleep? But these things were all imaginary phantoms of the mind, were they not? Darksome things that visit in dreams or sleep deprived hallucinations.

And yet, certainty plagued my weary mind, the certainty that a great toilet bowl waited to suck me to hell, as I had watched the proud philosopher, the Crucified as he called himself, swirl helplessly down, down into the pit of endless fire, ash and smoke. Did I dare think I deserved better? Was I smarter, more rational than Nietzsche? I was, at least, thinner than Chesterton, but what would that count for in the vastness of eternal torment? Did it really await me? Or, was it all a delusion? The blue of that church ceiling matching the blue of her eyes. Had that been a coincidence, as well? Of course, it was! Why would my mind try to connect the color of a church ceiling with the color of those eyes, once so deep and serious, and then so quickly dead, and lightless? And now, buried in the cold ground.

I sat in the green room for *The City, Today,* the clock ticking down to the time of my interview. I had neither showered nor shaved. Maury casually snacked on a Danish and motioned me to join him, but I had no appetite. The orange logo for the show colored the place in an anything-but-green glow. I feared my complexion might be the only green in the room except for a couch or two, some of the grapes laid out on the table, and the friggin' Christmas tree in the corner. It was January, folks. Time to move on to Valentine's day. I knew the Catholics would point out that the Kings from the east had not come yet, but friggin' screw them!

I stared at the clock. Ticking, ticking, on and on, the moments passing accumulating toward my forty-day limit. My mind raced with contradictions against all I had stood for. The grief of an undeserved death, a willing sacrifice to save me, sparing me from a second death, only deepened my anguish and my doubt. Perhaps no one could prove there was no god, but at least, there should be some better argument than, "I don't know." I only had the weak solace of ignorance and stupidity to justify my disbelief, but at least it was something. The last refuge, the final retort. "I don't know, but it can't be God." But my soul seemed to know it was winning the battle, my mind having taken refuge in such flimsy cover. How could God do this? How could God do that? But, if he were God, of course, he could do...whatever. What kind of God would he be if he couldn't? The weakness of my flesh and blood shivered as it sought to judge the unworthiness of the Almighty, if He were almighty, because He did not do things my way. I looked over at Maury. He looked worried.

"Are you okay, Carlton?" he asked.

"Huh? What? Oh, yeah, yeah..."

"'Cuz if you're not okay, we can call this whole thing off, if you're gonna #?@! it up."

"Huh? Call it off? I can't call it off!" I said, then muttered on to myself, "Forty days, it's almost up. What am I going to do?"

"That's the spirit! What a pro! The show must go on!" I don't think Maury heard my muttering.

"What's that? Go on? Yes, yes."

One of the producers of *The City, Today* came into the green room.

"Carlton? You're on in two."

"Yes, yes, I'm on in two..."

The producer shook his head and walked me to the set.

Morgan Shaunessey, the hot redhead, sat in a chair, with another chair opposite her. She stood up as we approached. She stuck her hand out toward me.

"Good morning, Mr. St. Michael. Morgan Shaunessey, of *The City, Today.*"

I shook her hand, then looked around at all the bright lights. Not even that smoking hot redhead could snap me out of it. My conscious mind hid behind weeds of unawareness, while my subconscious mind took over. But, my subconscious mind was not used to being in charge.

"Yes, yes, *The City, Today,*" I stammered.

"Yes, *The City, Today.* We're on as soon as we get back from commercial. Please, take a seat."

She glanced at the producer, who shrugged. The producer motioned with his fingers as he said, "You're on in three, two, one..."

Morgan Shaunessey looked into the camera and read off the teleprompter. I glanced around, blinking my eyes in the brightness of the set.

"Welcome back to *The City, Today.* Well, about a month ago, we had booked a very special guest, funny man Carlton St. Michael, for an interview. But a funny thing happened on the way to the studio. Carlton was hit by a truck! As I understand it, Carlton was actually dead for some twenty full minutes before doctors were able to revive him. And, then, on New Year's Eve, he was nearly run over, again. This time by a drunk driver, who struck the woman he was with, and killed her. But now, he's back. A little worse for wear, perhaps, but here he is, the man they call the Miracle Man, Carlton St. Michael. Good morning, Carlton."

"Good morning." I blinked and turned my head to look at Morgan.

"First, I just wanted to say how sorry I am about your friend, Charlise Jameson, who was tragically killed on New Year's Eve."

I closed my eyes. She had to hit me with that one, first.

"Charlie, that's what she went by, she saved me. She knew if she were drowning, I would try to save her, and that's how she saved me."

Morgan looked at me quizzically.

"She was drowning? Wait, wasn't that from *It's a Wonderful Life?*"

"Yes, it is a wonderful life! And, it's great to be back!"

The audience laughed, but Morgan didn't let it go.

"No, what you said? That's what Clarence said, in the movie, isn't it?"

"Yeah, well, get me, I'm giving out wings!"

The audience laughed again. I didn't want to talk about taking Charlie to an AA meeting. After all, it is Alcoholics *Anonymous.* She started a new line of questions.

"So, the last time we planned to have you on was about a month ago."

"What's that? A month! Holy *shuh*, crap, has it been that long? What day is today?"

The audience laughed. I smiled, shrugging my shoulders.

"It's Thursday, January fifth, Carlton. So, you have a show opening next Friday night. I guess the opening was delayed because of the accident, but why don't you tell us about it?"

"January fifth? So, that means I have nine more days..."

"Nine more days? I thought the show opens next Friday night? That's eight more days?"

"Show? Show? Oh, yeah, the show. Yeah, that's next Friday night. I was thinking of something else. I'm sorry. I'm still a little rattled. Did you know I died a month ago? Something like that is bound to throw you off your game a bit."

The audience laughed. Morgan assumed my strange behavior was just part of the act, but it was just strange.

"Yes, I'm sure it would. So, Carlton, just how dead were you?"

"Well, they hadn't put me in the ground yet, but I was pretty darn dead! As I understand it, I had no pulse, wasn't breathing, no blood pressure. Pretty darn dead!"

"Wow, that's something. So, what was it like, being dead?"

"Awful! Wouldn't wish it on my worst enemy!"

The audience laughed a bit louder.

"Well, as I understand it, there was a little hero involved in bringing you back."

"Yes, not to mention St. Luke and the Virgin Mary. At least that's how the boy tells it."

I slapped my hand over my mouth. The audience laughed. What the hell was I saying? St. Luke and the Virgin Mary? Jeez!

"I can't believe I just said that!" I shrugged again.

"Why, Carlton, have you had a religious experience? That might not go so well with your act."

"Well, you know, the kid put a tourniquet on my leg and started CPR, so that's probably what saved me, but there's also the possibility that Saint Mary and Saint Luke interceded to save my life. Who can tell?"

I slapped my hand over my mouth again. The audience laughed. I shrugged again.

"So, you're leaving open the possibility of divine intervention?"

"Who can say? I mean there's always a rational explanation, but there's always an irrational explanation, as well."

I slapped my hand over my mouth, again. The audience laughed. The gesture was becoming a comic motif. I closed my eyes and shook my head. What would come out of my mouth next?

"Well, Carlton, we just have a few minutes left. Just one more question. If you have had a religious experience, won't you have a little trouble doing your act next week? After all, I understand you have some pretty anti-religious themes in there."

"Do not prepare what you will say beforehand, because the holy spirit will supply the words when the time comes." Yes, I, Carlton St. Michael, was spouting scripture like some Bible-believing buffoon.

"Carlton, isn't that a Bible verse?"

"Why, yes, I believe it is..." I was just as confused and surprised by the words coming out of my mouth as anyone else.

"Well, it has been really great talking with you, Carlton. And good-luck with your show next week. Once again, that's Carlton St. Michael opening at the New City Theater, next Friday night, January thirteenth. What was the title again?"

"Mystery Solved: Nonsense and the Catholic Faith."

I paused. I must have looked like some wandering lunatic trying to unlock a door with a banana.

"Well, it was just a working title. How about, Miracle Man: Back From the Dead." I said, doing my best to cover for the ironic juxtaposition of the interview and the title.

"Well, I'm sure we're all looking forward to the show. We'll be back after this."

The cameras turned off, as the show went to commercial. I looked around, not knowing what to do next.

"Carlton, that was amazing!" Morgan shook my hand. "What a great interview. Every answer was just so, well, unexpected."

I ignored her, got up and headed backstage. Maury greeted me, excited and smiling.

"Carlton, Carlton! Miracle Man: Back From the Dead? Genius! That was great! They'll be beating down the doors to get in. I'm telling you, I see cable specials here."

"Maury, just shut up! I'm out of control! I don't know what's going to come out of my mouth next!"

"Yes, yes, and neither does anybody else. That's what makes it exciting. This angle you're playing is brilliant!"

"Maury, you stupid putz, I'm not playing an angle! I think I'm heading for a breakdown."

"Yes, that's what makes it so exciting! The public loves a train wreck. How else do you explain the popularity of NASCAR?"

"Those are car wrecks, not train wrecks, you idiot! This is my friggin' life here. I don't know if I can do this."

"Carlton, you listen to me. We already put these guys off once. You blow this off and you're through. Especially after this interview. I don't care what you do, you've got to pull it together and get out there next Friday or else."

"Or else what?"

"Or else you're done, I'll make sure you don't get another job in this business. All you've worked for is flushed down the crapper. You said you wanted me to make you rich and famous? Well, this is it, boy. Here's your chance."

"I gotta get outta here. See you 'round, Maury."

I pushed past Maury and headed out the door.

22

Sinner Repent

I limped out of the building into the street. My mind flitted here and there. A kind of panic seized me. I had to get this figured out. I had to get back in control. I had to get a drink. But it was morning. The city was alive and bustling with commercial activity. Cars, buses, taxis, subways all making their special noises and fuming their exhausts stinking up the air. Commuters hurried toward their jobs. Shop owners readied their stores for business. Everybody seemed to have a goal and a purpose. My only goal was to find a bar and get a drink. I had to calm down. One thing about Manhattan, finding a bar was like finding a turd in a toilet; they were everywhere, and they were hard to miss.

I ducked into the first one I found, the Mana a Mano. I walked into the place. A dimly lit place, with a colored, metallic decor that likely would become brilliant in places, once the lights came up, but would cast weird shadows and never be too bright. The lights at the bar were on, and the liquor bottles glowed invitingly, the overhead rack of glasses glittered. Clearly, the place was styled as a kind of hedonistic sex club, the lighting carefully designed to enhance and stimulate, without revealing too closely the features of the guests. Yeah, looked like the kind of place where people got involved with people they would never want to see again nor recognize in the light of day, just my kind of place. The acrid odor of disinfectant and floor wax assaulted me, as I waded deeper into the artificial darkness. Likely, they had hosed the whole place down, washing away the sins of the previous evening.

A bartender wiped down the bar. He looked to be in his twenties, clean-shaven and dressed in a white tuxedo shirt, with his black bow tie dangling around his neck. Thin and well-groomed, no doubt he fit well here and likely did well with the ladies. He looked like he was getting things ready for lunch, which surprised me a little; this place was built for the evening. But then, there were no windows letting in the outside light, so any hour of the day seemed like night, once the doors were shut.

"You open?"

"Just about. Can I help you?"

"Sure, Jameson, straight up. Make it a double."

"A little early to be hitting the hard stuff, isn't it?"

"Just pour me a drink and keep 'em coming."

"Okay, okay, just cool your jets, sweet-cheeks." He set a glass down in front of me and filled it with the whiskey.

I downed the drink and looked around. The neon Mana a Mano sign featured two men...well, let's just say it featured two men.

"Holy $#!!! This is a gay bar!"

The bartender looked around.

"Why, yes, so it is! Got something against gay bars?"

"No, no! I don't have anything against gays. Except when they try to say that homosexual acts aren't sinful."

I clapped my hand over my mouth. Why the frig would I say that! It was still happening.

"Are you calling me a sinner?" The bartender glared at me indignantly.

"No, No! Not at all! But, we all do fall short of the glory of God."

I clapped my hand over my mouth, again. How could I stop this?

"So, you *are* calling me a sinner!"

"Listen, buddy, we're all sinners. No one's a bigger sinner than me. You can't imagine the magnitude of my sin. I've blasphemed the name of the Lord and ridiculed his Church. I have driven people away from God. I am no better than one of that scoffing, jeering crowd calling for Christ's crucifixion and mocking him with the crown of thorns. Only, I'm even worse, because I knew what I was doing! I don't even have ignorance as an excuse. Do you think I condemn you? Your sins are petty little self-indulgences. Nothing compared to mine. I'm the biggest sinner you'll ever meet. Now, give me another drink."

"I think you better go. This is no place to talk religion."

A large, muscular bouncer stepped forward menacingly.

"Oh, come on! How 'bout I buy you a drink? One sinner to another?"

"I don't think we serve sinners here? Bruno, do we serve sinners here?"

"Never have," the bouncer answered.

"That's what I thought. Would you please show this sinner to the door?"

The big oaf ushered me out the door with a shove. I stumbled forward and fell on the sidewalk. The bartender threw my cane at me.

"Repent, sinner!" he said, laughing and high-fiving Bruno. The two of them went back into the bar.

I reached into my pocket for my bottle of Vicodin and took a handful. I stumbled down the sidewalk, looked up and saw St. Malachy's Catholic Church. I stumbled up the steps and opened the door. Wandering through the narthex, then through the nave, I cowered before the altar and the cross, the tabernacle that stored the Eucharist, the body, blood, soul and divinity of Christ. I gasped and turned to the left. I staggered and there she was, the statue of the Lady in flowing robes, hands together in a posture of prayer, eyes looking downward to the left in humility, and the picture behind her, the angel bringing the news that she would bear the Christ. The Mother of God, the Ever Virgin Mother, the Immaculate Conception conceived without sin, the Mother of the Crucified, the portal through which God entered His own creation as man, She who the Catholics venerated and even most protestants scoffed at, thinking her just some teen-aged girl, special for only a moment then lost in the greatness of Her son, the great mystery Herself. She was praying for me; my soul was certain of it. But she was only a great hunk of stone, carved and polished, my mind protested. Not a mother, not a virgin, not a portal, not even the teenaged star of a Christmas fantasy, just a hunk of rock. She was not real. She could not be real. That crazy story could not be true. Superstitious nonsense! But, something in my soul knew, and I fell to the floor on my knees. I reached into my pocket and felt the rosary beads there that the kid had given me. I took them out of my pocket and shook them at the statue.

"No, no!" I shouted, "I don't want your prayers. There was no immaculate conception. There was no virgin birth. You don't exist. Now, leave me alone!"

Then, everything went black.

23

Healing with Fr. Murphy

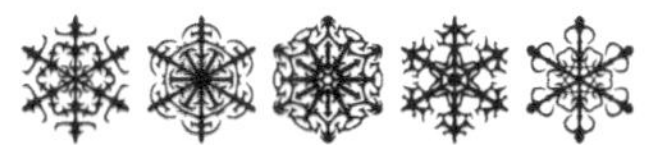

My entire body burned like hellfire when I awoke. Had I died? Was I with Nietzsche, coughing up ash and smoke, tormented by that goat-horned whatever-it-was that had clawed and chomped at me? My head pounded, and I blinked and gagged, spitting out the coffee someone was forcing me to drink. I blinked again, struggling to get my eyes to focus.

"Easy, Easy, my son." I recognized the voice. That damned priest from the hospital, Father Murphy, blurred into view in my burning eyes.

"What happened? Where am I?"

"Easy, easy. You're in the rectory of St. Malachy's Church. I had a couple of Knights carry you here."

"Knights?" I had a vision of armored men, with shields and swords carrying me on a bier to some dark place to be burned to ash.

"Knights of Columbus."

Father Murphy pointed to two men waiting to assist him. They were ordinary looking middle-aged guys, wearing sport jackets and slacks, and smiling like goof balls. I looked around the rather ordinary carpeted living room. The couch I laid on reminded me of the psychiatrist's office, especially with Father Murphy sitting on the chair close by. Everything was still hazy, and I felt hot, agitated, and completely on edge.

"Father Carey, the pastor here, said I could care for you here, but if you got worse to call the ambulance. Apparently, you staggered into the church, denied the existence of a statue, and passed out. Looks like you've taken too many of these."

Father Murphy shook my bottle of Vicodin.

"Oh..."

"I counted what was in the bottle, twenty-six. Looks like you took at most four. Not likely enough to kill you, and I figured you'd rather avoid the publicity of being rushed to the hospital."

It hurt to open my eyes, but I did. "Thank you, Father."

Father Murphy fed me some more coffee. I started to gag again.

"Easy, Easy. There, now. Well, is there anything you would like to talk about?"

"Yes, father, you know, there is. I don't know what's happening to me. I'm no longer in control of myself. I'm saying things I don't believe. I just told a couple of gay guys that they were sinners. I don't believe that! I mean it's just a lifestyle choice, isn't it? You have to be crazy to believe that homosexual sex is sinful, but somehow, I know it's true. But I don't believe it! At least, I don't want to believe it."

"Yes, well, Carlton, sometimes when the truth enters a man's heart, he is given an opportunity to accept it, but to accept it he must deny everything he thought he knew and give himself over to it. It takes effort to maintain disbelief, once you know the truth."

Nietzsche's words as he got flushed out of heaven rang clearly in my ears: "*If anyone supposes that he knows anything, he has not yet known as he ought to know.* Learn this, Carlton, or I'll see you in hell."

I shuddered, feeling a sudden chill that did not seem to lessen the burning sensation I felt all over and pulled the blanket the priest had wrapped over me closer. "But I don't believe these things. What do I care about whether these guys sleep with each other? Why is it my business? I'm an atheist, Father. I don't even believe in sin!"

"Carlton, you've been given a great gift."

"Gift? Father, I'm going insane!"

"Yes, maintaining disbelief in the face of the truth is a form of insanity. And the booze and drugs are only going to make matters worse. Oh, you might be able to suppress the truth within you, but consider the cost!"

"Cost? I have plenty of money, Father."

Father Murphy laughed. "Not the monetary cost, Carlton. The god of booze and drugs doesn't want your money. He wants your soul."

"I'm an atheist, Father. I don't believe in any gods."

"Oh, don't you? Have you not made yourself your own god? Only, now, faced with your own inadequacies, you're looking to booze and drugs to take your place. Carlton, sooner or later, you will be faced with a choice. You will have to make a decision."

"It's not exactly a fair decision, is it, Father? I keep myself and risk losing my mind, or I believe in your God, lose myself, and suffer humiliation and scorn, and how do I know I won't have lost my mind, anyway? It's like I'm a protagonist in some bizarre story, trying to make something of my life, and God Himself is the antagonist, blocking me at every step, forcing me to go where I don't want to go, to believe what I don't want to believe. But, everything I've ever believed tells me that He is not there at all, and it's just some invisible phantom of my imagination, a psychological delusion that I must overcome."

"If a man stands on the beach and denies the existence of tidal waves, he's quite safe and sane, until he sees a tidal wave coming. Once he sees the wave coming, he has a chance to change his beliefs and find shelter. If he holds to his old beliefs, is he still sane? As the wave approaches, he must make a decision. Will he stand on the beach shouting to the wave that it does not exist? Or, will he come to his senses and head for higher ground?"

I paused to consider his words. He seemed kind, and, in a way, wise, but I still thought him a superstitious fool out to hoodwink me.

"Well, Father, that's a nice story about the wave and all, but I'm an atheist."

Father Murphy took a business card from his pocket and handed it to me.

"Here's my card, Carlton. Call me if you ever want to talk. My parish is across the river, in Jersey City. I used to be assigned here, so I visit here whenever I can to help out Father Carey."

"Jersey, huh? Between you and me, that's purgatory, right?"

Father Murphy laughed. "Always the comedian, Carlton. But, comedy works when there is some truth in it. I'm a New Yorker at heart."

"I died in Jersey, you know. I'm hoping to do better next time."

"Well, maybe it's better to die in Jersey than to *live* there."

I laughed. "Who's the comedian now?"

Father Murphy chuckled again, then he got serious. "They do have a good substance abuse program here, too, if you think that might help? I can talk to Father Carey."

"No thanks, Father. I'm just not ready to give myself over to a higher power."

"Not yet, not yet." The old priest shook his head.

24
Diagnosis: Catholic

I left the rectory of St. Malachy's Church, still shaking from the withdrawal symptoms, my head aching. I had to figure this out from a scientific basis. Sure, the priest was telling me the answer was to give in and believe what he does. That's not just human nature, that's his job. But if ever there was something that could be called mental illness, having no control over what you say, and not believing a word of it? Well, they have doctors for that kind of thing. I took my cell phone out and called Dr. Freundheim's office.

"Hello, yes, this is Carlton St. Michael. I'd like to make an appointment with Dr. Freundheim."

The receptionist answered. "Well, looks like the earliest we can fit you in would be a week from next Thursday."

"A week from next Thursday? No, that won't do at all."

"Well, that looks like the earliest opening I have."

"Well, I'll most likely be burning in hell by then, so I would really appreciate it if you could get me an appointment a little sooner."

"I understand. We'll try to get you in as soon as possible. Could you make it here in half an hour?"

"Sure, I'm on my way."

I entered the waiting room at Dr. Freundheim's office and greeted the receptionist.

"Hi, I'm Carlton St. Michael."

She glanced up at me, anxious dread lined across her face like a deranged suicide note, like she expected me to try to jump out the window. "Oh, hi, Mr. St. Michael. Please take a seat. The doctor will be with you momentarily."

"Well, that's much better. I don't think I could have waited two weeks."

"Please, Mr. St. Michael, try to stay calm. The doctor will be with you in a moment."

I rolled my eyes. "Okay, I'll try to stay calm."

The nurse opened the waiting room door from the office. Yeah, she had that same please-don't-stab-me look about her, again. Likely, it had become a permanent feature, an occupational hazard of working with the insane day after day.

"Mr. St. Michael?"

"That's me," I said, standing up.

"Dr. Freundheim will see you, now."

"Well, thank-you. It's about time!" I cast a snide glance at the receptionist. A week from next Thursday.

I entered the disturbing, falsely ordinary room that Dr. Freundheim called an office, knowing full well that it was where he evaluated nutjobs. I glanced quickly at the desk and then the closet, places I suspected the involuntary patient restraint devices might be stashed.

"Good morning, Mr. St. Michael." Dr. Freundheim stood up from behind his desk and motioned for me to take a seat on the chair on the opposite side. I was relieved that he did not assume I needed the couch or the straitjacket.

"Good morning, Dr. Freundheim." I shook his hand then sat in the chair. I wondered if the pictures behind his desk were really his family, or if they were part of the weirdly normal vibe he was trying to send out. The family looked too cute to be his, and his wife too pretty for a shrink. They looked like models in a magazine. The guy was likely a bachelor trying to make himself look more normal. He didn't wear a wedding ring, anyway. But none of that mattered. My head needed shrinking or unshrinking or something. The diplomas and certifications behind the desk looked legitimate, and that was what mattered.

"So, now. What's all this I hear about you being suicidal?"

I twisted my face in surprise.

"Suicidal? What, do you think I'm crazy or something?"

"No, Carlton. Nobody thinks you are crazy."

"Nobody, except me. But I'm not suicidal."

"Well, my receptionist said that I had to see you right away because you were suicidal."

"Well, I don't know where she got that idea. All I said was that in two weeks I'd most likely be burning in hell."

The doctor cocked his head. I was sure he heard this kind of crazy sass all the time. Why disappoint him. I was likely bonkers anyway.

"Well, now, Mr. St. Michael, you're an atheist. You don't even believe in hell."

"No, I don't. That's just the problem."

"How's that?"

"I don't believe in hell, but I believe that in two weeks I'll most likely be burning there."

"I see..."

"You don't see anything! Listen, Doc, I'm off my nut. I keep saying all kinds of things I don't believe. I told a couple of gay guys that homosexual acts were sinful. I don't believe that! I don't even believe in sin."

"I see..."

"You don't see anything! I told a statue that it didn't exist."

Dr. Freundheim raised an eyebrow and turned his head.

"I..., uh, how did that make you feel?"

"How did it make me feel? How did it make me feel? Like I'm going crazy! Listen, aren't there some kind of pills or something you could give me?"

"I think you're probably taking enough pills."

"Very funny, Doctor."

"Now, Carlton, try to relax. You have had quite a traumatic experience. You nearly died, and you had a near-death experience. Many times, when people have these experiences, they find religious meaning in them."

"Doctor, I'm not a religious person. I don't believe in God. I didn't have some pleasant experience of walking into the light and being called back. I was being pulled apart by demons and was saved when I called on Jesus. I don't even believe in Jesus! I was taking His name in vain, as the Catholics say. It doesn't make any friggin' sense!"

"Maybe you believe in Jesus more than you think."

"What do you mean? You either believe or you don't believe. And, I don't believe."

"Yes, Carlton. Consciously, you consider yourself an atheist. But perhaps your subconscious mind is not so convinced."

"Well, what do I have to do to convince my subconscious mind?"

"Well, we could try hypnosis, but I wouldn't recommend it."

"Hypnosis? Yeah, sure. Just don't make me act like a chicken or something."

Dr. Freundheim rolled his eyes. I figured I must be a real jerk to have earned this reaction from a psychiatrist who was used to keeping his head when dealing with the insane. "Now, Carlton, this is not some night club act. I'll have the receptionist make an appointment with you in a couple of weeks."

He turned to write something on my chart.

"A couple of weeks! I'll most likely be burning in hell by then!"

"Now, Carlton."

"I'm serious, Doctor. I can't wait. According to my dream, my time is up next weekend. I don't know what's gonna happen. I'll pay you anything you want."

"Okay, okay."

Dr. Freundheim hit the intercom button. "Betty, Please cancel my next two appointments."

"Okay, Dr. Freundheim."

"Thank you, Betty."

Dr. Freundheim motioned for me to move to the couch, so I limped over and sat down.

"Okay, Carlton, I want you to relax. Just lie back and relax." He sat down in the chair next to the couch.

I turned my body and lay on the couch, looking up at the ceiling.

"Just turn your head toward me, Carlton."

I turned and looked at Dr. Freundheim. He held up some kind of spinning gizmo.

"Okay Carlton, I want you to relax and watch this device. As you watch, your eyes will get heavy and you will become more and more relaxed. You are descending into a relaxed, peaceful state, falling deeper and deeper into sleep. Your eyes are closing now, and you are falling deeper and deeper into a peaceful, dreamless sleep.

"Okay, Carlton, you are in a very deep state of hypnosis. I want you to listen to me, and only me. All the things you have been experiencing are just your mind's way of coping with fear. There is no God, no heaven, no hell. You just had a very bad dream, a delusion, a fantasy. There is no meaning to existence. There is no life after death. No God, no devil, no heaven, no hell. Just here and now, on planet earth. Only what you consciously see, hear, smell, taste, and feel. Now, repeat after me, there is no God."

"There is a God."

"No, no, Carlton. There is no God. Now, repeat after me. There is no God."

"There is a God."

"Listen carefully, Carlton. There is no meaning behind existence."

"There is a meaning behind existence."

There was a pause for a few moments, then the doctor continued.

"What is the meaning behind existence?"

"God made me to know him, to love him, and to serve him in this world and to be happy with him forever in the next."

"Listen carefully, Carlton. There is no God. There is no life after death. Now, Carlton, is there life after death?"

"Yes."

"Why do you believe there is a life after death?"

"I don't."

"But you just said there is a life after death?"

"There is. I have seen it."

"But you don't believe it? Do you believe there is a God?"

"No. I don't believe that there is a God, but there is a God."

"If there is a God, why don't you believe in Him?"

"Because I'm an atheist."

"So, you know there is a God, but you choose to believe that there is no God?"

"Yes."

"Okay, Carlton. You are slowly coming back to consciousness. You will feel better than you ever have but you will slowly wake up as I count to ten. When I get to eight, your eyes will open and when I get to 10 you will be fully awake and feel better than you have ever felt. One, two, three, four, five, six, seven, eight your eyes are opening, nine, ten. You are fully awake and feeling better than you ever have."

"Wow, Doc, I feel great!"

"You believe you are an atheist."

"I *am* an atheist."

"No, Mr. St. Michael. You *believe* you are an atheist. But you *know* you are a Catholic."

"What do you mean, 'I *know* I'm a Catholic?'"

"Well, Mr. St. Michael, your subconscious mind is a Catholic."

"What do you mean my subconscious mind is a Catholic?"

"You are experiencing what we call a cognitive dissonance. You believe consciously that you are an atheist, but you know, subconsciously, that you are a Catholic. That subconscious knowledge is much stronger than your conscious belief. That's my diagnosis. You're a Catholic."

My heart raced. It just could not be true! How could I be Catholic? I didn't believe any of that crap. Mysteries? Hooey!

"Well, can't you cure me of it?" I was frantic.

"It's not a pathological condition. I suggest that you talk to a priest."

"Not a pathological condition? What the frig does that mean?"

"It means there's nothing wrong with you. You're just Catholic."

"But I don't want to be a Catholic!"

"A part of you, perhaps a majority of who you are, already is Catholic. In your case, it is more than what we normally encounter as faith. You don't just believe in God, you know there is a God, just as surely as you know your name is Carlton, or that the sky is blue. It is really quite extraordinary."

I was *elfed!* I didn't know any such thing!

"No, Doctor! I don't believe in God at all! I'm not a Catholic! I can't be!"

"Mr. St. Michael, you will have to come to resolve this cognitive dissonance, or there is a risk of a psychotic break, which could be quite serious."

"You mean I might go mad?"

"Yes, in common language, you may very well go mad."

I paused, thinking about it. The memory of Chesterton and Nietzsche flashed through my mind. Chesterton said, "And what did you get for putting your faith in your own sense of rationality? Only madness. Writing letters calling yourself 'the Crucified.' What folly." Word-for-word it rang in my mind. And I was going mad. I knew it was true. Putting faith in rationality would make me irrational? That's what happened to Nietzsche? The Crucified? Would I start raving nonsense like that? And, now, he was coughing up ash in hell? If there was a hell? Holy $#!!! Unholy $#!!! But, how could the rational make you irrational? It made no sense. A mystery! Another friggin' mystery! But I couldn't be Catholic! I just couldn't.

"Now, Mr. St. Michael, this is not really a very big problem, as psychological problems go. Just accept that you are a Catholic. Embrace it! There's nothing wrong with being a Catholic. Many Catholics live happy and fulfilled lives."

Embrace it? No friggin' way! If I was going down, I was going down fighting. "But there is something wrong with being a quack, now isn't there? You're asking me to believe a lot of superstitious nonsense. Virgin births! Immaculate conceptions! And, you call yourself a man of science?"

I must have struck a nerve because the psychiatrist snapped back at me, "And, you call yourself an atheist? Would an atheist crawl up to a statue and argue with it?"

I opened my mouth, but nothing came out. I huffed, got up and hobbled out of the office. I regretted that I had not first smacked him with my cane.

25

This Century vs. Last Century

I went back to my apartment. In my hobbled condition, still shaky from my withdrawal symptoms from the Vicodin, the last friggin' thing I needed was Doctor Friend Home diagnosing me as Catholic. Not a pathological condition? What was it then? Telling me to just embrace and accept it? What a dick!

I was exhausted and did the worst thing I could have done. I should have gone out for a drink. I should have gone to the Laugh Out Loud for some jokes or something. I should have paid a prostitute for the night, so I wouldn't be alone. But, being exhausted, I went to bed. The thing about going to bed when you are in a weird emotional state? You dream.

"And, now! Let's get ready to rumble!" The announcer revved himself up into a froth, spitting into the microphone. "Live, from Madison Square Garden, the main event of the evening, the championship bout with no rules and no time limit, the fight of this century against last century! Ladies and gentlemen, let us present in the blue corner, standing an even 6 feet in height and weighing in at a svelte one hundred and seventy pounds, fighting out of New York City, a self-styled comedian and atheist with a record of questionable jokes, blasphemes and assorted sins of the flesh, fighting to prove it's all a dream and there's no afterlife, the challenger Carlton, 'The Miracle Man,' St. Michael."

Impossibly, a large crowd of people cheered as I entered the ring with boxing gloves on my hands dressed in boxing trunks and wearing a robe proclaiming me as, "The Miracle Man." I could not help but wonder if Nietzsche had had this dream and wore a robe saying, "The Crucified."

I raised my gloved hands, and the crowd cheered. At least, in my dream I was not hobbling around on a cast with my arm in a sling. That would hardly seem a fair fight.

The announcer continued, "And in the red corner, fighting out of Heaven, by way of Kensington England, a self-styled philosopher and Catholic apologist, writer and author of bad jokes at the expense of no one, with a record of making a monkey out of the great Clarence Darrow, and summoning Nietzsche out of Hell to scare the crap out of people, standing a stately six feet four inches tall and weighing in at a prodigious twenty stone, six pounds, fighting to prove the world is not quite as regular as it seems, that there is a heaven and hell, and all that superstitious religious bull crap, G. K. 'Fat Boy' Chesterton."

Chesterton entered the ring and held his hands up showing off his more than ample belly. He made a point of rubbing it with his boxing gloves. I went to my corner. My corner man, Clarence Darrow, had no encouraging words to offer. "Son, he's way out of your weight class."

Well, no duh! I figured I had slightly more than half the stones he had, but stones I had. And David had only needed one to take down Goliath. I was going to *murderlize* the bum.

The bell rang, and I sprang out into the ring.

"Okay, Fat Boy, let's see what you got!"

I took my best shot, but the fat man slipped the punch and I felt one right in my gut. I gasped and doubled over. I heard the crowd respond, "Oooh!"

"I'm sorry, Carlton. Did I hurt you?" He bent down to try to see my face. I used the opportunity to throw a sucker punch uppercut, but he slipped that punch as well. I lost my balance and nearly fell.

"Carlton, you need to work on your balance. You're flailing out of control."

I regained my stance. I would need to be more careful. He was quick for a fat man. And, he had iron in his words. I meant hands, but I thought of Charlie and how her words had slapped me. I was out of balance. And he was beating me with his words. I was flailing against his words, but I hadn't laid a glove on him. It *melted my snowballs off!* If I couldn't beat him with words, I should at least be able to beat the paunchy pedant with my fists.

I lunged at him again, and he quickly sidestepped, and I staggered under my own unbalanced momentum. He shook his head. He was such a large target, I did not understand how I could miss.

"Is that the best you can do?"

The crowd started chanting that line from the Karate Kid movie. "Sweep the leg! Sweep the leg!"

But I didn't know karate, so I went in again for a frontal attack. I swung at him again, and again he slipped the punches and I staggered unbalanced until I felt his fist buried once again in my gut, and then the leather of his other glove directly into my face. Bright stars flashed everywhere.

26

Doubting Carlton

Sat Jan 7, 2012 The Thirty-third day

Knocked out cold in my dream, I returned to the nightmare of my waking reality with a start. "Holy crap! I can't believe the fat load beat the snot out of me!"

I needed to be more balanced in my attack. More methodical. But, less direct. *Sweep the leg.* I couldn't go straight at Chesterton. I had to go for his foundation. Back to basics. Another day had dawned, and I had a new line of attack.

On the bookshelf, somewhere, a Bible collected dust. Yeah, it was time to get back to basics. I planned to use logic to prove it was all bull $#!!. How hard could it be? I found the Bible, a leather-bound King James version, not an officially Catholic Bible, but it would have to do.

I liked the King James with all the thees and thous because it made it easier to make it all sound like an ancient pile of bull crap, archaic and past its sell-by date, like a carton of curdled milk. I particularly loved all the "pisseth against the walls." Yeah, that was my favorite part. The Israelites were instructed to kill everything that pisseth against the wall, so since I used a toilet, I felt safe. I wasn't sure how they would have counted a urinal that hung on the wall? Sure, that was likely good enough to get your throat slit or head bashed in or however the good old Heavenly Father wanted them to do it.

But, was all that old testament killing enough to disprove my dream, and put this behind me? Many of my atheist brethren made lots of hay about how unjust God would have to be to order the slaughter of people He created whose only crime was that they had been born into a culture opposed to the Israelites. Wasn't that an unjust act that the God of Justice could not commit?

The argument gave some solace that there was evidence that a loving God, if He existed, would not do such things. But, was that enough to claim that, therefore, God does not exist? I hadn't even opened the Bible yet, and my soul already countered with arguments from the other side. If this God had commanded one group to slaughter another group to lay the ground for His ultimate purpose, He also had given his son to be tortured and killed, an innocent for the sake of many.

I had met Jesus in my dream. He suffered when I sinned. I saw it happen. And that experience was so much more real to me than some ancient judgment that I might question, without full knowledge of the supposed innocence of ancient pagan cultures worshiping their phony gods, sanctioning the sacrifice of their children to their idols of stone. Could I judge God for injustice without all the evidence, while not admitting that He had allowed Himself to be falsely judged by men and condemned? And His own words rang in my head, *Judge not, lest ye be judged?* In order to prove God did not exist by contradiction, I had to first assume He did exist. And, if He did exist, where could I find someone qualified to judge Him? Where would I find a jury of His peers? From my perspective, could I evaluate God's actions? And dared I? Could I judge God and not be judged by God? And, how could I withstand His judgment?

Yeah, it seemed extreme to kill everything that "pisseth against the wall," but was it more extreme than giving your son to be sacrificed, tortured horribly, and crucified for all the sins of humanity? Had He not sent Jesus as a guide to teach us how to live, how to sacrifice ourselves for God and for others? If we judged God as harsh, cruel and unjust, had He not entered His own creation and subjected Himself to the same cruel and unjust punishment? And, when He came to guide us as the Good Shepherd, He never told anybody to kill anything as far as I could tell. *A bruised reed He did not break; a smoldering wick He did not quench.*

Sure, He told parables with violent consequences, with lots of wailing and gnashing of teeth. And, people being tortured until they paid the last penny. And the guy burning in hell begging for a drop of water. But, I had witnessed this last one. A matter of justice, Nietzsche burned in torment. But don't we beg God for justice when we see injustice? How can we say God does not love, when he condemns the guilty, and then He is unjust if He does not condemn the guilty? How would a loving God balance the scales of justice with the concept of mercy? Could I, from where I sat on the recliner in my living room, judge God that He did not love or was unjust? I could not shut my soul up but endured the torrent of Christian arguments I did not want to hear thrown back at me with each judgment I wished to make of God. I figured it was likely a good idea to use the stalls rather than the urinals, though, just to be safe. The way my life was going, some old Israelite would surely cut my head off for using the urinal. Likely, he'd look a lot like Lenny. Maybe, he'd have a Chucky dummy wield the sword?

I turned on the reading lamp and struggled to push the recliner back with my good leg. I glanced at the leather cover of the Bible. Sure, it would be daunting to disprove the Bible with logic, but I was out of my mind and didn't much care. My soul seemed ready to counter everything I could come up with, no matter how much I wanted to remain a committed atheist. I had to come up with something, or I would have to give in. And I wasn't about to give in. I was going down swinging if I was going down. I had to start somewhere, so I started with, "In the beginning..." It seemed like a good place to start.

I worked through the day and into the night, looking for something, something more than the "Why would God do this or that?" Those traps in which many atheists thought they caught God required a box in which to fit the Almighty, but the Almighty, if He existed, was infinite and not easily fitted into a box. The Creator of all, if He existed, was a master of paradox and not so easily trapped with words.

Even if they could prove God was a hypocrite, that did not disprove His existence. And, if He existed, He made the rules. That would be His job. And, even if God, by His own rules, were judged a murderer, a psychopathic serial killer, that did not prove He did not exist. If God were untrustworthy, or crazy or whatever, He still *was.* I liked to think that God would not have allowed my brother to be struck dead by a lightning bolt, that there could not be a God, if things like that happened. But that really didn't prove He didn't exist. Only that if He did exist, He allowed random, science-based cruelty to happen, as if He did not exist or did not care. There wasn't anything mysterious about a kid on the top of a hill killed by a thunderbolt. It would have been mysterious if he had survived.

None of the arguments seemed convincing anymore. It was, after all, like the clay judging the potter. Atheists like to claim that the clay created the potter, but any pot that was clever enough to create a God surely was designed by some intelligence. A pretty darn bold assertion, my friends made, saying that chaotic random forces were responsible for the intricate designs of the universe. I wondered what kind of slap Michelangelo would have for the critic who claimed his Sistine Chapel ceiling came about as a result of random accidents? Or, even, that the act of creation he attempted to depict was really just a great cosmic accident?

And, freakin' Jesus, they were always trying to trap Him with these kinds of arguments, and He made them look like fools. And, the darn stories. That parable of the prodigal son that my father had corrupted so badly when he threw me out? Well, that one just *Kringled my Christmas Tree* off. If I had actually asked for my inheritance and squandered it, it would make sense. But I never asked. He just figured he had raised a complete jerk and sent me packing. And now, as wrong as he might have been in doing that, I was being drawn back into believing all the crap he had drilled into me.

But I hadn't squandered my inheritance. I was on the verge of breaking out, hitting it big. I was getting back at him, by mocking his God, proving I could do it. But I couldn't disprove any of the miracles. All I could do was scoff at them. I especially could not disprove my own miracle, coming back from the dead. That was a good trick. Why me? Why would it have to be me? It was like my father had created an all new parable: the parable of the pain-in-the-butt-son. I was the reluctant protagonist, and now the ridiculous ending was coming out just the way he had planned. I must have fallen asleep, finally, sitting in that reclining chair reading the Bible, desperately searching for the smoking gun that had killed God.

Dreams are evidence of truths beyond the reach of logic. If nobody important ever said that, I just did. I dreamed I was St. Thomas, you know, doubting Thomas. My kind of Apostle. I faced the other Apostles and called them out on their B.S. "Oh, come on, guys!" I said, "You're telling me that the Lord came back from the dead and ate with you?" Zombie bull $#!!. Freaking lunatics, all of them!

"Yes," St. Peter said, "it was the Lord! Risen from the dead!"

Now, Peter was supposed to be this big shot, but he was still all busted up about having denied the Lord three times. That's the kind of guilt that can make you hallucinate.

"This is a lot of bull!" I said, "Look, I'm not believing this unless I stick my fingers in the holes in His hands, and my hand in His side!"

Then, the freaking guy walked right through the door. I mean, you know, I watched Him walk right *through* the locked door, and He looked just like He did before. Yeah, He was all cleaned up from all the blood, and He didn't have all the scars you would expect, except the holes in His hands, feet, and side. He didn't look like a freaking zombie like I thought He would, if He had risen from the dead. I mean, they scourged the crap out of the dude! He should have been a mess of rotting busted flesh, but there He was, standing there all cleaned up, just a few holes, making it clear that it was Him, the one Who was nailed to the cross, died and rose again. Not some spirit, some ghost, and not some phony impostor.

"Holy $#!!!"

"Carlton, put your fingers in the nail holes and your hand in my side. Do not persist in your unbelief but believe."

"No freakin' way! I'm not sticking my fingers anywhere!" I turned away in revulsion.

But stick my finger in, I did. And my hand, too. Now, I knew the script. I was supposed to say, "My Lord and my God." But I didn't. Instead, I said, "I still don't believe!"

27

Epiphany

Sun Jan 8, 2012 Day Thirty-four, The Feast of the Epiphany

My heart pounded with the dread of certainty that only a dream can confer. I blinked a few times to get my bearings. I looked at the Bible on my lap. "Holy $#!!! I don't believe this. My subconscious is Catholic. And it's driving me insane! I gotta clear my head!"

I got up and threw on my coat. I grabbed my cane and hobbled out the door. I limped along in the cool, yet unseasonably mild, January air. The sun was up. It was morning. Sunday morning. I figured I'd have the street nearly to myself, but people were gathering for Mass at St. Joseph's Catholic Church, just a couple blocks away. The same church I was going to with Charlie to the AA Meeting. *No, I can't go in! I can't!*

I walked up the steps to the church. The greeters welcomed me, shaking my hand, as I entered. I sat in the back. People settled in as Mass was preparing to begin. *No, no! I won't kneel down!*

I knelt down and prayed. *Lord, save me! I'm losing my mind. I know you are not real. I know none of this is true, and yet I'm on my knees praying to you! Forgive me, Lord. I just can't believe this stuff. I'm a terrible sinner, Lord! Free me of this! I can't bear it!*

Mass progressed to the scripture readings. The First Reading, from the Book of the Prophet Isaiah:

"...See, darkness covers the earth,

And thick clouds cover the peoples;

But upon you, the LORD shines,

And over you appears His glory..."

And, I felt the opening of my heart, as if that light had scattered the darkness within me. Something inexplicable rejoiced in my soul, and the words echoed in my ears. And then the psalm:

"...For he shall rescue the poor when he cries out,

And the afflicted when he has no one to help him..."

And I felt my heart cry out in my affliction, the affliction I had never known enough to acknowledge. The separation from the purpose and meaning meant for my life. The will to please this God who had created me. My soul cried out, "Lord, I want only to please you." And my conscious mind recoiled, my body physically cringed at the very idea of it.

And the second reading:

"...that the mystery was made known to me by revelation.

It was not made known to people in other generations,

as it has now been revealed..."

The word "mystery" clanged like a gong, blaring in my mind, so I covered my ears. Mysteries! Friggin' mysteries! And, my soul piled on the words of Chesterton to hammer home the reality of mysteries, "Life looks just a little more mathematical and regular than it is. Its exactitude is obvious, but its inexactitude is hidden." Mysteries, miracles, unfathomable, unexplainable revelations, were they real? Could a mystery be known by revelation?

And then, the Gospel reading, the words of Herod:

"...'Go and search diligently for the child.

When you have found him, bring me word,

That I too may go and do him homage...'"

The conviction of sin fell heavily upon my soul. Had I been Herod? Had I sought out the child, not to do Him homage, but to do Him harm? Had I not sought Him out, discovering all I could, so I could mock Him and His Church? And, even now, I grasped to hold onto my disbelief. I had no intention, having found Him, of paying Him homage, even as my heart yearned within me to do just that.

The mass progressed to the liturgy of the Eucharist, and I felt crushed under the weight of it.

"...Take this, all of you, and drink from it,

For this is the chalice of my Blood,

The Blood of the new and eternal covenant,

Which will be poured out for you and for many

For the forgiveness of sins.

Do this in memory of me."

I closed my eyes, recalling my mocking routine with the wine glass. Had I really joked about this most solemn part of the Mass? I recalled my dream, my vision of being pulled into heaven by Jesus, how He could hardly stand the sight of me, but He had saved me. And, there, at the Mass for the Feast of the Epiphany, I could no longer deny the truth of my personal epiphany. The mystery had been made known to me by revelation. No reasoning or trick of the mind could undo the knowledge in the depth of my soul. I could no longer deny any of it, though I could not understand most of it. Atheists are free to reason and hypothesize because they don't know. It's all very reasonable. But I saw the tidal wave coming and it was not reasonable any longer to stand on the beach denying it. I could not reject what I knew to be true and stay sane. If I held to what I had always felt was reasonable, I would become a madman like Nietzsche, writing ranting letters claiming to be "The Crucified," or maybe "The Resurrected," and share his fate in hell. And, I saw that it was, after all, a great gift, as the priest in the hospital had said. A greater gift than any of the gold, frankincense or myrrh of the magi. A knowledge of my purpose and meaning in life, the most important thing I could know. And all the other things I thought I had known paled with the realization that I had "not known as I ought," convicted as I was by the scripture Nietzsche had quoted. I blubbered like a baby.

I felt a hand on my shoulder. A young religious sister in a gray habit with an oversize set of rosary beads at her side peered down at me. Even in my distress and weird emotional state, I noticed she was just too darn attractive to be dressed in a habit. The twinkle in her green eyes, the delicate curve of her cheeks, the perfect symmetry of her plump lips and slight nose, unadorned and enhanced by no makeup, but needing none, she was a picture of loveliness. Her hair hidden under her headdress, with just a peak of dark hair slipping past onto her right cheek. An added weight of conviction fell upon me, as my sinful flesh questioned why such a vision of beauty would opt for such an austere life.

"Are you alright?" she asked.

I looked up at her, through my tears. "No, sister. I'm anything but all right! I'm a Catholic!"

"I know what you mean." She chuckled. "Let's get a cup of coffee and talk about it."

"But the Mass isn't over."

"There'll be another one in an hour."

28

Cleaning Up My Act

I left the church with the religious sister, who introduced herself as Sister Theresa. We walked across the street to the nearest restaurant.

"It doesn't look like it's opened," I said, feeling a bit of relief that I might have a way out. I did not want to talk to this woman in the gray habit, with the large rosary beads hanging at her side. She had caught me at a vulnerable moment, and now I felt trapped.

"Knock, and the door shall be opened." She smiled, the innocent, confident smile of a nun. Some artist might use her one day as a model for the Virgin Mary with the kids at Fatima.

"Bible believin' scripture quotes aside, Sister, the place is closed."

Sister Theresa knocked.

A young woman opened the door. "I'm sorry, Sister. We don't open until 11:30."

"Oh, yes, I know. But, we'd just like a cup of coffee and a little privacy. Do you think you could accommodate us? We would really appreciate it."

The woman smiled.

"Sure, Sister, I don't see how that could do any harm. We've got some coffee made for the set-up crew."

Another Christmas miracle, the sarcasm dripped in my inner voice. The woman showed us in and seated us at a table.

"Now, see, sometimes doors do open when you knock."

I rolled my eyes, and she smiled. The woman came back with two cups of coffee and placed them in front of us on the table.

"Sister?" I asked, "What did you mean, in the church, when you said you knew what I meant?"

Sister Theresa looked puzzled for a moment, and I realized my question was anything but clear, but, she seemed to catch on, "Oh, about discovering you're Catholic? Well, do you think I always wanted to be a religious sister?"

I shrugged my shoulders. I had memories of nuns from my days in Catholic school. The nuns at school didn't really seem completely human, we were all so afraid of them. They were mostly crotchety old women who, if I had ever thought about it, I would have guessed just came out of the womb in a habit, ready to rap kids' knuckles with a ruler. I never heard about any of the kids actually getting whacked by one of them, but I remember we all were afraid that we would be. I always figured if a woman could do anything else besides being a nun, she would likely do it.

"No, no!" she said, shaking her head, emphatically, "If only people who wanted to be nuns by their own choice became nuns, there would be far fewer of us, I dare say. Not that there are that many of us. It's more of a calling, a subconscious yearning to be closer to God, and to do service for Him. I mean, who would choose to do such a thing? I wanted to be a pop singer, of all things, fame and fortune, you know."

"So, why did you become a nun?"

"Because I realized that what I wanted was not the best thing for me. There is a verse in the Bible that says, 'You are the potter, we are the clay.' You can't exactly expect the potter to listen to the clay when the clay says I want to be this or that."

"But I'm not clay. I'm a human being, with free will."

"Yes, you have free will. You can deny God. You can deny what is best for you, and what is best for humanity. You can choose to go to hell. But, I think God may be trying to save you from that path. Just as He saved me. Eternity is a long time and hell is a very bad place."

"You're telling me, Sister! But it seems like I don't have a choice. God just won't let me do what I want to do."

"And why do you suppose that is? When you make God your enemy, you don't expect Him to fight back now and then? But He doesn't want to be your enemy."

"But He doesn't fight fair!"

"My, you have some ego! Do you really think you could win a battle with God, even if He fought fair?"

"Well, I might have a chance."

Sister Theresa laughed. "Listen to yourself! Why do you want a chance? If God made you for a purpose, to accomplish something for Him, why wouldn't you want to be what He made you to be? Seems to me that once you know that there is a God, you might want to try to get on His good side?"

I thought about that damn psychiatrist. My subconscious mind knew there was a God. If it were true, didn't I have to change? Wasn't that the smart thing to do? "I can't believe I'm losing an argument with a nun!"

"What do you say we make the next Mass?"

"That's the last thing I want to do!" I paused a moment. "Okay, let's go!"

We walked back across the street to St. Joseph's Church. I sat with Sister Theresa in the back and followed along with the Mass. It was not much different from when I was a kid, but I got this feeling like I was finally home. Like this was where I was meant to be. I was like the prodigal son, who had lived a life of dissipation, and returned home, to find myself welcomed and loved. And, the whole idea of it just really *merried the Christmas* off that part of me that still wanted to believe it was all superstitious nonsense, and I was being duped. The priest got to the closing prayer.

"Go in peace glorifying the Lord by your life."

The congregation responded, "Thanks be to God."

"Peace? I have no peace," I said, looking skeptically at Sister Theresa.

"Are you glorifying the Lord by your life?"

"Damn it! You did it to me again!"

"Carlton! We're still in church!" Sister Theresa glared with that stern, no-nonsense religious sister scowl that made me cover my knuckles.

"Oh, I'm sorry, Sister. I'm just not used to losing arguments."

"Now, Carlton, you've been losing arguments all your life. You've only just become aware."

"Please! Stop it, I don't want to curse in church again."

"So, what do you think you will do to love and serve the Lord?" Sister Theresa chuckled.

I thought for a moment. The future in my new reality, what would it mean?

"I have to revise my act. I mean, I can't do it the way it is."

"Sounds like a good place to start."

I went back to my apartment, and I looked over the pile of books by Chesterton, and my busted-up TV. I took a deep breath. I had six days to clean up my act. If it's enough to make the universe and everything in it, I should be able to do it. I can rest on the seventh day.

"Ok, Mr. G. K. Chesterton, give me some inspiration."

I opened one of the books and started reading. I had ideas popping into my head in no time. I had to change the whole thing. I started writing.

29

The Prodigal Phones Home

Tues, Jan 10, 2011 - The Thirty-sixth Day

Late into the night, night after night, I worked, researching and refining my new act. Finding out many new and surprising things to joke about. Oh, I was going to *rile the reindeer* off a whole different set of people, all the people I used to laugh with. No, it likely would not make me rich and famous, but that didn't seem to matter to me anymore.

But something else was gnawing at me. I had committed to change and to accept Jesus and His Church. I was fully Catholic, again, at least in my heart. There were still things to work out with the Church to be fully reconciled, like the long confession I would have to make, and I would need to complete whatever God-awful penance the priest might assign. The Labors of Hercules probably would not suffice.

But, the thing that really gnawed at me was my father. I was going to have to reconcile with him. And I dreaded it. He threw me out in hopes that I would come groveling back like the prodigal in the parable. It was totally unfair. I never asked him for my share of the inheritance. I ran the old episode over in my mind.

We were in his office in our home. A home he had architected himself and an office that naturally suited him perfectly. Three walls of bookshelves eclectically colored the room in random patterns of book spines and scented the room in the musk of old paper. A closet hid behind one of the bookcases that turned on a ball-bearing swivel and acted as a door. The books covered many subjects, but the most recent acquisitions were on religion and Catholicism, in particular.

He went to Mass every day since my brother, Tommy, had died, and had dragged me to Mass with him whenever he could, until I was eighteen. The old man valued education and sent me to Fordham University, the oldest Catholic University in the northeastern United States, and that was probably a mistake. That's where I learned to love New York and hate New Jersey.

His large desk was oak, his drafting desk was oak, the bookshelves were oak, and he might as well be an oak. And I? I was the acorn that had fallen too far from the tree. Or, maybe I was somehow an impossible maple? Or, maybe a buckthorn? Or, perhaps the fig tree that Jesus cursed because it bore no fruit, even though it was not the time for figs.

My father was not so hard a man as an oak might suggest. He was an oak that had been struck by lightning and now feared the rain. He had so hoped to instill his faith in me and had utterly failed. I had learned better how to mock his God and his Church at the very school he spent so much money to send me to and I was never shy in my disrespect of him. I had always thought it would be a pleasure that would not end. But he was done turning his cheek and had come up with another plan.

I sat in his office across from him at his oak desk and smirked. "So, what sermon do I get today, Pop? Perhaps a woman caught in adultery to spare from the stones? I've known many of them, in the biblical sense, not that I've thrown any rocks at them. That's not the biblical sense I mean."

My father closed his eyes. "No more sermons, son. I've taught you as much about the faith as I can. You know it all. You know everything God wants you to do and everything he doesn't. The problem is not that you don't *know*. It's that you don't *believe*. You've chosen your path and I can't alter it."

"You mean, you'll finally leave me alone? No more quizzing me on the Catechism? No more dragging me to Mass? I can finally live the way I want to live?"

"Yes, son that's the point of this meeting. Look, I know you've suffered, actually being there, seeing your brother die. That kind of thing, well, there's no easy way over that."

"Leave Tommy out of this. This is between me and you, old man." He ticked me off, bringing up my brother.

"I'm sorry, so sorry. How can I expect you to believe in God, when you saw that? I can't teach you that God is love, when God took your brother right in front of your eyes."

"Oh, man! Will you stop with the jive? It wasn't God, Pop. It was a discharge of electricity from a cumulonimbus cloud, striking the highest point, which happened to be Tommy, on the top of that hill. That's what lightning does. God had nothing to do with it. There is no God to have anything to do with it."

"I know that's what you believe, and I've been trying to change what you believe with education, but it can't be changed that way. You think you know something, and I think you're wrong, but I can't change what you think you know by arguing. It's a first principle for you that there is no God. You're going to have to figure it out for yourself."

"Well, hallelujah! Give the man a cigar!"

"Son, this is hard enough for me without the wisecracks. This is the hardest thing I've had to do since I watched the dirt cover up your brother's casket."

I bit my lip. I wanted to slap the old fool for bringing that up. "You keep trying to make this about Tommy, but it's not. It's about me and you. You tried to brainwash me with all that Catholic crap and you're finally giving up."

"It's more than that son. I'm saying good-bye. As surely as I said good-bye to your brother all those years ago. I'm what's keeping you from God, from faith, from Jesus. And, I can't be that obstacle to you any longer. I'm giving you your inheritance, now. So, you can make your way in the world. I've liquidated half my estate. Here's the cashier's check."

I took the paper from him and glanced dumbfounded at the number. It was a big number. I had no words. Something within me was breaking. My father considered himself dead to me. I thought I would have had many more years to kick him around. "Old man, you really suck, you know. I suppose you think I'll squander it like that dope in the parable and come crawling back one day? Like that's going to happen."

The old oak started to weep like a willow.

"I hope not son. I only want what's best for you. And what's best is that you make your way on your own. I can't hold you back any longer. Perhaps you will find the Lord? Or perhaps, He will find you? Or perhaps you will stay lost? I've done all I can for you. You're on your own, now."

And now, I would have to call him. What would I say? I had not squandered everything and been in want, feeding pods to hogs. I had been dragged back to faith through a revelation I could not deny. I had come back from the dead and been given forty days to make a decision. I had decided it was real, and I couldn't deny it. What he had tried to drill into me had been hammered home by a supernatural intervention in my life. I had hated him for trying to tell me the truth. I stared at the phone. I took a deep breath and dialed his number. The phone rang. I heard him pick it up.

"Hello?"

"Pop? It's Carlton."

There was a pause. "Carlton, I've been so worried. I saw on the news, the accident. I, uh, I wanted to go see you, but, you know, I just had to let you go."

"It's okay, Pop. You know, it's okay. I'd have thrown you out, if you tried to visit me in the hospital. I'm okay, now. I, uh, I've come back."

"They're calling you the miracle man. Say you came back from the dead."

"Yeah, but that's not what I mean. I'm Catholic again."

"Oh, son, that's great! The best news I could imagine." His voice cracked, and he sighed. "I've been praying every day. Have you gone to confession?"

I heard the anxiety in his voice when he spoke of confession.

"Not yet. I have an appointment on Saturday."

"Oh, go as soon as you can! If anything should happen before you go, you'll have that burden to bear."

That was Pop. Always worried about my soul.

"Yes, I know. But I have a work to complete first, something I feel called to do. Perhaps it's part of my penance? I have a lot to make up for."

"Okay, you're in God's hands. Let Him guide you and protect you."

"Yes, I think that's the idea."

"Will you come home, son? I've missed you terribly."

"Maybe Sunday. I'm heads-down working on revising my act for a show on Friday night, then I have my confession on Saturday. That will probably take a while."

I heard the old oak weeping again over the cellphone airwaves. A tear formed in my own eye.

"'It was his home now. But it could not be his home till he had gone from it and returned to it.'"

I paused, wondering at the odd third person structure of his sentence.

"What's that?"

"Oh, just something Chesterton wrote in one of his stories."

I gasped. Well, it figures he'd know his Chesterton.

"You'll have to show me that one. I've come to know Chesterton pretty well. He's like an old friend I used to hate."

"Sure! I have a library full of Chesterton, and that book, *The Coloured Lands,* is pretty rare."

"Yeah, well, I have forty of his books that I have to return to the library, but I don't have that one."

"Gee, son, I feel like I should kill the fatted calf. If I had one."

"Pop, I don't need any robes or rings or parties. I just want to come home."

30

The Big Show

❅ ❅ ❅ ❅ ❅

Fri, Jan 13, 2011 - The Thirty-ninth Day

All week, I worked on it. Writing, then, practicing, getting the phrasing and the timing down. It was still a bit rough and untested, but the big day was upon me. I hoped I was ready, but it would be a great leap into the unknown. Whatever the audience was expecting, they would not be ready for my new act. The phone rang. It was Maury.

"Hello? Yeah, Maury, I'm fine. Better than ever."

"Are you ready for the show, tonight?"

"Ready, sure, more ready than I've ever been."

"I like the sound of that!" His voice was even more gravelly and gangster-like when he got enthusiastic. I made a mocking face in the anonymity offered by the phone. "So, you're going with the standard set?"

"Well, I've made some modifications."

"Modifications? I don't think it's a good idea to go with untested material. What have you modified?"

"The whole thing."

"The whole thing! Are you crazy?"

"Maury, for the first time in my life I'm certain that I'm not crazy."

"I don't like the sound of that!"

I laughed. "Don't worry, Maury. I'll be fine."

"You need to be funny, not fine, Carlton. You pay me to worry. It's what I do best."

"Well, you don't need to worry anymore."

"I don't like the sound of that!"

"I'll pray for you, Maury."

"Now that's funny! I like the sound of that!"

"Good-bye, Maury."

I hung up the phone. "Putz!" I muttered to myself.

The New City Theater was a hot new venue in midtown that provided stand-up acts a place to perform on a large stage, with theater seating of some twelve hundred people or so. The new venue was gambling on big comedy acts being able to fill a large venue more like a theater act would versus some of the more exclusive and intimate comedy clubs that littered the Manhattan entertainment scene. We had gotten loads of free publicity from my various antics and foibles, so the place was packed. The New City had struggled at times to fill the place when newer acts were up, so we surprised them with our sell-out crowd. They were ready with an army of servers to sell drinks and make a killing. We had billed it as a one-night only affair, and it had made all the entertainment shows as a New York happening that no one wanted to miss. People were still talking about that crazy interview on *The City, Today.* The buzz was electric. It's not often a comedian comes back from the dead. Lots of people were expecting a train wreck. Maury was absolutely right about that. No one could predict what might come out of my mouth next, and that made it exciting.

Religious people did not know what to make of me, since the early reviews of my show, and the original title, indicated a satirical indictment of religion, but my interview seemed to indicate something else. Most thought it a brilliant publicity stunt, and Maury took credit as if it was. He retitled the show, "Carlton St. Michael, Back from the Dead." What would the resurrected comedian say? Well, that was a lot more interesting and had broader appeal than the original working title. Lots of people who caught my act at the Laugh Out Loud Club were there, expecting the old material, ready to cheer me on. Laughing with the sinners. I was one of *them.* Well, that's what they expected. I saw Chico on the way in. I wasn't sure if Lenny made it. But, it seemed like Manhattan was all abuzz about the live happening.

I waited backstage to be introduced. Maury had gotten a respectable, recovering warm-up act to go on before me. Maury trusted recovering acts more than up-and-comers. A guy who's been up and then down, well, that's a guy who works hard and tries not to make too many waves. Up-and-comers, those guys are trying to be noticed. Maury did not want any distractions like that. One train wreck at a time. The management made sure everyone who wanted a drink got one, and most had more than enough to lubricate their laugh muscles.

The emcee, a good-looking guy in his forties, wearing a tuxedo shirt, bow tie and denim jeans stepped out on stage to introduce me.

"Ladies and gentlemen, we have a real treat tonight. Carlton St. Michael will be performing for the first time since the accident that nearly took his life. Carlton's irreverent commentary against established religious and political institutions had been attracting quite a large and vocal following, more of a movement than a mere comedy act, before being temporarily derailed by that tragic accident. Now, he's back, and ready to pick up where he left off. So, without further ado, the guy who survived a bone-crushing altercation with a truck to be here, the guy who was counted out as dead for twenty minutes, but came back to be here tonight, the Miracle Man, who epitomizes the adage, 'The Show Must Go On.' Here he is, Carlton St. Michael, Back from the Dead!"

The audience stood up and applauded. My big moment had arrived.

"Thank you, thank you. You're too kind. But I need to correct some of the things in the intro. First of all, the accident did not *nearly* take my life. It *took* my life. I, Carlton St. Michael, have returned from the dead."

The audience laughed.

"No, No, it's true. I was actually dead for over twenty minutes! *Twenty* minutes. One third of an hour. Dead. And, you wanna know the worst thing about it?"

I paused and rolled my eyes.

"I was in friggin' Jersey!"

The audience laughed.

"You know, I used to say, 'I wouldn't be caught dead in Jersey?' But I found something out. It's better to be caught dead in New Jersey than to be *alive* in New Jersey!"

The audience laughed again.

"I friggin' know that from experience!"

The audience laughed again.

"Friggin' Jersey. Do we got any people here from Jersey?"

Some people cheered; a smattering raised their hands.

"Well, you have my condolences. Wait a minute? I was the one who was *dead* in friggin' Jersey. You should be giving *me* your condolences! Oh, wait, never mind. I forgot. They don't have funerals in Jersey. They just stuff you in a barrel and throw you in the river."

The audience laughed.

"I guess I was one of the lucky ones. I came back before they completed the Jersey funeral rights. After twenty minutes of being dead, I come back to life, and there's this goombah cramming me in a barrel."

I paused and rolled my eyes.

"And the guy says, 'Like, I thought you was dead? Hey, Paulie? Wasn't this guy supposed to be dead? We supposed to finish the job, if he ain't?'"

I laughed, "Just kidding, just kidding. I like kidding about Jersey because, well, because Jersey *sucks!*"

The people laughed.

"Okay, okay, enough of the Jersey jokes. So, what's it like being dead? Well, I'm here to tell you, strange things happen when you're dead."

I laughed and rolled my eyes, again.

"In the time I was dead, I went to heaven. That's no joke. I'm here to tell you it's true. I know from experience. I was there. And, like, there's the Lord, and He's like, 'Carlton? I've seen your act.' And I'm like, 'Holy $#!!, man, bummer for you!'"

The audience laughed.

"That's like running into George W. Bush, and he's like, 'I seen you on the internets; I think you're *misunderestimating* me.'"

I paused, letting the laughter die down. New Yorkers loved a good George W. Bush joke, even a bad one.

"Only it's worse, man, because this is like, *The Lord!* I mean, *strange* things happen to you when you're dead!"

The audience laughed.

"So, there I am, face to face with *The Lord of Lords,* J.C., Himself. And, He's like, 'Carlton? You have to clean up your act.'"

I shrugged and made a confused face, then pointed to myself.

"So, I'm like, no way, man, the act is working just fine! People are laughing, having fun, what's the problem? And He's like, 'Carlton? Ever hear of a comic named Harry Hoan?' And I'm, like, 'Harry Hoan? No Lord, never heard of him.' And the Lord gets animated talking about this guy. He says the guy's act was a lot like mine. The Lord says all the people were laughing, joking around, having a great old time with Harry Hoan. And I'm like, okay, maybe I'll check him out sometime. Oh, he's not around anymore. Oh, that's too bad. What happened to old Harry?"

I paused and rolled my eyes.

"And so, The Lord says, 'He drowned...' And, I'm like, 'Oh, that's terrible!' And the Lord's like, 'Yeah, and all the people laughing with him, they drowned too.'"

I scratched my head.

"I'm thinking, what the heck? You know, how does a comedian and all his audience drown? Was there no life guard on duty or something? Maybe they went down on a cruise ship or something? Which would really suck, you know. You're on vacation having a good time, laughing it up, and then, all of a sudden, you're throwing women and children out of the way to be first on the lifeboat."

I made motions like I was tossing people out of the way.

"Well, I know that sounds bad, but I've been dead, once. I think that entitles me to cut the line. I'm just kidding, ladies. I wouldn't throw you out of the way to get on the lifeboat first. It's just a joke. But, maybe kids? They're smaller and easier to throw."

I made like I was throwing a kid.

"No, no. Just another joke." I laughed.

"So anyway, I ask the Lord, 'Did a cruise ship sink or something?'

"And, He's like, 'No, and if I ever catch you throwing women and children out of the way to get on a lifeboat, you'll be going to a place where the least of your worries will be *drowning*.'"

I make my, *oh-my* face, with my hands on my cheeks.

"So, I'm wondering what happened? I mean, how did this comedian and his whole audience drown? So, I ask Him, 'So what happened, Lord? How'd they all drown?'

"So, the Lord is staring at me like I shouldn't have to ask. Now, what you have to understand about the Lord and comedy is, He's not a comedian. I mean He's a straight man all the way. Always a deadpan, and sometimes you have to think about it. I mean, He told me they don't have any good comedians in heaven, and I believe Him. So, I know you're waiting for this really great punchline. But there isn't one.

"The Lord glances down at His feet and says, 'There wasn't any room for them on the ark.'"

I slowly go from a smile into my *oh-my* face, with my hands on my cheeks.

There was less laughter, as I expected. Well, I knew that was a weak joke, but it went with the theme. I kept going.

"Yeah, well, now I'm a little worried. I mean, if I don't change my act, might I drown you all? We're right near the ocean here in New York, will some great tsunami come rolling in and wipe us all out, if I use the old material? Because, that would really suck! Whoosh! Does this place have life boats? I guess there won't be any use in throwing women and children out of the way!

"Anyway, I figured I better not take any chances. So, I had to change my act a bit. You know I've had a lot of fun razzing Catholics."

The audience applauded. A rowdy contingent started chanting, "Holy \$#!!! Holy \$#!!!"

"Yeah, yeah, holy \$#!!. That was the bit. But I can tell you now, that when I was dead, I saw something a whole lot more disturbing. Unholy \$#!!!"

The audience murmured.

"Have you ever thought about what death would be like if the Catholics were right? Unholy \$#!!, man. Unholy \$#!!."

Uncomfortable laughter sputtered from the audience.

"Now, the Catholics believe that Jesus came to earth, both fully God and fully man, and died as a sacrifice for our sins."

"Yeah, it doesn't make any #?@!ing sense," a drunk heckler interrupted.

"Yeah, yeah, I used to joke about that, but think about it. God, the almighty creator of the universe, sent His only son to earth to suffer and die, so that a sinner like me can be redeemed from my sins. God must friggin' be crazy!"

"Yeah, it's a mystery," the heckler said, sarcasm dripping from each word.

The audience laughed.

"Yeah, I know." I shrugged. "It doesn't make any friggin' sense."

A vocal, drunken contingent cheered and applauded.

"That's right, it's a friggin' mystery that makes no sense. I used to joke about that, but what a wonderful mystery! Through the suffering of Christ, we can all be redeemed and reunited with God. Even the a-holes from Jersey!"

"Yeah, and what about the holy $#!!?" the heckler asked, confused and annoyed.

Now, back in the day, I would have handled this heckler with a put-down, like "Hey buddy, just because God gave you a little pecker, doesn't mean you can come here and be a big dick." Yeah, always dick jokes for hecklers. Even that one I Godded up a bit. But I'm going the way of heaven, and no put-downs, so I just rolled my eyes and continued.

"Now, let's suppose that archaeologists on a dig in a site in Israel, found a holy $#!!, still steaming and with no discernible smell."

The crowd cheered.

"What would an atheist do?"

The audience murmured.

"Why, I'll tell you what he would do. He'd come up with some pseudo-scientific psycho-babble explaining that it happened by accident. 'Well, yes, it appears to be an ancient stool sample, still emanating heat, with no discernible odor. Obviously, there must have been some kind of missing link hominid, who through a super-evolved digestive system could generate feces with no discernible odor and a perpetual heating bio-mechanism, that must have been rendered extinct by the surrounding tribes of lesser hominids, with their smellier feces.'"

I scratched my chin, pondering the scientific mystery.

"You gotta love these scientists. They make their wild-ass guesses almost sound reasonable. Just throw in a lot of Latin or Greek based words, and stroke your chin, and it all makes sense. And then they send the article for peer review, and as long as the peer reviewer has no idea how to interpret all the indecipherable jargon, it passes the review."

I stroked my chin again.

"'Yeah, sure, I have no idea what you're talking about, so it must be scientifically correct! I mean, I might look stupid, if I said it wasn't, so sure. But, it sounds a little bit like they found a \$#!! that don't stink, but it can't be that! Whose \$#!! doesn't stink?'

"I can imagine some kid raising his hand, and asking, 'But, golly gee, Mr. Science, there's like no fossil or bone evidence of this tribe of super \$#!!-producers, so where do you suppose it came from?' And, the science guy would scratch his head and say something like, 'Well, Johnny, perhaps it was just some kind of genetic accident, some freak mutant, who laid a still steaming turd, that has no smell? Some accidental creature whose \$#!! doesn't stink?' And, little Johnny, the Christian kid, says, 'They've dated the thing back to like 20 AD, that's the time of Jesus? Maybe it's Jesus' turd. I don't think a Jesus turd would stink.'"

I made an innocent face for the kid, then turned and made an angry face representing the science guy. "'Now, Johnny, this is science class! There's no Jesus in science class! I will see you in detention!'

"Yeah, I spent a lot of time in detention as a kid. These days, I don't think I'd fit in so well there, with all the Christians they're locking up there."

Not many laughs for that one.

"I mean, these science guys, they can't think for a moment that some religious miracle happened. The Big Bang Theory, you know that one? That's the accepted scientific theory that the entire universe, all the billions of galaxies, with billions of stars in each galaxy, the whole shooting match, used to be the size of an atom, something you could only see with an electron microscope, only you couldn't have an electron microscope because the universe wouldn't be big enough for one to exist, and you would be in the universe."

I physically tried to scrunch myself down to atom size, which got a few laughs.

"Yeah, try wrapping your noodle around that one! Well, anyway, science tells us that one day, for no particular reason, this infinitesimally small universe just blew up, Kaboom!"

I started my hands and legs in close and then simulated an explosion by suddenly spreading my body out.

"And, then, over billions of years, that exploding tiny thing became everything we see. Now, that incredible story, from atom size, to the entire universe, with all the galaxies long ago, and far, far away, all the Luke Skywalker and Darth Vader drama, all the UFO's and earthmen, and all the people, doing their things, moving and grooving, living and dying, getting run over by trucks, and cars, texting on iPhones, you know, everything, yeah, it all started as a tiny atom sized thing, that one day, for no particular reason that anyone can figure out, just decided to explode and form into everything there is over billions of years. No, that's not some crazy religion creating some ridiculous idea for how the universe was formed. That's, da, da-da, da! Science!

"No, the screwball, far-fetched religious theory is that one day God, the creator of all things said, 'Let there be light', and then there was light.

"But if you say that to a scientist, he'll say, 'You're nuts! The whole universe started out as an atom size proto-universal-primordial-element that one day, totally by chance, underwent an exponential cosmic expansion.'"

I scratched my head.

"And so little Johnny might ask, 'Golly gee, Mr. Science, before this proto-universal-primordial element underwent this exponential cosmic expansion, was there any light?'

"And Mr. Science would answer, 'Well, no, Johnny, everything would have been fused into a single element before the expansion.'

"And, little Johnny would ask, 'But, after the expansion started, there would be light?'

"'Oh, yes, a tremendous release of energy and light.'

"'Well, golly gee, Mr. Science, it sounds like the difference between the scientific theory and the religious one is only in the, 'God said' part?'"

I made the innocent face, then turned and made the angry one again.

"'Now, Johnny, we've been through this before. I'll see you in detention.'"

I paused a moment, shaking my head. "It used to be kind of cool and rebellious to get sent to detention. Now, it's probably like a prayer session. So, it's like..."

I positioned myself to one side. "'Hey, Johnny? What are you in for?' And Johnny's like..."

I positioned myself as if I were the other party in the conversation. "'I prayed before taking a quiz.'"

Moving back to the other side, "'Oh, that's nothing! I told the science teacher she was too good-looking to be descended from apes.'"

Back again, "'Whoa, you complimented a woman on her looks *and* defied the teachings on evolution? *YOU* are a *BAD*, uh, *butt!*'"

I rolled my eyes. A few people laughed. The New York crowd seemed to be squirming in their chairs like bound hostages trying to break loose. It got worse. Likely, heaven was rubbing off on me because my routine, whether in time I would have been able to hone it into something really funny, veered more into a sneering lecture, mocking science-based atheism. Some in the audience had come to hear ridicule, but ridicule of religion. No one had come to hear my not-so-funny, fact-based attack on the scientific perspective. And, the drinks that increased the jolly-effect with the right material, increased the angry-effect with the wrong material.

"Did you know that the Big Bang Theory was first proposed by a Catholic Priest? A guy named Georges Lemaitre, a French guy. He called it the hypothesis of the primeval atom. I bet you didn't know that. And, the first reaction of the men of science was like, 'No way, Father! Why don't you go say a Rosary and leave the science to us professionals? The universe always existed. Don't give us this, *Let there be light, crap.'* But, they did all the observations, and they were like, 'Holy crap, man, the priest dude is right!' So, now the Big Bang theory is accepted as science, as long as it all happened by accident. You see, that's the key, for science. Everything is an accident. And, they get real sensitive when things start lining up with something in the Bible.

"There was this other dude, J. Harlen Bretz, who looked at the geology of Washington State and found evidence of a great flood. And, all the scientists laughed and mocked the dude. 'Hey, man, don't go selling us that Noah, jive. There was no great flood!' And the guy's like, 'No, man, look at the rocks! They look like they were carried and weathered by water, see the deep gouges? That only happens with fast running water. See the granite boulders on the basalt rock way above any possible water line? How did they get there? There had to have been a really big flood, like hundreds of feet of water rushing across the land.' And the scientists are like, 'Hey buddy, go build an ark or something, we're not buying your jive.' But, now, the theory is that when all that ice from the ice age was melting, an ice dam formed and gave way, causing billions of gallons of water to flood over the land and rush into the Pacific Ocean, a great flood."

I rolled my eyes and shrugged. "Well, that's *science!*

"It's like there's a kind of religious dogma around scientists. Thou shalt not produce scientific evidence that something happened the way it says it did in the Bible!

"When science is your religion, you have to have a lot of tolerance for accidents and coincidences. I mean, everything has to be an accident and coincidence. Things just happen by chance. Everything happens by chance. And we are the luckiest friggin' critters. I mean, if I ever thought I was that lucky, I'd be cleaning up at the craps table in Vegas somewhere.

"The latest theory is that there is a multiverse of millions of universes, most of which have crazy unworkable rules, so all kinds of impossibly screwed up things happen, and we just happen to live in a universe where the physical laws work out pretty darn well and make a whole lot of sense. You see, if we live in a universe with order and if there is no creator to have made things work in a sensible way, why then there must be millions of totally effed up failed universes, and we're just coincidentally part of one of the few universes where things make sense.

"So somewhere out there, there's another universe where everything is totally effed up, I mean infinitely more than our universe is effed up. Like, maybe everything is made out of cellophane or polyester or something. And some polyester creature is asking a cellophane based creature.

"'Golly gee, Mr. Cellophane Science, our universe sure is all effed up.'

"'Yes, Johnny, but out there somewhere there must be a better universe where things actually friggin' work in the most basic ways. Like there's something called light and energy and mass and physics and chemistry that holds everything together in an ordered and coherent way. But, completely by chance, our universe is just $#!!-out-of-luck, because there's no God to have built any sense into it.'

"That's science! There's no God, so there must be an infinite amount of other unbelievable crap.

"That's the kind of bull you end up with when you put your faith totally in science. It's a whole lot crazier than believing in God. Scientists will make up any amount of fantasy to explain how there must not be a creator God, but the much simpler solution is that a God of infinite wisdom and intelligence created this marvelous universe, and whether he did it in six days or billions of years, he certainly deserved a day off when he was done.

"Like, yeah, so science says, all creation just sort of accidentally happened? At least Catholics admit when they can't explain something, by calling it a mystery. An atheist has blind faith in accidents!"

A few nervous laughs echoed from the audience.

"See that great ball of energy in the sky there? Happened by accident. See those clouds in the sky raining fresh water down on the land and making all those plants grow? Another accident. See all those life forms all over the world from the deepest depths of the oceans to the highest mountain peaks? Just sort of happened. And the funny thing is, just how certain they are that it all happened by accident! Oh, they'll come up with explanations of how things change over time, how this life form just sort of evolved into that life form. How they are certain that all life came from some single cell somewhere and by accident after accident evolved into all the multitude of life on the planet. And it never even occurs to them that this series of accidents might even be more miraculous than the Bible story of creation where God created the universe in seven days!"

More nervous laughter.

"And, you know, they never quite get around to explaining that accident that caused that first cell of life to form. When you think about it, it doesn't make any #?@!ing sense!"

The audience began booing.

"Hey, don't boo me! I'm just an accident! That's another thing about atheists; they like to scoff and make fun, but they don't like it when it comes back at them. After all, they're the ones with the rational explanations. But just because you comfort yourselves that an explanation is rational, doesn't mean that it is true. There is always a rational explanation for everything, but there is always also an irrational explanation. How do you know that the rational explanation is the right one? An atheist thinks that he can fit the whole universe inside his head, and know everything, and know that everything is rational. But what if the most rational thing that one can fit in one's mind is God?"

The crowd started throwing things at me. Fights broke out as security tried to stop people from throwing stuff.

"You see the difference between Catholics and atheists? When I used to be a Catholic and made fun of Catholics, they didn't throw stuff at me. Now that I used to be an atheist and make fun of atheists, you want to crucify me!"

I ducked as a bottle nearly hit me in the head. I limped as fast as I could off the stage. I bumped into Maury.

"Carlton, this is great! We'll be bigger than ever when this hits the news!"

"Maury, I can't do this anymore."

"What are you saying? We're gonna be huge!"

"I'm saying I quit, and you're fired. Sorry, Maury."

I hobbled out as fast as I could. Passing a garbage can, I took the bottle of Vicodin out of my pocket and threw it in. "I've got the opiate of the masses, now. Won't be needing these anymore."

31

Back to McGinty's

I slipped out the back door of the theater and miraculously was able to hail a cab. I got in.

"Ugh, take me to McGinty's Tavern, down in the village."

"Hey, you that zombie dude?"

I laughed.

"Just you remember. I got my nine in the glove box, and gets you one in the brain, you tries to bite me."

The cab driver put the car in gear and started to drive.

"Whoa, what's the action in there?" the cabbie asked, seeing the police arriving to break up the near riot.

"Some idiot was making fun of atheists. He said something about the resurrection of the dead," I said.

The cab driver laughed. "Some peoples gots no sense of humor."

The driver shook his head, "Hey, ain't something like that happen in the Bible? Like, people causing a big blow when St. Paul say something like that?"

"Nothing new under the sun, my friend."

The cabbie dropped me off at McGinty's. I knew it was the right place to go. I was keyed up from the performance, and it was my usual place to relax after a show, though I never had a show that big, or that crazy. The place just felt like home, right down to the pictures on the walls. I was happy to see Lenny sitting at the bar, nursing his drink. No, he had not come to the performance and was clueless.

"Hey, Lenny!" I said, tapping his shoulder.

Lenny turned toward me and rolled his eyes. "I'd say break a leg, Carlton, but you already did."

"Is that you talking or the dummy?"

"You haven't returned my dummy, yet. Remember? You used Tony to crash the funeral?"

"I almost got pummeled by a guy who looked a bit like Tony."

"Would have been better publicity if you had."

"Now, you're thinking like Maury."

"I can be ruthless too, you know. Just because I helped you crash a funeral, doesn't mean I'm a pushover."

"Hey, Lenny. Don't be like that! You're like the best person I know."

Lenny rolled his eyes. If Lenny could make his dummy make that gesture, he wouldn't have to speak for it. "So, what do you want, Carlton? To gloat about your big show, and Maury taking you to the top or whatever? You really are a putz."

I laughed. "No, the show was a full-on Jerry Springer disaster, with people throwing stuff at me and the cops breaking things up."

Lenny laughed. "Bet Maury will be thrilled with the publicity."

"I told him to *tinsel* off."

Lenny cocked his head. "Really?"

"Yup."

"So, you just quit and walked out on Maury?"

"Yup."

"Oh, Carlton, he'll make sure you never work again! I've seen him do it. He's that connected."

"Yup."

"I can't help you, Carlton. I don't have the juice to dig you out of that one."

"I know. But, I can't be his latest train wreck. I'm out of the game, Lenny. No more mocking Catholics, no more fake blessings, no more holy $#!!. I'm done."

"Really?"

"Yup. I can't do this anymore. Everything has changed for me. When I look back, I see what a putz I've been. I can't believe I ever viewed the world the way I did. I am totally a new person."

"Well, I always knew you were a $#!!, but you were a $#!! with potential, a talented $#!!."

"Well, I was really a jerk to you and I apologize. You were always looking out for my interests and were always a good friend. I was just too much of a self-absorbed schmuck to appreciate it."

"I am so happy for you, that you were able to get out. They were set to use you up and spit you out. You were all set to be the latest side-show freak. I was trying to keep you from that."

"I know you were, Lenny. You were a good friend and a great manager. I'm so sorry."

"It's okay, Carlton, but what will you do now?"

"I don't know. I really don't know. I feel that there is a reason this has happened to me, that there is something special and important that I am supposed to do, but not for me. I don't think it's about me anymore. I guess the first thing I have to do is get right with the Church. It starts with going to confession tomorrow."

"I imagine that will take a while," Lenny said.

"I'm blocking off the whole day."

A tipsy blond staggered up to me. She pointed at the picture of me behind the bar, and then at me.

"Hey, that looks like you?"

"Yes, that used to be me."

"Hey, I remember you! You wanted to see today show tomorrow." She slurred her words and wobbled.

"Yes, that was me."

"Weren't you hit by a truck or something?"

"You have to excuse me, I don't remember your name. I'm Carlton St. Michael."

"Oh, uh, Sally, Sally Petruski." The "u" in her name lasted way too long, as she slurred her words.

"Sally, I'm not sure you even remember, but I treated you very badly about a month ago, and I want to apologize."

"Really?" She blinked and swayed. "Oh, lots of guys treat me badly. It's okay."

"Well, I'm just not that guy anymore."

32

Decisions, Decisions

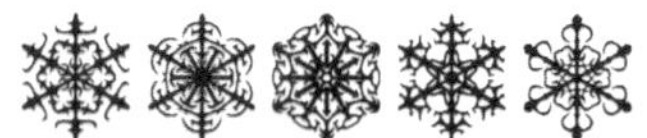

Sat, Jan 14, 2012 - The Fortieth Day

The fortieth day had arrived, and I had made my decision. I figured I had made my decision days ago, and had acted on it, but today, I would make it official. I made my way over to Jersey. I had to make my confession after many years of sin. I wanted to confess to a priest I knew and trusted, and Father Murphy was the only one I could think of. I used to say I wouldn't be caught dead in Jersey, but I guess I already had been. I was scared, I tell you. I had lots of sins to confess. Oh, man, how could I even remember them all? I'm sure there were lots of things I didn't even know what to call. As I followed the directions, I realized Father Murphy was assigned to the Church associated with David King's school, St. Nicholas. Can you imagine? The church of the fat guy in the red suit with all the ho-ho-hos. I was right back to the scene of the crime, so to speak. The place of my first death. And, here, I would be reconciled to a new life in Christ, repairing the damage done to my soul by years of rebellion against God. In Jersey, of all places. And just in time, forty days since the accident.

I looked up at the stone church, with its single spire and portal entrance. A heavy wooden door blocked the entrance through the rounded arch under a peaked portico, atop the concrete steps, with the large rose window overtop, the crosses atop each peak. Chesterton's quote rang in my head, "The outsiders stand by and see, or think they see the convert entering with bowed head a sort of small temple which they are convinced is fitted up inside like a prison, if not a torture chamber." I chuckled to myself. The place looked like a place of torture, with its forbidding facade.

I recalled how tortured I had felt by the mural across the parking lot to the left of the church. But, the old fat boy said inside is like the light of day, so let's see. I limped up the stairs and opened the heavy main door. I entered the church with trepidation. Passing through the narthex into the nave, I was surprised at how bright it was. The ivory-colored walls reflected light from large chandeliers hanging down from the vaulted ceiling and augmented the sunlight glowing through the stained-glass windows, revealing an inviting worship space. I was seized by a sense of holiness, an aura of blessedness, as my eyes were drawn forward to the altar, and beyond it, the tabernacle that seemed to glow. Above it, the crucifix, Jesus nailed stiffly to the cross, and above a symbol of the Holy Spirit descending.

To the left of the altar, stood the statue of Saint Nicholas, himself. Not the jolly, old, fat Saint Nick of legend, but the long gray-bearded, statuesque figure of a saint, wrapped in the red ecclesial robes of a bishop celebrating a martyr's feast day. He looked not at all jolly and fat, but rather dour and svelte, standing grimly with his shepherd's crook, the symbol of a bishop's authority.

To the right of the altar, the statue of the Virgin holding her child, in her blue robes, gazing humbly downward. I took it all in, but I wasn't exactly sure what to do. Father Murphy came in from the front of the church and motioned me to come forward. I limped up the main aisle and met him in front of the altar.

"Hi, Father Murphy. Thank you so much for doing this for me."

"Carlton, it is a pleasure. A day of great joy, when a lost sheep comes home."

"I was worried Saint Nick over there might reach out and hook me around the neck with that thing."

Father Murphy laughed. "More likely, he'd clunk you over the head."

"I guess I deserve worse than that. You know, I once got coal in my stocking?"

"Why am I not surprised?"

"I guess I deserve that as well. Now, Father, this might take a while. It's been a long time, and I've done some pretty crappy stuff. I mean, I used to go out of my way to eat meat on Friday."

"That's okay, Carlton. Take all the time you need. And, we only require people to abstain from meat on certain holy days now, not every Friday. We allow other forms of penance or sacrifice on Fridays, rather than requiring abstention."

"Well, I guess things have gotten easier since I left."

"Some things, maybe. Come this way, to the confessional."

The confessional consisted of two chairs facing each other, and a screen with a kneeler. I wasn't exactly sure what to do.

"You can either kneel behind the screen or sit in the chair. It's up to you."

I knelt behind the screen. Father Murphy put a purple stole over the back of his neck and sat in the chair beyond the screen.

"Bless me, Father, for I have sinned. It has been fifteen years or so since my last confession, probably more since my last valid confession. I used to make things up to see if I could shock the priest with sins I would never have committed. I guess that's a sin I should include."

"Go ahead."

I went through everything I could remember. All the blasphemies, the women, the booze, the drugs, the conniving, the disrespecting, the lying, well, you get the idea. Lots and lots of sin. I even confessed that I had bad thoughts about Father Murphy, himself. And, Sister Theresa. And then, I stopped.

"Is there anything else, my son?"

"Isn't that enough?"

Father Murphy laughed. "Yes, Carlton, that's quite enough. For your penance, I'd like you to say the rosary."

"That's it? Come on, Father, I had a lot of sins there!"

"I'm not finished. Just one more thing. I would like you to perform one act of self-sacrifice."

"Self-sacrifice? Like what?"

"Opportunities for selfless acts present themselves every day. I would like you to start taking them. You are only required to do one for your penance, but you might find you like doing them. Just try to think about someone else before thinking of yourself. You'll figure it out."

"Ok, Father. But I'm not sure I remember how to say the rosary. It's been a long time."

"There are some free rosary beads by the statue of the Blessed Mother in the front of the church. There are instruction cards included in the packages."

"Thank you, Father."

"God, the Father of mercies, through the death and resurrection of his Son has reconciled the world to himself and sent the Holy Spirit among us for the forgiveness of sins; through the ministry of the Church may God give you pardon and peace, and I absolve you from your sins in the name of the Father and the Son and the Holy Spirit. Go in peace, my son."

I walked over to the statue of the Blessed Mother and picked up one of the packets with rosary beads and instruction cards. I noticed that they were the same kind of homemade, plastic beads that the kid had given me.

"I guess you do exist, after all," I said to the statue.

I pulled one of the instruction cards out of the packet of rosary beads and took the rosary beads that the kid gave me out of my pocket.

"I only need the filling. I'll use these for my first rosary."

I knelt down in a pew, and said the rosary, following the instructions on the card. The Joyful Mysteries for Saturday. I laughed that I was meditating on the mysteries I had so roundly mocked. The Annunciation, the Visitation, the Nativity. I scandalized myself recalling how I had called the Christ Child the "little brat in the hay." What a total jerk. Then, the Presentation, and finally the Finding in the Temple. I liked the Finding in the Temple. Jesus was a bit sassy with his parents. It's a bit of an edgy mystery. His parents have been looking for him for three days, and they finally find him in the temple in Jerusalem, and he's like, why were you looking for me? Didn't you know I'd be about my Father's business? Little Jesus was pushing the envelope on that one. My father likely would have started storing up coal for my stocking, if I'd given him that kind of sass. When I finished, I got up and headed for the door with a spring in my step. I felt like a great weight had been lifted off me. I glanced up at the rose window over the pipe organ at the entrance to the church featuring St. Nicholas in the center. I imagined he was more jolly than the statue in the front had been, but still not the bowl-full-of-jelly of legend. Now, for an act of self-sacrifice. But first, I had to return the beads to that kid.

I left the church. A soccer ball bounced in the street and an athletic, boy hopped the retaining wall from the park and chased it down, crossing the street with more care than last time. David King. I couldn't believe it. The kid was right there! I held up the rosary beads and called to him.

"David!"

The kid looked up as he grabbed the ball in the street and got his foot caught in the storm drain grate. He fell, and his body lay in the street with his foot caught in such a way that he could neither stand up and get out of the way, nor swivel his position so he lay over the sidewalk rather than the street, though he struggled desperately to do either. I looked up the avenue and saw the truck, with the driver's head turned toward the park and not toward the road or even the side of the road where David lay. The truck braked not at all, honked not at all, slowed not at all.

"Holy $#!!!" I limped toward him with my cane, as fast as I could manage. I was a step late, the truck would surely run him over, crushing him under its tires before I could reach him. I quickly stretched the cane out to him. The kid grabbed it. I pulled as hard as I could, and heard the sickening sound of his ankle snapping, as I pulled him onto the sidewalk. But the force of pulling him to safety caused me to lose my balance and I fell forward. The brakes screeched. The horn blared. A great light flashed. Pain streamed through my body, and all went dark.

"No, mister, no!" I heard the kid say as I opened my eyes and gasped for breath. Everything was so bright, like I was looking through some strange camera filter. I blinked and gasped again. It hurt to breathe. I turned to look toward the kid, his foot was still caught in the grate, his ankle impossibly twisted. He struggled to free himself, to get to me, but the force of the collision had carried my body some distance away. I looked up at the truck that hit me, "Red Devil Paints."

"It figures," I gasped.

I blinked and struggled for a breath. Father Murphy? Was that him? My head lolled to one side. I saw the unlit Christmas lights that seemed to glow with an unnatural light dancing around St. Nicholas Church, and blinked several times to steady my vision. A revelation of the great gift of love, the child given to a broken world, the man to give his life, the star lighting the way, filled my spirit. I blinked again, and there was the mural painted on the wall across the parking lot. The star, the stable, the sun, the cross, the tomb, the Savior, and the Eucharist. The mystery unsolved but accepted completely on faith.

"Somebody call an ambulance!" I heard his muffled shout, almost like I was underwater.

I turned my head to face the voice. The face, I recognized. "Merry Christmas, Father Murphy." I sputtered warm blood from my lips.

"Merry Christmas, Carlton."

I heard mumbled words in Latin, then swallowed something placed on my tongue.

"I didn't...get a...chance," another painful, sucking gasp, "to complete...my penance."

"I saw you praying the rosary?"

I gasped for another breath, pain filled my lungs.

"Act of self-sacrifice," I barely managed to whisper.

"I'd say this counts, Carlton. You saved the boy. I saw it."

I reached out my hand, still holding the kid's rosary beads.

"Rosary? No time for that, now, Carlton." Father Murphy didn't understand.

Sucking in air like razor blades, pain streamed through my body.

"For the boy." One last pain-filled gasp. "He'll need them more than me, now."

I felt the beads slip from my fingers into the priest's hand.

I saw my brother, Tommy, waiting on the top of the hill, on that bike he loved so much.

"Hurry Carlty! We have to beat the storm."

I saw the flash and heard the instantaneous crash of thunder.

Yup. You got it. Welcome to my second death.

33

Solving the Mystery

Thank God I didn't have to take another breath! There was no gray haze this time. I found myself directly in a large banquet hall, or something like one. Souls rejoiced at a big reception. I wandered in, with no limp nor cane. It was like a full-on party, with everyone having a great time. And they all cheered and applauded when I entered. I looked around. I shielded my eyes from a sudden brilliant light and I marveled as the angel's wings retracted.

"Well done, Carlton! Well done," he said, "It was such a pleasure guarding you."

The strangest thing, his voice sounded familiar. Like, I had known him all my life.

"Guarding me? What are you talking about?"

The angel laughed, a mystical shimmering laugh that seemed to surround me with sound. "I was your guardian angel. All those little words that did not seem quite like your own? Just me. That and I made sure you didn't get into too much trouble. Couldn't have you ending up in a barrel at the bottom of a river in Jersey. Not when we had such special plans for you."

I shook his hand. "You'll have to excuse me, I'm still a little disoriented. I think I was just run over by a truck?"

The angel laughed, again. "Sorry, couldn't save you from that one."

He slapped my back. "Here comes someone I think you'll want to talk to."

Chesterton, that fat know-it-all, greeted me. He was all cheerful and enthusiastic like he had won the lottery or something.

"Carlton, Carlton, how you astound!" The fat guy was as jolly as a corner Santa Claus ringing a bell.

"Well, I do my best."

"You do your best? Do you realize what you have done?"

"I saved the boy, I think?"

"Yes, yes, you saved the boy! But do you know who that boy is? Pope Michael the First!"

"Pope? But he's just a boy."

"Well, you have to understand, time is not exactly chronological here. Maybe you would understand better if I say he *will be* Pope Michael the First, the first American Pope. He took Michael from your last name. Very unusual. Michael is an archangel, so no previous pope would dare to take that name. But, we couldn't exactly have a Pope Carlton, now could we? Here's his picture."

Chesterton showed me a picture of an old man dressed as pope, with the blood-stained rosary beads I had given back to the boy draped over his fingers.

"Notice the rosary beads? He never goes anywhere without them. Every photo you will ever see of Pope Michael the First will include those rosary beads. He says he uses them so that as he meditates on the life of Him who gave His life that he may have life in the hereafter, he may also remember the man who gave his life that he may have life in the here and now."

"Oh, that kid." I wiped a tear from my eye.

"And, look closely, you see? The beads are still stained with your blood. A genuine relic of Carlton St. Michael!"

"So, I made it, then? Does this make me the funniest man in heaven?"

"Well, Carlton, there is just one more step. Your final purification."

"Oh, yeah. Purgatory. Couldn't we just skip that part?"

"No, no, Carlton. Purgatory is a good thing. Anyway, your soul was pretty darn clean when you passed. You had just gone to confession and received last rites. It counts for a lot that you sacrificed your life for the boy. So, the Lord came up with a purgation activity to fit you perfectly. Just one final act of humility for you."

And that's when Chesterton handed me the toilet brush.

"Oh, no. You don't mean?" I said.

"Yes, Carlton. You get to clean up the Holy, uh, feces. But don't worry. It's still steaming but has no discernible smell."

I looked to the left and the right. An endless line of toilets stretched in each direction. Don't tell me God doesn't have a sense of humor. I suppose once I've cleaned them all, I may just be the funniest man in heaven.

Well, like I told you, my life is the most popular program on the Undying Rerun Network. If there's one thing they love in heaven more than some Bible-believing trucker reaching for a Perry Como Christmas CD, I think it's got to be a no-good, dirty sinner repenting and sacrificing his life to save a kid, a future pope no less.

When I look back on it all, now that I've written it all down, it all kind of makes sense, you know. If there was a God who loved a fool like me who ranted and raved about how there was no God and mocked him so roundly, wouldn't he run me over with a truck? And, if he loved me, wouldn't he give me another chance? And then, being this really great story teller, wouldn't he make me part of a bigger story, so that when I repented, I would save some kid who would turn out to be a pope? And, think of all the souls that would hear that pope tell my story, every time he explained the bloodstained rosary beads? Wouldn't they be touched and moved, and maybe repent? Wouldn't a great story-telling God do something like that? Use His former greatest enemy as His great evangelizing tool? Kind of like St. Paul, the great persecutor of the Church becoming its greatest advocate and writing all those letters that now make up so much of the Bible? It all seemed to fit so well.

I was still puzzled about my brother, though, senselessly struck by lightning at so young an age. But, if there is everlasting life, maybe an early death is a blessing? When we think that there is only earthly life, losing that life is insufferably tragic. But, if there is more, and better life on the other side? Well, that perspective changes everything.

The one thing that didn't seem to fit was all these friggin' toilets I have to clean. I mean, *holy feces*, as that oaf Chesterton called it. I made that crap up to mock God. There shouldn't be any holy feces if there really is a God. So how does it make any sense?

And, I heard the voice, as if it came from my own soul, but it couldn't have. "It's a mystery."

And I laughed to myself. A mystery? Yeah, sure, Colonel Mustard in the living room with a candlestick. Wait, maybe that was it? No, not a Catholic mystery? Maybe, it was a mystery to be figured out? And I had figured it out. I had not taken a dump since I got here, so there were no holy feces! Just some doubt I had been holding onto. Something from my life on earth I had to let go of. Something that didn't belong here in the afterlife. I looked up into the endless haze above me.

"Lord," I said, "I believe it all. It all happened. I repented. I was saved and redeemed. You made of me a great story, better than I could ever have written, myself. You made my life something fantastic, better than I ever could have deserved. And you did it all for love, even when I hated you. I get it, now. I renounce this idea that you don't exist, that you may not exist, and all this foolishness about holy excrement. I want only to know you, to love you, to serve you and to be happy with you."

I looked around and the endless line of toilets was gone. I felt a part of me burn away, as through fire, so that only the part of me that loved remained. And, I felt a deep love for all the people I had known in my life, Pop, Tommy, Lenny, Chico, Sally, Charlie, Father Murphy, J.C. Wiley, Nicholas Penneymoore, David King, the doctors and nurses who cared for me, the reporters and the librarian, even Maury, and Chesterton, my Clarence-like angel who had turned me from my path toward the pit. And, all the others. And I felt a deep regret that I had not loved more in my life. And a most deep regret that I had missed loving my father, as he deserved to be loved.

I saw my father. The grief of my brother's loss tearing his soul. His overcompensation into a strict Catholicism and his grief-warped love for me driving him to drive me away. My own feeling of loss from my brother's death driving me from God, and to resent my father, I understood it fully, now. The irreconcilable conflict between father and son, between strict believer and strict unbeliever. The incredible grief as the revelation came to him that the only way to save the soul of his remaining son was to cast him away. And the assurance that the prodigal would return, not to him, but to God. His grief at my funeral, thinking I may not have fully completed my reconciliation. His relief, joy and wonder when Father Murphy told him of my reconciliation with the Church and my self-sacrificing penance. My martyrdom to save a future Pope, something they would not realize for many years.

Then, all the stories of all the intersecting characters in my life became clear and distinct. I knew them completely, their motives, their goals, their desires, their personalities, everything that they chose to do, and everything they chose not to do. And, each other person impacted by my life, the tremendous good this loving God had brought from my foolishness.

I knew Lenny, and his struggles to keep his act going, his vow to try to protect other performers from the abuses he had experienced. Chico, the struggles with his family's health that had led to his fear of germs. Sally, how she had turned to drink and promiscuity to numb the pain of the sexual abuse she had suffered as a child.

And, Charlie, Nurse Jameson, her struggles with addiction, her descent into despair, and her emergence into that serious person, dedicated to helping others beat their addictions. Her wild inspiration to try to save me by allowing herself to fall again. An inspiration not her own, but ordered to a divine plan to save me from my self-destructive course, to lead me to where I needed to be. Her resistance and struggle with the idea, but finally submitting to the divine call to self-sacrifice, though she only thought she would get me to a meeting. The full extent of her call to sacrifice was only revealed when she saw the car coming and reacted almost instinctively. And, I knew the special love God had for her, and I had for her. Her gift beyond the measure of value.

Father Murphy, how he had broken his leg skiing, by avoiding a collision with a kid, the accident that led him into the hospital, where he would meet me. And, the strange savior, Mr. J.C. Wiley, who had cleared the elevator of the serial killer who would have ended my story in Jersey City, as he came down the elevator, and later so improbably saved me at the New York Public Library. A man so singularly in tune with the Holy Spirit that he just knew where he needed to be to cooperate with the plans of the great story writer, never knowing why, just going where he felt the inspiration lead him. If I could still feel shame, I would have been ashamed that I feared he would be the one who would harm me.

Sister Theresa, her early career as a promising singer and songwriter. Her remarkable stage presence and charm and then the tragic death of one of the musicians in her band of an overdose. The reexamination of her life in light of that tragedy and her resistance to the call to her religious vocation. The pressure from her management as she desexualized her act and tried to focus on the music. And her final capitulation to her call to an austere lifestyle as a Franciscan Religious Sister, working with some of the most wretched of the poor, though none more wretched than myself.

Then, Maury, well, Maury's story got real interesting, ending in a barrel tossed in a river in Jersey, having tried to bully the wrong client, one connected with some folks in Jersey who do those kinds of things.

And, of course, the miraculous life of David King, the boy who would become the first American Pope, or North American, anyway. How Father Murphy took to him after the accident, discovering his mystical prophetic power, and nurturing him as his spiritual director. I saw how that boy had a special awareness to know that I would need those rosary beads more than him, and the significance of the forty days in my story. How he could glimpse the Eternal Rerun Network through prayer and meditation, and have insights into souls like mine, who crossed his path.

The stories and events of all their lives, and countless other lives, interconnecting and interweaving with my own in an impossibly complicated tapestry made visible to me in a startling clarity and complete understanding, each one beckoning to be experienced in a greater and more vivid way, to be, in way, lived and known completely through the Undying Rerun Network. Knowing, and experiencing each person and every interaction with far more intimacy than the experience of watching and listening, and at the same time having the omniscient perspective to know beyond what any person could possibly know about himself or others he encountered.

I marveled at how very many lives intersected and connected with my own, all directed toward that one little act of self-sacrifice, my willing penance for a life of sin, made visible in the focused clarity of the Undying Rerun Network, and I understood why my story was so popular. God had intervened more in my life than most, sacrificing an innocent sending me off on a life of rebellion and folly, then striking me down and bringing me back from the dead by a miracle of His own hand. An extraordinary, inexplicable occurrence beyond His normal hiding in rationality, He moved His hand to make this incredible story. The least deserving of such a miracle, and yet the recipient, saved despite my full will not to be saved. Mercy beyond all telling. A soul so irredeemably destined for hell, hellbent, you might say, saved in the most merciful and entertaining way. All that persistence and holding to disbelief, just so terribly entertaining to all the souls here, could be experienced with the full knowledge of the great mercy of God, so impossible and unreasonable, so filled with love for a soul so wretched.

And for the first time in my life, I could not think of anything funny to say. I was as serious as Nurse Jameson. All the humor that had been based in anger, cynicism, and hate was gone, not a sarcastic jot, nor bit of snark remained. And I knew, however funny I might have thought myself, or actually had been, while on earth, I would never be the funniest man in heaven. My humor was not fit for the place and had to be left behind. Only love could remain, and so little of my humor was based in love. The brilliant light shown all around me as I felt the love of God, and the eternal embrace of billions upon billions of souls, enveloping me with their love. Each knew me and knew my story. Each loved my story and loved the great author of the Undying Rerun Network who had worked through me such a marvelous tale. I fell down upon what were my knees and wiped the tears from what were my eyes.

I had thought that God was the antagonist of my story, keeping me from my goals, blocking me at every turn. But, it wasn't my story at all. It was His, and I was the antagonist, and not even a very serious kind of antagonist, but a hapless, comic villain. A Wile E. Coyote kind of villain, persistently searching the ACME catalog for some new trick in which to catch the Creator of all things, only to have it backfire and wind me into His ultimate plan, providing endless entertainment for the countless souls in heaven. And as I would learn, my brother Tommy most of all. He lived my story over and over and relished his small but integral part in it, knowing that it was my love for him that had driven me to hate God, and it was that love, and that hate, that had shaped such an entertaining piece in the great puzzle of life.

But, despite all my efforts and fury, I had been defeated by the great hero with the only weapon that matters, love. All my efforts to defy him, all the blasphemes, the sins of the flesh, the pride and arrogance, the unbalanced flailing against the truth, had not laid a glove on Him. All of it had resulted in an act of repentance that had led to my penance, the act of self-sacrifice that had inspired a boy who would be pope. In His miraculous wisdom He had turned me unwittingly to His service to do the one thing I was meant to do in all my life. In reparation for all the sins I had confessed, the one thing that was the meaning and purpose for my existence I accomplished when I pulled that boy out of the way of that truck, and in my last gasps before my second death returned the bloody rosary beads. Everything had led to that moment of service.

So, now my service in this life completed and the remnants of worldly desires and doubts dispelled, and the truth fully revealed, all that remains is to be happy with Him in heaven. And, I know, that whether or not my story is true, this is how true stories end. Not in death, but in unending, eternal life.

Acknowledgments

Merry Friggin' Christmas borrows quotes liberally from various works of G. K. Chesterton, the source of which are indicated with the quotes. The author is indebted to Mr. Chesterton for his genius and inspiration and apologizes for putting words in his mouth in his interactions with the main character in the afterlife and in his dreams. The author is completely confident that Mr. Chesterton is thoroughly enjoying his afterlife, and if he is not the funniest man in heaven, the author's sincere hope is that he retains his sense of humor. The television program, *G.K. Chesterton: The Apostle of Common Sense* can be viewed on the Eternal Word Television Network (EWTN) and the author encourages readers to check it out. The author requests anyone who has questions about the Catholic perspective in this work to consult the works of Chesterton with the full warning that there is a risk of conversion.

Merry Friggin' Christmas also borrows from the Frank Capra classic movie of 1946, *It's a Wonderful Life,* and incorporates some quotes from the iconic Clarence character. The author wholeheartedly disagrees with the main character in the present work and assesses *It's a

Wonderful Life to be one of the all-time best Christmas movies. Christmas is hardly Christmas without watching Clarence save George by having George save him.

The author would also like to recognize the television show, *Monty Python's Flying Circus,* for the line, "No one expects the Spanish Inquisition." Please check out this wonderful classic television show.

And, of course, the Author would like to thank the authors of the Holy Bible, the compilers of the Catholic Liturgy and prayers which have been referenced in this work.

The author would also like to thank Warner Brothers for their marvelous character, *Wile E. Coyote, Super Genius*, that industrious, comic model of persistence who has provided us all with endless hours of entertainment in his steadfast pursuit of an impossible goal we all know he will never attain.

Author Notes

M*erry Friggin' Christmas: An Edgy Christmas Comedy* is based on my first screenplay, *Carlton St. Michael in the Afterlife.* Having accepted a challenge from a Hollywood producer, something along the lines of, "If you don't like the movies you are seeing, write your own," I undertook to write a screenplay. My idea was to create a compelling story that used the Catholic faith as a backdrop, something assumed to be true, rather than something to be doubted and questioned. I wished to instill within my work a faith in an unambiguous truth, rather than the predictable questioning and doubting, if not outright hostility, that always seemed to underly Hollywood's treatment of religion.

However, I quickly found I had no idea how to write a screenplay, so I purchased a book on the subject. The book, *Television and Screen Writing, Fourth Edition: From Concept to Contract* by Richard A. Blum, provided a road map for how to create a story and write a screenplay. Its discussion of character arcs led me to attempt the biggest character arc I could conceive, which was the St. Paul conversion story, where the greatest enemy of the Church and Jesus Christ became their greatest defender. So, I conceived the premise of an anti-Catholic atheist stand-up comic having a near-death experience in which he found that the Catholics were right, "right about everything!"

The original screenplay was not specifically a Christmas story, though it was set around Christmas time. In fact, *Merry Friggin' Christmas* is not really a Christmas story, in that the centerpiece of the story is not Christmas, though it takes place in the Christmas season. The story is rather like Frank Capra's, *It's a Wonderful Life*, in that respect. The original screenplay focused more on general dislike for all things Catholic rather than the more specific dislike for Christmas in the present work.

The screenplay also did not include the Undying Rerun Network. The Undying Rerun Network is a device created to enable the telling of a first-person narrative in which the first-person dies. The screenplay begins with Carlton's act at the Laugh Out Loud Club and ends with Chesterton assigning him the task to clean the toilets. These additions add a depth and extra twist to the story in the novel that is missing from the screenplay.

Also included in the novel are much more developed characters and the addition of characters like J. C. Wiley. Nicholas Penneymoore appeared in the original story as the truck driver, but I added his scene dressed as Santa Claus in the hospital in the novel, as well as the scenes with Nurse Jameson outside the hospital.

I owe a debt of gratitude to K. M. Weiland, who I have never met but have had breakfast with for many mornings via her podcast at helpingwritersbecomeauthors.com. Many of her ideas on writing have seeped into my rework of *Carlton St. Michael in the Afterlife* into a novel. Most notably is the addition of Carlton's "ghost," his brother Tommy and his tragic death. The original story was about an up-and-coming stand-up comedian who was virulently anti-Catholic, but I never really explained why he was so anti-Catholic. I also did not explain very well how he could afford to live in Manhattan as a comedian on the verge of success with no other source of income. The addition of Carlton's father and the large inheritance mitigated that concern and added another layer of depth to the story.

I find that the reworking of the original story into a novel has added depth and meaning and resulted in a better story. Were I to make the story into a movie now, I would likely incorporate the new material and scenes from the novel into the script.

MERRY FRIGGIN' CHRISTMAS!

Joseph Cillo Jr.

Also by Joseph Cillo, Jr.

Blind Prophet, Episode 1: A Prophet Is Born

Blind Prophet, Episode 2: Spiritual Warfare

Blind Prophet, Episode 3: The Prophet Goes to Washington

Blind Prophet, Episode 4: The Great Demon of Pride

Blind Prophet, Part I

Get *Blind Prophet, Episode 1: A Prophet Is Born* for **FREE!** For details, please visit:

www.edgycatholic.com

COMING *SOON...*
When the Wood Is Dry
An Edgy Catholic Thriller
By
Joseph Cillo, Jr.

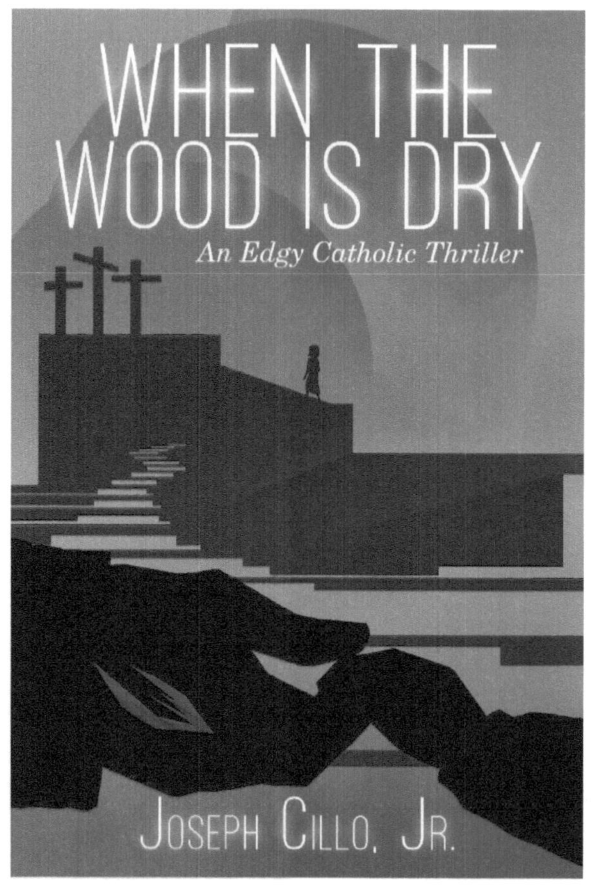

"...a chilling, unpredictable, fascinating story..."